MARK TWAIN was born Samuel Langhorne Clemens in Florida, Missouri, in 1835, and died at Redding, Connecticut, in 1910. In his person and in his pursuits he was a man of extraordinary contrasts. Although he left school at twelve, when his father died, he was eventually awarded honorary degrees from Yale University, the University of Missouri, and Oxford University. His career encompassed such varied occupations as printer, Mississippi riverboat pilot, journalist, travel writer, and publisher. He made fortunes from his writing, but toward the end of his life he had to resort to lecture tours to pay his debts. He was hot-tempered, profane, and sentimental—and also pessimistic, cynical, and tortured by self-doubt. His nostalgia for the past helped produce some of his best books. He lives in American letters as a great artist, the writer whom William Dean Howells called "the Lincoln of our literature."

MARK TWAIN

The Mysterious Stranger
And Other Stories

With a Foreword by EDMUND REISS

Revised and Updated Bibliography

A SIGNET CLASSIC

SIGNET CLASSIC
Published by New American Library, a division of
Penguin Putnam Inc., 375 Hudson Street,
New York, New York 10014, U.S.A.
Penguin Books Ltd, 80 Strand,
London WC2R 0RL, England
Penguin Books Australia Ltd, Ringwood,
Victoria, Australia
Penguin Books Canada Ltd, 10 Alcorn Avenue,
Toronto, Ontario, Canada M4V 3B2
Penguin Books (N.Z.) Ltd, 182–190 Wairau Road,
Auckland 10, New Zealand

Penguin Books Ltd, Registered Offices:
Harmondsworth, Middlesex, England

Published by arrangement with Harper & Row, Publishers

35 34 33 32 31 30 29

Cover painting *Carnival and Lent* (detail) by Peter Bruegel, Kunsthist, Museum,
Vienna. Courtesy Art Resource,

 REGISTERED TRADEMARK—MARCA REGISTRADA

Library of Congress Catalog Card Number: 89-063813

Printed in the United States of America

Contents

Foreword

As the most significant of the significant stories in this collection, *The Mysterious Stranger* represents Mark Twain's final attempt to put into fictional form the misanthropic ideas of his old age, ideas that render incongruous the appellation of humorist usually given to him. The work stands in all its bitterness and scorn at the end of a long line of stories and novels beginning with the jocular "Celebrated Jumping Frog of Calaveras County." Although the differences between these two pieces are immeasurable, one may see developing through the Twain corpus the *Weltschmerz* explicit in *The Mysterious Stranger*.

Sometimes this changing attitude toward life is revealed in the world created in each work. In "The Celebrated Jumping Frog of Calaveras County" the world is one of pleasant memories, of anecdotes, of the folk hero Jim Smiley. The world shown has little meaning to a reader, for even with its con-man's tricks and exaggerated tall tales it still is innocent, not a true reflection of life. Although similar in appearance to the Faulknerian world seen, for example, in the horse-trading episode of *The Hamlet,* it is essentially different; for there is an implicit evil in Faulkner's world that never touches or taints the frontier Arcadia of "Jumping Frog."

We read such works as "The Stolen White Elephant" and "Luck" for their humor and only as an afterthought think that the stories may contain out-and-out satire. They continue to have a detachment from life and, although not to be termed escape literature, they nevertheless tend to exist in a world of their own. In "The £1,000,000 Bank-Note" Twain's world is more than humorous; it is truly comic, revealing an inherent faith in the outcome of human achievement and an abiding belief in the success of life. The story is a romantic idyl showing the poor hero, down on his luck, eventually gaining through a *deus ex machina* reputation, position, wealth, and the woman he loves. It is the American dream of success come to life. One really need not worry about the future; the benevolent hand is outstretched around the next corner. Man is important and will be cared for.

In "The Man That Corrupted Hadleyburg" the faith begins to shatter. Mankind's goodness is merely skin-deep, and the benevolent hand may really be attached to the body of a demon, or perhaps to the body of a confidence man who has changed from the folksy stranger of "Jumping Frog" to a deceiver who tricks men into revealing hidden faces, or perhaps even to the body of someone like the new Mark Twain, who intends to reveal to public eyes his discovery of the ignobility and greed of man. Nevertheless, Twain still offers man the opportunity to change. Hadleyburg is able to change its name and become "an honest town once more" because its citizens finally realize that rather than sit back and feel self-satisfied and have faith in man's future, they must get up and make the future. One word is deleted from the town's official seal to make it read, "Lead Us Into Temptation." There is still hope for man but only if he understands what he is and that he is responsible for what he becomes. One must, says Twain, shun the benevolent hand, not the hard road away from the hand.

A similar theme appears in "The Five Boons of Life." Here man again takes from the outstretched hand, and again he suffers, now because, having to make a choice, he chooses the wrong boon, not once but four times. Of all the gifts—Fame, Love, Riches, Pleasure, and Death—only Death is valuable, and man loses even this blessing. All that is left for him is "the wanton insult of Old Age," an empty barren existence shot through with memories of waste, frustration, and nonachievement, an existence as horrible as that portrayed by Jonathan Swift in Book III of *Gulliver's Travels* when he shows the *Struldbrugs*, the deathless ones, who have nothing left but existence.

"Was It Heaven? Or Hell?" continues the theme as

Twain here states explicitly what man must do if he is to be saved: "Reform! Drop this mean and sordid and selfish devotion to the saving of your shabby little souls, and hunt up something to do that's got some dignity to it! *Risk* your souls! risk them in good causes; then if you lose them, why should you care? Reform!" Thus pulpit oratory, used to render an antipulpit thought, heightens the paradox that, for Twain, the saving of man may be quite different from the saving of man's soul. But again Twain gives man no promises. His main characters, by lying for the good of someone else and at the risk of their own salvation, do "reform"; but the story, ending on a Lady-or-Tiger note, leaves unanswered the fate of their souls, the question stated in the title. By negating the value of the soul here Twain approaches the view of man and of life he finally gives in *The Mysterious Stranger*.

In this work Twain again asserts the value of death, again negates the comic view of life, and again reveals human greed and hypocrisy. The responsibility is again man's; no force or deity is on his side to make things ultimately turn out right for him. At the end even existence is taken away from man as Twain in the guise of the Stranger—a reincarnation of the figures in "Jumping Frog" and "Hadleyburg," but now openly supernatural or demonic—asserts that "nothing exists; all is a dream." Man may "dream other dreams, and better"; he may re-create as the citizens of Hadleyburg re-created their town. But Twain does not show how re-creating will help. As in "Was It Heaven? Or Hell?" he promises nothing, but here Twain goes further, denying man a soul, an afterlife, even a present life: "there is no God, no universe, no human race, no earthly life, no heaven, no hell. It is all a dream—a grotesque and foolish dream." Man is "but a *thought*—a vagrant thought, a useless thought, a homeless thought, wandering forlorn among the empty eternities!" Perhaps dreaming and seeking will be of value but perhaps not. Nothing is given to man, not "the wanton insult of Old Age," not even existence.

By wiping the slate clean in *The Mysterious Stranger* Twain is, however, doing more than denying the existence of man. Rather than merely turn his back on the human race, he asks man to rid himself and his life of all illusions. In making free will and predestination meaningless terms, in asserting that the world around man is one of his own making and that man may change this world that has failed him—just as it failed Twain in his personal life—he gives to man the supreme compliment. Man must answer only to himself; he must in fact accept the responsibility of being both asker and answerer or, in other words, of assuming the roles of both familiar hero and stranger.

The changing attitude of Twain to the world around him may also be seen in the quality of the laughter which appears in his narratives and that which the reader brings to the writings. In "Jumping Frog" the laughter is innocent, a chuckle at a joke; in "The Stolen White Elephant" it is rollicking burlesque, not yet the horse-laugh and jocular scorn directed at the famous hero of "Luck" who is really "an absolute fool." In "The Man That Corrupted Hadleyburg" the laughter is bitter, derisive, sarcastic, angry, discomforting, even frightening. Laughter has no part in the narration of such stories as "The Stolen White Elephant." In fact Twain is careful to make his narrator there unconscious of the ridiculousness of the episode. The narrator is a straight man, one not in on the joke; and the laughter results from the reader's realizing the difference between his own reaction and that of the narrator. The laughter is, in other words, the result of dramatic irony. In "The Man That Corrupted Hadleyburg," however, laughter forms a continuous backdrop to the central scene of the story, the scene revealing the hypocrisy of the solid, self-righteous citizens of the town. Here the reader does not laugh; he realizes that the laughter is not at something humorous but at man in all his weakness. Perhaps the reader wonders how he himself would have reacted to the money, and if he is honest, he may feel that the laughter is also being directed at him.

Laughter can be a deadly weapon in the hands of a bitter writer. Besides reducing its object to shambles, it also succeeds in disturbing the reader, in making him feel uncomfortable. The dry laugh is really like the thrust of a dagger; the uncontrollable laugh makes one's hair stand on end—the fiend who laughs is more horrible than he who roars. In *The Mysterious Stranger* Twain shows the Stranger, Philip Traum or Satan, laughing "in the most unfeeling way," and has him speak of the power of laughter:

> . . . your race, in its poverty, has unquestionably one really effective weapon—laughter. Power, money, persuasion, supplication, persecution—these can lift at a colossal humbug—push it a little—weaken it a little, century by century; but only laughter can blow it to rags and atoms at a blast. Against the assault of laughter nothing can stand. You are always fussing and fighting with your other weapons. Do you ever use that one? No; you leave it lying rusting. As a race, do you ever use it at all? No; you lack sense and the courage.

But Twain is not able to laugh here as he could in "The Man That Corrupted Hadleyburg." For him there is only the hope that mankind can laugh and "dream other dreams, and better." For him nothing is left. With his life almost over, with an increasing understanding of the waste that hovers over man, he realizes that if his laughter, the laughter of one man, is to be effectual, one must first have something at which to laugh; for him there is only a void.

Twain is in many ways similar to his contemporary, Henry Adams, who entered the new century conscious mainly of the multiplicity in life, of the lack of direction and lack of unity in the world, of the machine—the Dynamo—that had become man's new god. He is also like another contemporary, Henry James, who insisted throughout his writings on the ambiguity of human existence and experience. For James the end of man's life is less likely to be achievement and success than it is waste, frustration, and grayness. None of these writers denies the emptiness of life: Adams makes multiplicity the norm; James presents man as gray in the grayness; and Mark Twain shows that this world and man are perhaps not the permanent, real things we think them to be. None of these views represents an answer—they are more statements of the problem than anything else—but by stating the problem, or rather, by calling up statements in the reader, they are all successful.

While the bitterness and pessimism of the later writings of Twain are in part the result of personal misfortunes, they are also states of mind present in Twain all his life but largely dormant. Such a story as the relatively unfamiliar "Facts Concerning the Recent Carnival of Crime in Connecticut," written in 1876, is somewhat anomalous when viewed in the light of the stories chronologically contiguous to it but perfectly understandable when seen as part of Twain's complete works. In this story of a man's coming to grips with his conscience and then destroying it Twain seems to sway back and forth between pure farce and cynical questioning, not able to decide exactly what he wants to do. The title of the piece is meaningful only because of the last few sentences, but both title and ending give the impression of being superfluous and irrelevant to what would seem to be the theme of the story. The work finally ends as a farce, just as "Hadleyburg," "Was It Heaven? Or Hell?" and *The Mysterious Stranger* also could easily have tipped over at the last minute, ending as little more than curious pieces of humor. Nevertheless, "Carnival of Crime" shows that the capability for questioning was in Twain throughout his life.

The pessimistic spirit was active in Twain, however, after the death in 1896 of his favorite daughter, Susy. After a long illness his wife, Livy, died in 1904; and Twain wrote to his friend, William Dean Howells, "I am tired and old; I wish I were with Livy." Soon after, another daughter, Clara, suffered a nervous collapse and had to remain in a sanitarium for a year. At the same time his youngest daughter, Jean, was hospitalized after an accident, and within a few months news came to him of the death of his sister, Pamela. During the following years Twain, filled with self-reproaches, exclaimed several times that he was to blame for the misfortunes that had come to his family. In 1908, a favorite nephew died and shortly after, Twain suffered what may have been the first of several heart seizures. In 1909, he had an actual heart attack; his daughter Jean experienced recurrent attacks of epilepsy; and his private secretary was found to be an embezzler. He also received news on two consecutive days of the deaths of two good friends, and on Christmas Eve, Jean died of an epileptic convulsion. Less than four months later Twain himself died.

It was in these final years of his life that Twain wrote "The Man That Corrupted Hadleyburg," "The Five Boons of Life," "Was It Heaven? Or Hell?" and *The Mysterious Stranger*. In 1899, Twain expanded an earlier sketch into what is now known as the Hannibal Version of *The Mysterious Stranger*, a story different in setting, characters, and aims from the final version of 1905-1906 when he left off writing the piece. During the years between these versions, however, Twain overhauled the work at least twice; but even at the time of his death, he had not attached the ending. The great final chapter was "found" by Albert Bigelow Paine, Twain's literary executor, in a heap of fragmentary papers, selected as the intended ending, and attached to the work, which was first printed posthumously in 1916. Whether or not Paine's discovery represents the ending Twain intended for the piece, it nevertheless brings the work together and gives it direction.

Although beginning auspiciously, the novelette tends to become disjointed. The questions of the worth of man, of the ambiguity of good and evil, of free will, of the Moral Sense, begin to fade into the background as Twain emphasizes the adventurous part of the story. The wonderful irony of the boy-angel, Satan, in the earthly paradise, Eseldorf (Jackassville), of his being both the creator and destroyer of life, fades as Twain makes his narrator, Theodor Fischer, the center of his attention. Father Peter's freedom becomes a dominant issue, and we see Theodor almost become the boy-hero-rescuer—the Tom Sawyer freeing Jim from the bedpost—who is a stock character in a stock scene in Twain's fiction. Incidents that are interesting but distracting begin to appear. In not contributing much to the whole work, many of

Theodor's adventures, which may have been designed earlier as part of an initiation of sorts, are comparable to those of Faustus and Mephistophilis in the middle scenes of Marlowe's play—satirical, curious, but yet, as they stand, not really necessary. It is with the final chapter that *The Mysterious Stranger* regains the intensity of its opening episodes.

One must note, however, that Twain's works are rarely tied up neatly in packages of the right shape and the proper color; and usually the string around them is somewhat loose. The works rarely achieve the organized direction and unity found in *Huckleberry Finn*, but at the same time they also rarely achieve the intensity of language and general effect seen in *The Mysterious Stranger*. Moreover, while Twain had a tendency to concentrate on matters of momentary relevance at the expense of basic philosophical problems, he has here written a work unhurt by topical allegory or by matters belonging on the editorial page of a newspaper.

Still, one might question the effectiveness of the overt didacticism throughout and at the end of *The Mysterious Stranger*. Although the work is effective because of its philosophizing, it falls short of the artistic achievement of "The Man That Corrupted Hadleyburg." There Twain does not have to intrude into the story to announce his theme. Everything from the beginning of the story leads to the end, and the reader is swept along and made to see the theme and feel the author's attitude without the author's having to throw away his narrative garb and come out in front of the footlights to address him. "Hadleyburg," even with all its narrative art, is, however, tame and undramatic beside *The Mysterious Stranger*, especially beside its memorable and really tormenting conclusion. "Hadleyburg" is like the first two books of *Gulliver's Travels*—controlled and well organized—and Twain is like the Swift of these books—calm, detached, and objective. But *The Mysterious Stranger* suggests the account of Gulliver's fourth voyage, the voyage to Houyhnhnmland, with its bitter invective against mankind. Twain begins in full control but ends with a violent burst suggestive of the savage frenzy of Swift in this section of the *Travels*.

The Mysterious Stranger, along with the other late writings of Twain, is not the work of an author sitting back in a comfortable easy chair dispassionately viewing life. It is rather the struggle of a man in the midst of life trying desperately to understand what he is and what he is a part of, what life is and why it is so bad. Twain is more than a *fin de siècle* writer fashionably mourning his fate; his cry is similar to that of all who have ever questioned and not been answered.

EDMUND REISS
Western Reserve University

The Celebrated Jumping Frog
of Calaveras County

IN compliance with the request of a friend of mine, who wrote me from the East, I called on good-natured, garrulous old Simon Wheeler, and inquired after my friend's friend, *Leonidas W.* Smiley, as requested to do, and I hereunto append the result. I have a lurking suspicion that *Leonidas W.* Smiley is a myth; that my friend never knew such a personage; and that he only conjectured that, if I asked old Wheeler about him, it would remind him of his infamous *Jim* Smiley, and he would go to work and bore me nearly to death with some infernal reminiscence of him as long and tedious as it should be useless to me. If that was the design, it certainly succeeded.

I found Simon Wheeler dozing comfortably by the barroom stove of the old, dilapidated tavern in the ancient mining camp of Angel's, and I noticed that he was fat and bald-headed, and had an expression of winning gentleness and simplicity upon his tranquil countenance. He roused up and gave me good-day. I told him a friend of mine had commissioned me to make some inquiries about a cherished companion of his boyhood named *Leonidas W.* Smiley—*Rev. Leonidas W.* Smiley—a young minister of the Gospel, who he had heard was at one time a resident of Angel's Camp. I added that, if Mr. Wheeler could tell me anything about this Rev. Leonidas W. Smiley, I would feel under many obligations to him.

Simon Wheeler backed me into a corner and blockaded me there with his chair, and then sat me down and

reeled off the monotonous narrative which follows this
paragraph. He never smiled, he never frowned, he never
changed his voice from the gentle-flowing key to which he
tuned the initial sentence, he never betrayed the slightest
suspicion of enthusiasm; but all through the interminable narrative there ran a vein of impressive earnestness
and sincerity, which showed me plainly that, so far from
his imagining that there was anything ridiculous or
funny about his story, he regarded it as a really important
matter, and admired its two heroes as men of transcendent genius in finesse. To me, the spectacle of a man drifting serenely along through such a queer yarn without
ever smiling, was exquisitely absurd. As I said before, I
asked him to tell me what he knew of Rev. Leonidas W.
Smiley, and he replied as follows. I let him go on in his
own way, and never interrupted him once:

There was a feller here once by the name of *Jim*
Smiley, in the winter of '49—or maybe it was the spring
of '50—I don't recollect exactly, somehow, though what
makes me think it was one or the other is because I remember the big flume wasn't finished when he first came
to the camp; but anyway, he was the curiousest man
about always betting on anything that turned up you
ever see, if he could get anybody to bet on the other
side; and if he couldn't, he'd change sides. Any way that
suited the other man would suit him—any way just so's
he got a bet, *he* was satisfied. But still he was lucky, uncommon lucky; he most always come out winner. He was
always ready and laying for a chance; there couldn't be
no solit'ry thing mentioned but that feller'd offer to bet
on it, and take any side you please, as I was just telling you. If there was a horse race, you'd find him
flush, or you'd find him busted at the end of it; if there
was a dogfight, he'd bet on it; if there was a cat-fight,
he'd bet on it; if there was a chicken-fight, he'd bet on
it; why, if there was two birds setting on a fence, he
would bet you which one would fly first; or if there was a
camp meeting, he would be there reg'lar, to bet on Parson Walker, which he judged to be the best exhorter
about here, and so he was, too, and a good man. If he
even seen a straddlebug start to go anywheres, he would

bet you how long it would take him to get wherever he was going to, and if you took him up, he would foller that straddlebug to Mexico but what he would find out where he was bound for and how long he was on the road. Lots of the boys here has seen that Smiley, and can tell you about him. Why, it never made no difference to *him*—he would bet on *anything*—the dangdest feller. Parson Walker's wife laid very sick once, for a good while, and it seemed as if they warn't going to save her; but one morning he come in, and Smiley asked how she was, and he said she was considerable better—thank the Lord for his inf'nit mercy—and coming on so smart that, with the blessing of Prov'dence, she'd get well yet; and Smiley, before he thought, says, "Well, I'll risk two-and-a-half that she don't, anyway."

Thish-yer Smiley had a mare—the boys called her the fifteen-minute nag, but that was only in fun, you know, because, of course, she was faster than that—and he used to win money on that horse, for all she was so slow and always had the asthma, or the distemper, or the consumption, or something of that kind. They used to give her two or three hundred yards start, and then pass her under way; but always at the fag end of the race she'd get excited and desperate-like, and come cavorting and straddling up, and scattering her legs around limber, sometimes in the air, and sometimes out to one side amongst the fences, and kicking up m-o-r-e dust, and raising m-o-r-e racket with her coughing and sneezing and blowing her nose—and always fetch up at the stand just about a neck ahead, as near as you could cipher it down.

And he had a little small bull pup, that to look at him you'd think he wan't worth a cent, but to set around and look ornery, and lay for a chance to steal something. But as soon as money was up on him, he was a different dog; his underjaw'd begin to stick out like the fo-castle of a steamboat, and his teeth would uncover, and shine savage like the furnaces. And a dog might tackle him, and bully-rag him, and bite him, and throw him over his shoulder two or three times, and Andrew Jackson—which was the name of the pup—Andrew Jackson would never let on but what *he* was satisfied, and hadn't expected nothing else—and the bets being doubled and doubled on the other side all the time, till the money was all up; and then all of a sudden he would grab that other dog jest by the j'int of his hand leg and freeze to it—not chaw, you understand, but only jest grip and hang on till they throwed up the sponge, if it was a year. Smiley always come out winner on that pup, till he harnessed a dog once that didn't have no hind legs, because they'd been sawed off by a circular saw, and when the thing had gone along far enough, and the money was all up, and he come to make a snatch for his pet holt, he saw in a minute how he'd been imposed on, and how the other dog had him in the door, so to speak, and he 'peared surprised, and then he looked sorter discouraged-like, and didn't try no more to win the fight, and so he got shucked out bad. He give Smiley a look, as much as to say his heart was broke, and it was *his* fault for putting up a dog that hadn't no hind legs for him to take holt of, which was his main dependence in a fight, and then he limped off a piece and laid down and died. It was a good pup, was that Andrew Jackson, and would have made a name for hisself if he'd lived, for the stuff was in him, and he had genius—I know it, because he hadn't had no opportunities to speak of, and it don't stand to reason that a dog could make such a fight as he could under them circumstances, if he hadn't no talent. It always makes me feel sorry when I think of that last fight of his'n, and the way it turned out.

Well, thish-yer Smiley had rat-tarriers, and chicken cocks, and tomcats, and all them kind of things, till you couldn't rest, and you couldn't fetch nothing for him to bet on but he'd match you. He ketched a frog one day, and took him home, and said he cal'klated to edercate him; and so he never done nothing for three months but set in his back yard and learn that frog to jump. And you bet you he *did* learn him, too. He'd give him a little punch behind, and the next minute you'd see that frog whirling in the air like a doughnut—see him turn one summerset, or may be a couple, if he got a good start, and come down flatfooted and all right, like a cat. He got him up so in the matter of catching flies, and kept him in practice so constant, that he'd nail a fly

every time as far as he could see him. Smiley said all a
frog wanted was education, and he could do most anything—and I believe him. Why, I've seen him set Dan'l
Webster down here on this floor—Dan'l Webster was
the name of the frog—and sing out, "Flies, Dan'l, flies!"
and quicker'n you could wink, he'd spring straight up,
and snake a fly off'n the counter there, and flop down on
the floor again as solid as a gob of mud, and fall to
scratching the side of his head with his hind foot as
indifferent as if he hadn't no idea he'd been doin' any
more'n any frog might do. You never see a frog so modest
and straightfor'ard as he was, for all he was so gifted.
And when it come to fair and square jumping on a dead
level, he could get over more ground at one straddle than
any animal of his breed you ever see. Jumping on a dead
level was his strong suit, you understand; and when it
come to that, Smiley would ante up money on him as
long as he had a red. Smiley was monstrous proud of his
frog, and well he might be, for fellers that had traveled
and been everywheres, all said he laid over any frog that
ever *they* see.

Well, Smiley kept the beast in a little lattice box, and
he used to fetch him downtown sometimes and lay for a
bet. One day a feller—a stranger in the camp, he was—
come across him with his box, and says:

"What might it be that you've got in the box?"

And Smiley says, sorter indifferent like, "It might be a
parrot, or it might be a canary, maybe, but it an't—it's
only just a frog."

And the feller took it, and looked at it careful, and
turned it round this way and that, and says, "H'm—so 'tis.
Well, what's *he* good for?"

"Well," Smiley says, easy and careless, "he's good
enough for *one* thing, I should judge—he can outjump ary
frog in Calaveras county."

The feller took the box again, and took another long,
particular look, and give it back to Smiley, and says, very
deliberate, "Well, I don't see no p'ints about that frog
that's any better'n any other frog."

"Maybe you don't," Smiley says. "Maybe you understand frogs, and maybe you don't understand 'em;
maybe you've had experience, and maybe you an't only

a amature, as it were. Anyways, I've got *my* opinion, and I'll risk forty dollars that he can outjump any frog in Calaveras county."

And the feller studied a minute, and then says, kinder sad like, "Well, I'm only a stranger here, and I an't got no frog; but if I had a frog, I'd bet you."

And then Smiley says, "That's all right—that's all right —if you'll hold my box a minute, I'll go and get you a frog." And so the feller took the box, and put up his forty dollars along with Smiley's, and set down to wait.

So he set there a good while thinking and thinking to hisself, and then he got the frog out and prized his mouth open and took a teaspoon and filled him full of quail shot—filled him pretty near up to his chin—and set him on the floor. Smiley he went to the swamp and slopped around in the mud for a long time, and finally he ketched a frog, and fetched him in, and give him to this feller, and says:

"Now, if you're ready, set him alongside of Dan'l, with his fore-paws just even with Dan'l, and I'll give the word." Then he says, "One—two—three—jump!" and him and the feller touched up the frogs from behind, and the new frog hopped off, but Dan'l give a heave, and hysted up his shoulders—so—like a Frenchman, but it wan't no use—he couldn't budge; he was planted as solid as an anvil, and he couldn't no more stir than if he was anchored out. Smiley was a good deal surprised, and he was disgusted too, but he didn't have no idea what the matter was, of course.

The feller took the money and started away; and when he was going out at the door, he sorter jerked his thumb over his shoulders—this way—at Dan'l, and says again, very deliberate, "Well, *I* don't see no p'ints about that frog that's any better'n any other frog."

Smiley he stood scratching his head and looking down at Dan'l a long time, and at last he says, "I do wonder what in the nation that frog throw'd off for—I wonder if there an't something the matter with him—he 'pears to look mighty baggy, somehow." And he ketched Dan'l by the nap of the neck, and lifted him up and says, "Why, blame my cats, if he don't weigh five pound!" and turned him upside down, and he belched out a double handful of shot. And then he see how it was, and he was the maddest man—he set the frog down and took out after that feller, but he never ketched him. And—

[Here Simon Wheeler heard his name called from the front yard, and got up to see what was wanted.] And turning to me as he moved away, he said: "Just set where you are, stranger, and rest easy—I an't going to be gone a second."

But, by your leave, I did not think that a continuation of the history of the enterprising vagabond *Jim* Smiley would be likely to afford me much information concerning the Rev. *Leonidas W*. Smiley, and so I started away.

At the door I met the sociable Wheeler returning, and he buttonholed me and recommenced:

"Well, thish-yer Smiley had a yaller one-eyed cow that didn't have no tail, only jest a short stump like a bannanner, and—"

"Oh! hang Smiley and his afflicted cow!" I muttered, good-naturedly, and bidding the old gentleman good-day, I departed.

The Facts Concerning the Recent
Carnival of Crime in
Connecticut

I WAS feeling blithe, almost jocund. I put a match to
my cigar, and just then the morning's mail was handed
in. The first superscription I glanced at was in a hand-
writing that sent a thrill of pleasure through and through
me. It was Aunt Mary's; and she was the person I loved
and honored most in all the world, outside of my own
household. She had been my boyhood's idol; maturity,
which is fatal to so many enchantments, had not been
able to dislodge her from her pedestal; no, it had only
justified her right to be there, and placed her dethrone-
ment permanently among the impossibilities. To show
how strong her influence over me was, I will observe
that long after everybody else's "*do*-stop-smoking" had
ceased to affect me in the slightest degree, Aunt Mary
could still stir my torpid conscience into faint signs of life
when she touched upon the matter. But all things have
their limit, in this world. A happy day came at last, when
even Aunt Mary's words could no longer move me. I was
not merely glad to see that day arrive; I was more than
glad—I was grateful; for when its sun had set, the one
alloy that was able to mar my enjoyment of my aunt's
society was gone. The remainder of her stay with us that
winter was in every way a delight. Of course she pleaded
with me just as earnestly as ever, after that blessed day,
to quit my pernicious habit, but to no purpose whatever;
the moment she opened the subject I at once became
calmly, peacefully, contentedly indifferent—absolutely,
adamantinely indifferent. Consequently the closing weeks

24

of that memorable visit melted away as pleasantly as a dream, they were so freighted, for me, with tranquil satisfaction. I could not have enjoyed my pet vice more if my gentle tormentor had been a smoker herself, and an advocate of the practice. Well, the sight of her hand-writing reminded me that I was getting very hungry to see her again. I easily guessed what I should find in her letter. I opened it. Good! just as I expected; she was coming! Coming this very day, too, and by the morning train; I might expect her any moment.

I said to myself, "I am thoroughly happy and content, now. If my most pitiless enemy could appear before me at this moment, I would freely right any wrong I may have done him."

Straightway the door opened, and a shriveled, shabby dwarf entered. He was not more than two feet high. He seemed to be about forty years old. Every feature and every inch of him was a trifle out of shape; and so, while one could not put his finger upon any particular part and say, "This is a conspicuous deformity," the spectator perceived that this little person was a deformity as a whole—a vague, general, evenly blended, nicely adjusted deformity. There was a foxlike cunning in the face and the sharp little eyes, and also alertness and malice. And yet, this vile bit of human rubbish seemed to bear a sort of remote and ill-defined resemblance to me! It was dully perceptible in the mean form, the countenance, and even the clothes, gestures, manner, and attitudes of the creature. He was a farfetched, dim suggestion of a burlesque upon me, a caricature of me in little. One thing about him struck me forcibly, and most unpleas-antly: he was covered all over with a fuzzy, greenish mold, such as one sometimes sees upon mildewed bread. The sight of it was nauseating.

He stepped along with a chipper air, and flung him-self into a doll's chair in a very free-and-easy way, with-out waiting to be asked. He tossed his hat into the waste-basket. He picked up my old chalk pipe from the floor, gave the stem a wipe or two on his knee, filled the bowl from the tobacco box at his side, and said to me in a tone of pert command:

"Gimme a match!"

I blushed to the roots of my hair; partly with indignation, but mainly because it somehow seemed to me that this whole performance was very like an exaggeration of conduct which I myself had sometimes been guilty of in my intercourse with familiar friends—but never, never with strangers, I observed to myself. I wanted to kick the pygmy into the fire, but some incomprehensible sense of being legally and legitimately under his authority forced me to obey his order. He applied the match to the pipe, took a contemplative whiff or two, and remarked, in an irritatingly familiar way:

"Seems to me it's devilish odd weather for this time of year."

I flushed again, and in anger and humiliation as before; for the language was hardly an exaggeration of some that I have uttered in my day, and moreover was delivered in a tone of voice and with an exasperating drawl that had the seeming of a deliberate travesty of my style. Now there is nothing I am quite so sensitive about as a mocking imitation of my drawling infirmity of speech. I spoke up sharply and said:

"Look here, you miserable ash-cat! you will have to give a little more attention to your manners, or I will throw you out of the window!"

The manikin smiled a smile of malicious content and security, puffed a whiff of smoke contemptuously toward me, and said, with a still more elaborate drawl:

"Come—go gently, now; don't put on *too* many airs with your betters."

This cool snub rasped me all over, but it seemed to subjugate me, too, for a moment. The pygmy contemplated me awhile with his weasel eyes, and then said, in a peculiarly sneering way:

"You turned a tramp away from your door this morning."

I said crustily:

"Perhaps I did, perhaps I didn't. How do *you* know?"

"Well, I know. It isn't any matter *how* I know."

"Very well. Suppose I *did* turn a tramp away from the door—what of it?"

"Oh, nothing; nothing in particular. Only you lied to him."

"I *didn't!* That is, I—"

"Yes, but you did; you lied to him."

I felt a guilty pang—in truth I had felt it forty times before that tramp had traveled a block from my door—but still I resolved to make a show of feeling slandered; so I said:

"This is a baseless impertinence. I said to the tramp—"

"There—wait. You were about to lie again. *I* know what you said to him. You said the cook was gone downtown and there was nothing left from breakfast. Two lies. You knew the cook was behind the door, and plenty of provisions behind *her*."

This astonishing accuracy silenced me; and it filled me with wondering speculations, too, as to how this cub could have got his information. Of course he could have culled the conversation from the tramp, but by what sort of magic had he contrived to find out about the concealed cook? Now the dwarf spoke again.

"It was rather pitiful, rather small, in you to refuse to read that poor young woman's manuscript the other day, and give her an opinion as to its literary value; and she had come so far, too, and *so* hopefully. Now *wasn't* it?"

I felt like a cur! And I had felt so every time the thing had recurred to my mind, I may as well confess. I flushed hotly and said:

"Look here, have you nothing better to do than prowl around prying into other people's business? Did that girl tell you that?"

"Never mind whether she did or not. The main thing is, you did that contemptible thing. And you felt ashamed of it afterward. Aha! you feel ashamed of it *now!*"

This was a sort of devilish glee. With fiery earnestness I responded:

"I told that girl, in the kindest, gentlest way, that I could not consent to deliver judgment upon *any*one's manuscript, because an individual's verdict was worthless. It might underrate a work of high merit and lose it to the world, or it might overrate a trashy production and so open the way for its infliction upon the world. I said that the great public was the only tribunal competent to sit in judgment upon a literary effort, and therefore it must be best to lay it before that tribunal in the outset, since in the end it must stand or fall by that mighty court's decision anyway."

"Yes, you said all that. So you did, you juggling, small-souled shuffler! And yet when the happy hopefulness faded out of that poor girl's face, when you saw her furtively slip beneath her shawl the scroll she had so patiently and honestly scribbled at—so ashamed of her darling now, so proud of it before—when you saw the gladness go out of her eyes and the tears come there, when she crept away so humbly who had come so—"

"Oh, peace! peace! peace! Blister your merciless tongue, haven't all these thoughts tortured me enough without *your* coming here to fetch them back again!"

Remorse! Remorse! It seemed to me that it would eat the very heart out of me! And yet that small fiend only sat there leering at me with joy and contempt, and placidly chuckling. Presently he began to speak again. Every sentence was an accusation, and every accusation a truth. Every clause was freighted with sarcasm and derision, every slow-dropping word burned like vitriol. The dwarf reminded me of times when I had flown at my children in anger and punished them for faults which a little inquiry would have taught me that others, and not they, had committed. He reminded me of how I had disloyally allowed old friends to be traduced in my hearing, and been too craven to utter a word in their defense. He reminded me of many dishonest things which I had done; of many which I had procured to be done by children and other irresponsible persons; of some which I had planned, thought upon, and longed to do, and been kept from the performance by fear of consequences only. With exquisite cruelty he recalled to my mind, item by item, wrongs and unkindnesses I had inflicted and humiliations I had put upon friends since dead, "who died thinking of those injuries, maybe, and grieving over them," he added, by way of poison to the stab.

"For instance," said he, "take the case of your younger brother, when you two were boys together, many a long year ago. He always lovingly trusted in you with a fidelity that your manifold treacheries were not able to shake. He followed you about like a dog, content to suffer wrong and abuse if he might only be with you; patient under these injuries so long as it was your hand that inflicted them. The latest picture you have of him in health and strength must be such a comfort to you! You pledged your honor that if he would let you blindfold him no harm should come to him; and then, giggling and choking over the rare fun of the joke, you led him to a brook thinly glazed with ice, and pushed him in; and how you did laugh! Man, you will never forget the gentle, reproachful look he gave you as he struggled shivering out, if you live a thousand years! Oho! you see it now, you see it *now!*"

"Beast, I have seen it a million times, and shall see it a million more! and may you rot away piecemeal, and suffer till doomsday what I suffer now, for bringing it back to me again!"

The dwarf chuckled contentedly, and went on with his accusing history of my career. I dropped into a moody, vengeful state, and suffered in silence under the merciless lash. At last this remark of his gave me a sudden rouse.

"Two months ago, on a Tuesday, you woke up, away in the night, and fell to thinking, with shame, about a peculiarly mean and pitiful act of yours toward a poor ignorant Indian in the wilds of the Rocky Mountains in the winter of eighteen hundred and—"

"Stop a moment, devil! Stop! Do you mean to tell me that even my very *thoughts* are not hidden from you?"

"It seems to look like that. Didn't you think the thoughts I have just mentioned?"

"If I didn't, I wish I may never breathe again! Look here, friend—look me in the eye. Who *are* you?"

"Well, who do you think?"

"I think you are Satan himself. I think you are the devil."

"No."

"No? Then who *can* you be?"

"Would you really like to know?"

"*Indeed* I would."

"Well, I am your *Conscience!*"

In an instant I was in a blaze of joy and exultation. I sprang at the creature, roaring:

"Curse you, I have wished a hundred million times that you were tangible, and that I could get my hands on your throat once! Oh, but I will wreak a deadly vengeance on—"

Folly! Lightning does not move more quickly than my Conscience did! He darted aloft so suddenly that in the moment my fingers clutched the empty air he was already perched on the top of the high bookcase, with his thumb at his nose in token of derision. I flung the poker at him, and missed. I fired the bootjack. In a blind rage I flew from place to place, and snatched and hurled any missile that came handy; the storm of books, inkstands, and chunks of coal gloomed the air and beat about the manikin's perch relentlessly, but all to no purpose; the nimble figure dodged every shot; and not only that, but burst into a cackle of sarcastic and triumphant laughter as I sat down exhausted. While I puffed and gasped with fatigue and excitement, my Conscience talked to this effect.

"My good slave, you are curiously witless—no, I mean characteristically so. In truth, you are always consistent, always yourself, always an ass. Otherwise it must have occurred to you that if you attempted this murder with a sad heart and a heavy conscience, I would droop under the burdening influence instantly. Fool, I should have weighed a ton, and could not have budged from the floor; but instead, you are so cheerfully anxious to kill me that your conscience is as light as a feather; hence I am away up here out of your reach. I can almost respect a mere ordinary sort of fool; but *you*—pah!"

I would have given anything, then, to be heavyhearted, so that I could get this person down from there and take his life, but I could no more be heavyhearted over such a desire than I could have sorrowed over its accomplishment. So I could only look longingly up at my master, and rave at the ill luck that denied me a heavy conscience the one only time that I had ever wanted such a thing in my life. By and by I got to musing over the hour's strange adventure, and of course my human curiosity began to work. I set myself to framing in my mind some questions for this fiend to answer. Just then one of my boys entered, leaving the door open behind him, and exclaimed:

"My! what *has* been going on here? The bookcase is all one riddle of—"

I sprang up in consternation, and shouted:

"Out of this! Hurry! Jump! Fly! Shut the door! Quick, or my Conscience will get away!"

The door slammed to, and I locked it. I glanced up and was grateful, to the bottom of my heart, to see that my owner was still my prisoner. I said:

"Hang you, I might have lost you! Children are the heedlessest creatures. But look here, friend, the boy did not seem to notice you at all; how is that?"

"For a very good reason. I am invisible to all but you."

I made mental note of that piece of information with a good deal of satisfaction. I could kill this miscreant now, if I got a chance, and no one would know it. But this very reflection made me so lighthearted that my Conscience could hardly keep his seat, but was like to float aloft toward the ceiling like a toy balloon. I said, presently:

"Come, my Conscience, let us be friendly. Let us fly a flag of truce for a while. I am suffering to ask you some questions."

"Very well. Begin."

"Well, then, in the first place, why were you never visible to me before?"

"Because you never asked to see me before; that is, you never asked in the right spirit and the proper form before. You were just in the right spirit this time, and when you called for your most pitiless enemy I was that person by a very large majority, though you did not suspect it."

"Well, did that remark of mine turn you into flesh and blood?"

"No. It only made me visible to you. I am unsubstantial, just as other spirits are."

This remark prodded me with a sharp misgiving. If he was unsubstantial, how was I going to kill him? But I dissembled, and said persuasively:

"Conscience, it isn't sociable of you to keep at such a distance. Come down and take another smoke."

This was answered with a look that was full of derision, and with this observation added:

"Come where you can get at me and kill me? The invitation is declined with thanks."

"All right," said I to myself; "so it seems a spirit *can* be killed, after all; there will be one spirit lacking in this world, presently, or I lose my guess." Then I said aloud:

"Friend—"

"There; wait a bit. I am not your friend, I am your enemy; I am not your equal, I am your master. Call me 'my lord,' if you please. You are too familiar."

"I don't like such titles. I am willing to call you *sir.* That is as far as—"

"We will have no argument about this. Just obey; that is all. Go on with your chatter."

"Very well, my lord—since nothing but my lord will suit you—I was going to ask you how long you will be visible to me?"

"Always!"

I broke out with strong indignation: "This is simply an outrage. That is what I think of it. You have dogged, and dogged, and *dogged* me, all the days of my life, invisible. That was misery enough; now to have such a looking thing as you tagging after me like another shadow all the rest of my days is an intolerable prospect. You have my opinion, my lord; make the most of it."

"My lad, there was never so pleased a conscience in this world as I was when you made me visible. It gives me an inconceivable advantage. *Now,* I can look you straight in the eye, and call you names, and leer at you, jeer at you, sneer at you; and *you* know what eloquence there is in visible gesture and expression, more especially when the effect is heightened by audible speech. I shall always address you henceforth in your o-w-n s-n-i-v-e-l-l-i-n-g d-r-a-w-l—baby!"

I let fly with the coal hod. No result. My lord said:

"Come, come! Remember the flag of truce!"

"Ah, I forgot that. I will try to be civil; and *you* try it, too, for a novelty. The idea of a *civil* conscience! It is a good joke; an excellent joke. All the consciences *I* have ever heard of were nagging, badgering, faultfinding, execrable savages! Yes; and always in a sweat about some poor little insignificant trifle or other—destruction catch the lot of them, *I* say! I would trade mine for the small-pox and seven kinds of consumption, and be glad of the chance. Now tell me, why *is* it that a conscience can't haul a man over the coals once, for an offense, and then let him alone? Why is it that it wants to keep on pegging at him, day and night and night and day, week in and week out, forever and ever, about the same old thing? There is no sense in that, and no reason in it. I think a conscience that will act like that is meaner than the very dirt itself."

"Well, *we* like it; that suffices."

"Do you do it with the honest intent to improve a man?"

That question produced a sarcastic smile, and this re-ply:

"No, sir. Excuse me. We do it simply because it is 'business.' It is our trade. The *purpose* of it *is* to im-prove the man, but *we* are merely disinterested agents. We are appointed by authority, and haven't anything to say in the matter. We obey orders and leave the conse-quences where they belong. But I am willing to admit this much: we *do* crowd the orders a trifle when we get a chance, which is most of the time. We enjoy it. We are instructed to remind a man a few times of an error; and I don't mind acknowledging that we try to give pretty good measure. And when we get hold of a man of a pecul-iarly sensitive nature, oh, but we do haze him! I have known consciences to come all the way from China and Russia to see a person of that kind put through his paces, on a special occasion. Why, I knew a man of that sort who had accidentally crippled a mulatto baby; the news went abroad, and I wish you may never commit another sin if the consciences didn't flock from all over the earth to enjoy the fun and help his master exercise him. That man walked the floor in torture for forty-eight hours, without eating or sleeping, and then blew his brains out. The child was perfectly well again in three weeks."

"Well, you are a precious crew, not to put it too strong. I think I begin to see, now, why you have always been a trifle inconsistent with me. In your anxiety to get all the juice you can out of a sin, you make a man repent of it in three or four different ways. For instance, you found fault with me for lying to that tramp, and I suffered over that. But it was only yesterday that I told a tramp the square truth, to wit, that, it being regarded as bad citizenship to encourage vagrancy, I would give him nothing. What did you do *then?* Why, you made me say to myself, 'Ah, it would have been so much kinder and more blameless to ease him off with a little white lie, and send him away feeling that if he could not have bread, the gentle treatment was at least something to be grateful for!' Well, I suffered all day about *that.* Three days before I had fed a tramp, and fed him freely, supposing it a virtuous act. Straight off you said, 'O false citizen, to have fed a tramp!' and I suffered as usual. I gave a tramp work; you objected to it—*after* the contract was made, of course; you never speak up beforehand. Next, I *refused* a tramp work; you objected to *that.* Next, I proposed to kill a tramp; you kept me awake all night, oozing remorse at every pore. Sure I was going to be right *this* time, I sent the next tramp away with my benediction; and I wish you may live as long as I do, if you didn't make me smart all night again because I didn't kill him. Is there *any* way of satisfying that malignant invention which is called a conscience?"

"Ha, ha! this is luxury! Go on!"

"But come, now, answer me that question. *Is* there any way?"

"Well, none that I propose to tell *you,* my son. Ass! I don't care *what* act you may turn your hand to, I can straightway whisper a word in your ear and make you think you have committed a dreadful meanness. It is my *business*—and my joy—to make you repent of *every*-thing you do. If I have fooled away any opportunities it was not intentional; I beg to assure you it was not intentional!"

"Don't worry; you haven't missed a trick that I know of. I never did a thing in all my life, virtuous or otherwise, that I didn't repent of in twenty-four hours. In church last Sunday I listened to a charity sermon. My first impulse was to give three hundred and fifty dollars; I repented of that and reduced it a hundred; repented of that and reduced it another hundred; repented of that and reduced it another hundred; repented of that and reduced the remaining fifty to twenty-five; repented of that and came down to fifteen; repented of that and dropped to two dollars and a half; when the plate came around at last, I repented once more and contributed ten cents. Well, when I got home, I did wish to goodness I had that ten cents back again! You never *did* let me get through a charity sermon without having something to sweat about."

"Oh, and I never shall, I never shall. You can always depend on me."

"I think so. Many and many's the restless night I've wanted to take you by the neck. If I could only get hold of you now!"

"Yes, no doubt. But I am not an ass; I am only the saddle of an ass. But go on, go on. You entertain me more than I like to confess."

"I am glad of that. (You will not mind my lying a little, to keep in practice.) Look here; not to be too personal, I think you are about the shabbiest and most contemptible little shriveled up reptile that can be imagined. I am grateful enough that you are invisible to other people, for I should die with shame to be seen with such a mildewed monkey of a conscience as *you* are. Now if you were five or six feet high, and—"

"Oh, come! who is to blame?"

"*I* don't know."

"Why, you are; nobody else."

"Confound, you, I wasn't consulted about your personal appearance."

"I don't care, you had a good deal to do with it, nevertheless. When you were eight or nine years old, I was seven feet high, and as pretty as a picture."

"I wish you had died young! So you have grown the wrong way, have you?"

"Some of us grow one way and some the other. You had a large conscience once; if you've a small conscience now. I reckon there are reasons for it. However, both of us are to blame, you and I. You see, you used to be conscientious about a great many things; morbidly so, I may say. It was a great many years ago. You probably do not remember it, now. Well, I took a great interest in my work, and I so enjoyed the anguish which certain pet sins of yours afflicted you with, that I kept pelting at you until I rather overdid the matter. You began to rebel. Of course I began to lose ground, then, and shrivel a little—diminish in stature, get moldy, and grow deformed. The more I weakened, the more stubbornly you fastened on to those particular sins; till at last the places on my person that represent those vices became as callous as sharkskin. Take smoking, for instance. I played that card a little too long, and I lost. When people plead with you at this late day to quit that vice, that old callous place seems to enlarge and cover me all over like a shirt of mail. It exerts a mysterious, smothering effect; and presently I, your faithful hater, your devoted Conscience, go sound asleep! Sound? It is no name for it. I couldn't hear it thunder at such a time. You have some few other vices—perhaps eighty, or maybe ninety—that affect me in much the same way."

"This is flattering; you must be asleep a good part of your time."

"Yes, of late years. I should be asleep *all* the time, but for the help I get."

"Who helps you?"

"Other consciences. Whenever a person whose conscience I am acquainted with tries to plead with you about the vices you are callous to, I get my friend to give his client a pang concerning some villainy of his own, and that shuts off his meddling and starts him off to hunt personal consolation. My field of usefulness is about trimmed down to tramps, budding authoresses, and that line of goods, now; but don't you worry—I'll harry you on *them* while they last! Just you put your trust in me."

"I think I can. But if you had only been good enough to mention these facts some thirty years ago, I should have turned my particular attention to sin, and I think that by this time I should not only have had you pretty permanently asleep on the entire list of human vices, but reduced to the size of a homeopathic pill, at that. That is about the style of conscience *I* am pining for. If I only had you shrunk down to a homeopathic pill, and could get my hands on you, would I put you in a glass case for a keepsake? No, sir. I would give you to a yellow dog! That is where *you* ought to be—you and all your tribe. You are not fit to be in society, in my opinion. Now another question. Do you know a good many consciences in this section?"

"Plenty of them."

"I would give anything to see some of them! Could you bring them here? And would they be visible to me?"

"Certainly not."

"I suppose I ought to have known that, without asking. But no matter, you can describe them. Tell me about my neighbor Thompson's conscience, please."

"Very well. I know him intimately; have known him many years. I knew him when he was eleven feet high and of a faultless figure. But he is very rusty and tough and misshapen now, and hardly ever interests himself about anything. As to his present size—well, he sleeps in a cigar box."

"Likely enough. There are few smaller, meaner men in this region than Hugh Thompson. Do you know Robinson's conscience?"

"Yes. He is a shade under four and a half feet high; used to be a blond; is a brunet, now, but still shapely and comely."

"Well, Robinson is a good fellow. Do you know Tom Smith's conscience?"

"I have known him from childhood. He was thirteen inches high, and rather sluggish, when he was two years old—as nearly all of us are, at that age. He is thirty-seven feet high, now, and the stateliest figure in America. His legs are still racked with growing pains, but he has a good time, nevertheless. Never sleeps. He is the most active and energetic member of the New England Conscience Club; is president of it. Night and day you can find him pegging away at Smith, panting with his labor, sleeves rolled up, countenance all alive with enjoyment. He has got his victim splendidly dragooned, now. He can make poor Smith imagine that the most innocent little thing he does is an odious sin; and then he sets to work and almost tortures the soul out of him about it."

"Smith is the noblest man in all this section, and the purest; and yet is always breaking his heart because he cannot be good! Only a conscience *could* find pleasure in heaping agony upon a spirit like that. Do you know my Aunt Mary's conscience?"

"I have seen her at a distance, but am not acquainted with her. She lives in the open air altogether, because no door is large enough to admit her."

"I can believe that. Let me see. Do you know the conscience of that publisher who once stole some sketches of mine for a 'series' of his, and then left me to pay the law expenses I had to incur in order to choke him off?"

"Yes. He has a wide fame. He was exhibited, a month ago, with some other antiquities, for the benefit of a recent Member of the Cabinet's conscience, that was starving in exile. Tickets and fares were high, but I traveled for nothing by pretending to be the conscience of an editor, and got in for half-price by representing myself to be the conscience of a clergyman. However, the publisher's conscience, which was to have been the main feature of the entertainment, was a failure—as an exhibition. He was there, but what of that? The management had provided a microscope with a magnifying power of only thirty thousand diameters, and so nobody got to see him, after all. There was great and general dissatisfaction, of course, but—"

Just here there was an eager footstep on the stair; I opened the door, and my Aunt Mary burst into the room. It was a joyful meeting, and a cheery bombardment of questions and answers concerning family matters ensued. By and by my aunt said:

"But I am going to abuse you a little now. You promised me, the day I saw you last, that you would look after the needs of the poor family around the corner as faithfully as I had done it myself. Well, I found out by accident that you failed of your promise. *Was* that right?"

In simple truth, I never had thought of that family a second time! And now such a splintering pang of guilt shot through me! I glanced up at my Conscience. Plainly, my heavy heart was affecting him. His body was drooping forward; he seemed about to fall from the bookcase. My aunt continued:

"And think how you have neglected my poor protégé

at the almshouse, you dear, hardhearted promise-breaker!"

I blushed scarlet, and my tongue was tied. As the sense of my guilty negligence waxed sharper and stronger, my Conscience began to sway heavily back and forth; and when my aunt, after a little pause, said in a grieved tone, "Since you never once went to see her, maybe it will not distress you now to know that that poor child died, months ago, utterly friendless and forsaken!" my Conscience could no longer bear up under the weight of my sufferings, but tumbled headlong from his high perch and struck the floor with a dull, leaden thump. He lay there writhing with pain and quaking with apprehension, but straining every muscle in frantic efforts to get up. In a fever of expectancy I sprang to the door, locked it, placed my back against it, and bent a watchful gaze upon my struggling master. Already my fingers were itching to begin their murderous work.

"Oh, what *can* be the matter!" exclaimed my aunt, shrinking from me, and following with her frightened eyes the direction of mine. My breath was coming in short, quick gasps now, and my excitement was almost uncontrollable. My aunt cried out:

"Oh, do not look so! You appall me! Oh, what can the matter be? What is it you see? Why do you stare so? Why do you work your fingers like that?"

"Peace, woman!" I said, in a hoarse whisper. "Look elsewhere; pay no attention to me; it is nothing—nothing. I am often this way. It will pass in a moment. It comes from smoking too much."

My injured lord was up, wild-eyed with terror, and trying to hobble toward the door. I could hardly breathe, I was so wrought up. My aunt wrung her hands, and said:

"Oh, I knew how it would be; I knew it would come to this at last! Oh, I implore you to crush out that fatal habit while it may yet be time! You must not, you shall not be deaf to my supplications longer!" My struggling Conscience showed sudden signs of weariness! "Oh, promise me you will throw off this hateful slavery of tobacco!" My Conscience began to reel drowsily, and grope with his hands—enchanting spectacle! "I beg you, I beseech you, I implore you! Your reason is deserting

you! There is madness in your eye! It flames with frenzy!
Oh, hear me, hear me, and be saved! See, I plead with
you on my very knees!" As she sank before me my Conscience reeled again, and then drooped languidly to the
floor, blinking toward me a last supplication for mercy,
with heavy eyes. "Oh, promise, or you are lost! Promise,
and be redeemed! Promise! Promise and live!" With a
long-drawn sigh my conquered Conscience closed his
eyes and fell fast asleep!

With an exultant shout I sprang past my aunt, and in
an instant I had my lifelong foe by the throat. After so
many years of waiting and longing, he was mine at last. I
tore him to shreds and fragments. I rent the fragments
to bits. I cast the bleeding rubbish into the fire, and
drew into my nostrils the grateful incense of my burnt
offering. At last, and forever, my Conscience was dead!

I was a free man! I turned upon my poor aunt, who
was almost petrified with terror, and shouted:

"Out of this with your paupers, your charities, your
reforms, your pestilent morals! You behold before you a
man whose life-conflict is done, whose soul is at peace;
a man whose heart is dead to sorrow, dead to suffering,
dead to remorse; a man WITHOUT A CONSCIENCE! In my
joy I spare you, though I could throttle you and never
feel a pang! Fly!"

She fled. Since that day my life is all bliss. Bliss, un-
alloyed bliss. Nothing in all the world could persuade
me to have a conscience again. I settled all my old out-
standing scores, and began the world anew. I killed
thirty-eight persons during the first two weeks—all of
them on account of ancient grudges. I burned a dwelling
that interrupted my view. I swindled a widow and some
orphans out of their last cow, which is a very good one,
though not thoroughbred, I believe. I have also committed scores of crimes, of various kinds, and have enjoyed
my work exceedingly, whereas it would formerly have
broken my heart and turned my hair gray, I have no
doubt.

In conclusion I wish to state, by way of advertisement, that medical colleges desiring assorted tramps for
scientific purposes, either by the gross, by cord measure-
ment, or per ton, will do well to examine the lot in my

cellar before purchasing elsewhere, as these were all selected and prepared by myself, and can be had at a low rate, because I wish to clear out my stock and get ready for the spring trade.

The Stolen White Elephant[1]

I.

THE following curious history was related to me by a chance railway acquaintance. He was a gentleman more than seventy years of age, and his thoroughly good and gentle face and earnest and sincere manner imprinted the unmistakable stamp of truth upon every statement which fell from his lips. He said:

You know in what reverence the royal white elephant of Siam is held by the people of that country. You know it is sacred to kings, only kings may possess it, and that it is indeed in a measure even superior to kings, since it receives not merely honor but worship. Very well; five years ago, when the troubles concerning the frontier line arose between Great Britain and Siam, it was presently manifest that Siam had been in the wrong. Therefore every reparation was quickly made, and the British representative stated that he was satisfied and the past should be forgotten. This greatly relieved the King of Siam, and partly as a token of gratitude, but partly also, perhaps, to wipe out any little remaining vestige of unpleasantness which England might feel toward him, he wished to send the Queen a present—the sole sure way of propitiating an enemy, according to Oriental ideas.

[1] Left out of "A Tramp Abroad," because it was feared that some of the particulars had been exaggerated, and that others were not true. Before these suspicions had been proven groundless, the book had gone to press.—M. T.

This present ought not only to be a royal one, but tran-
scendently royal. Wherefore, what offering could be so
meet as that of a white elephant? My position in the Indian civil service was such that I was deemed peculiarly
worthy of the honor of conveying the present to Her
Majesty. A ship was fitted out for me and my servants
and the officers and attendants of the elephant, and in
due time I arrived in New York harbor and placed my
royal charge in admirable quarters in Jersey City. It was
necessary to remain awhile in order to recruit the animal's health before resuming the voyage.

All went well during a fortnight; then my calamities
began. The white elephant was stolen! I was called up at
dead of night and informed of this fearful misfortune.
For some moments I was beside myself with terror and
anxiety; I was helpless. Then I grew calmer and collected
my faculties. I soon saw my course—for indeed there was
but the one course for an intelligent man to pursue. Late
as it was, I flew to New York and got a policeman to
conduct me to the headquarters of the detective force.
Fortunately I arrived in time, though the chief of the
force, the celebrated Inspector Blunt, was just on the
point of leaving for his home. He was a man of middle
size and compact frame, and when he was thinking
deeply he had a way of knitting his brows and tapping
his forehead reflectively with his finger, which impressed
you at once with the conviction that you stood in the
presence of a person of no common order. The very
sight of him gave me confidence and made me hopeful.
I stated my errand. It did not flurry him in the least; it
had no more visible effect upon his iron self-possession
than if I had told him somebody had stolen my dog. He
motioned me to a seat, and said calmly:

"Allow me to think a moment, please."

So saying, he sat down at his office table and leaned
his head upon his hand. Several clerks were at work
at the other end of the room; the scratching of their
pens was all the sound I heard during the next six or
seven minutes. Meantime the inspector sat there, buried
in thought. Finally he raised his head, and there was
that in the firm lines of his face which showed me that his

brain had done its work and his plan was made. Said he
—and his voice was low and impressive—

"This is no ordinary case. Every step must be warily
taken; each step must be made sure before the next is
ventured. And secrecy must be observed—secrecy pro-
found and absolute. Speak to no one about the matter,
not even the reporters. I will take care of *them;* I will
see that they get only what it may suit my ends to let
them know." He touched a bell; a youth appeared.
"Alaric, tell the reporters to remain for the present."
The boy retired. "Now let us proceed to business—and
systematically. Nothing can be accomplished in this trade
of mine without strict and minute method."

He took a pen and some paper. "Now. Name of the
elephant?"

"Hassan Ben Ali Ben Selim Abdallah Mohammed
Moisé Alhammal Jamsetjejeebhoy Dhuleep Sultan Ebu
Bhudpoor."

"Very well. Given name?"

"Jumbo."

"Very well. Place of birth?"

"The capital city of Siam."

"Parents living?"

"No, dead."

"Had they any other issue besides this one?"

"None. He was an only child."

"Very well. These matters are sufficient under that
head. Now please describe the elephant, and leave out
no particular, however insignificant—that is, insignificant
from *your* point of view. To men in my profession there
are no insignificant particulars; they do not exist."

I described, he wrote. When I was done, he said:

"Now listen. If I have made any mistakes, correct
me."

He read as follows:

"Height, 19 feet; length from apex of forehead to insertion of tail, 26 feet; length of trunk, 16 feet; length
of tail, 6 feet; total length, including trunk and tail, 48
feet; length of tusks, 9½ feet; ears in keeping with these
dimensions; footprint resembles the mark left when one
upends a barrel in the snow; color of the elephant, a dull
white; has a hole the size of a plate in each ear for the

insertion of jewelry, and possesses the habit in a remarkable degree of squirting water upon spectators and of
maltreating with his trunk not only such persons as he is
acquainted with, but even entire strangers; limps slightly
with his right hind leg, and has a small scar in his left
armpit caused by a former boil; had on, when stolen, a
castle containing seats for fifteen persons, and a gold-
cloth saddle-blanket the size of an ordinary carpet."

There were no mistakes. The inspector touched the
bell, handed the description to Alaric, and said:

"Have fifty thousand copies of this printed at once
and mailed to every detective office and pawnbroker's
shop on the continent." Alaric retired. "There—so far, so
good. Next, I must have a photograph of the property."

I gave him one. He examined it critically, and said:

"It must do, since we can do no better; but he has
his trunk curled up and tucked into his mouth. That is
unfortunate, and is calculated to mislead, for of course
he does not usually have it in that position." He touched
his bell.

"Alaric, have fifty thousand copies of this photograph
made, the first thing in the morning, and mail them with
the descriptive circulars."

Alaric retired to execute his orders. The inspector
said:

"It will be necessary to offer a reward, of course. Now
as to the amount?"

"What sum would you suggest?"

"To *begin* with, I should say, well, twenty-five thousand dollars. It is an intricate and difficult business;
there are a thousand avenues of escape and opportunities
of concealment. These thieves have friends and pals
everywhere—"

"Bless me, do you know who they are?"

The wary face, practiced in concealing the thoughts
and feelings within, gave me no token, nor yet the reply-
ing words, so quietly uttered.

"Never mind about that. I may, and I may not. We
generally gather a pretty shrewd inkling of who our man
is by the manner of his work and the size of the game he
goes after. We are not dealing with a pickpocket or a hall
thief, now, make up your mind to that. This property

was not 'lifted' by a novice. But, as I was saying, considering the amount of travel which will have to be done, and the diligence with which the thieves will cover up their traces as they move along, twenty-five thousand may be too small a sum to offer, yet I think it worth while to start with that."

So we determined upon that figure, as a beginning. Then this man, whom nothing escaped which could by any possibility be made to serve as a clew, said:

"There are cases in detective history to show that criminals have been detected through peculiarities in their appetites. Now, what does this elephant eat, and how much?"

"Well, as to *what* he eats, he will eat *anything*. He will eat a man, he will eat a Bible, he will eat anything *between* a man and a Bible."

"Good, very good indeed, but too general. Details are necessary, details are the only valuable things in our trade. Very well—as to men. At one meal—or, if you prefer, during one day—how many men will he eat, if fresh?"

"He would not care whether they were fresh or not; at a single meal he would eat five ordinary men."

"Very good; five men; we will put that down. What nationalities would he prefer?"

"He is indifferent about nationalities. He prefers acquaintances, but is not prejudiced against strangers."

"Very good. Now, as to Bibles. How many Bibles would he eat at a meal?"

"He would eat an entire edition."

"It is hardly succinct enough. Do you mean the ordinary octavo, or the family illustrated?"

"I think he would be indifferent to illustrations; that is, I think he would not value illustrations above simple letterpress."

"No, you do not get my idea. I refer to bulk. The ordinary octavo Bible weighs about two pounds and a half, while the great quarto with the illustrations weighs ten or twelve. How many Doré Bibles would he eat at a meal?"

"If you knew this elephant, you could not ask. He would take what they had."

"Well, put it in dollars and cents, then. We must get at it somehow. The Doré costs a hundred dollars a copy, Russia leather, beveled."

"He would require about fifty thousand dollars' worth —say an edition of five hundred copies."

"Now that is more exact. I will put that down. Very well; he likes men and Bibles; so far, so good. What else will he eat? I want particulars."

"He will leave Bibles to eat bricks, he will leave bricks to eat bottles, he will leave bottles to eat clothing, he will leave clothing to eat cats, he will leave cats to eat oysters, he will leave oysters to eat ham, he will leave ham to eat sugar, he will leave sugar to eat pie, he will leave pie to eat potatoes, he will leave potatoes to eat bran, he will leave bran to eat hay, he will leave hay to eat oats, he will leave oats to eat rice, for he was mainly raised on it. There is nothing whatever that he will not eat but European butter, and he would eat that if he could taste it."

"Very good. General quantity at a meal—say about—"

"Well, anywhere from a quarter to half a ton."

"And he drinks—"

"Everything that is fluid. Milk, water, whisky, molasses, castor oil, camphene, carbolic acid—it is no use to go into particulars; whatever fluid occurs to you set it down. He will drink anything that is fluid, except European coffee."

"Very good. As to quantity?"

"Put it down five to fifteen barrels—his thirst varies; his other appetites do not."

"These things are unusual. They ought to furnish quite good clews toward tracing him."

He touched the bell.

"Alaric, summon Captain Burns."

Burns appeared. Inspector Blunt unfolded the whole matter to him, detail by detail. Then he said in the clear, decisive tones of a man whose plans are clearly defined in his head, and who is accustomed to command:

"Captain Burns, detail Detectives Jones, Davis, Halsey, Bates, and Hackett to shadow the elephant."

"Yes, sir."

"Detail Detectives Moses, Dakin, Murphy, Rogers,

Tupper, Higgins, and Bartholomew to shadow the thieves."

"Yes, sir."

"Place a strong guard—a guard of thirty picked men, with a relief of thirty—over the place from whence the elephant was stolen, to keep strict watch there night and day, and allow none to approach—except reporters—without written authority from me."

"Yes, sir."

"Place detectives in plain clothes in the railway, steamship, and ferry depots, and upon all roadways leading out of Jersey City, with orders to search all suspicious persons."

"Yes, sir."

"Furnish all these men with photograph and accompanying description of the elephant, and instruct them to search all trains and outgoing ferryboats and other vessels."

"Yes, sir."

"If the elephant should be found, let him be seized, and the information forwarded to me by telegraph."

"Yes, sir."

"Let me be informed at once if any clews should be found—footprints of the animal, or anything of that kind."

"Yes, sir."

"Get an order commanding the harbor police to patrol the frontages vigilantly."

"Yes, sir."

"Despatch detectives in plain clothes over all the railways, north as far as Canada, west as far as Ohio, south as far as Washington."

"Yes, sir."

"Place experts in all the telegraph offices to listen to all messages; and let them require that all cipher despatches be interpreted to them."

"Yes, sir."

"Let all these things be done with the utmost secrecy—mind, the most impenetrable secrecy."

"Yes, sir."

"Report to me promptly at the usual hour."

"Yes, sir."

"Go!"

"Yes, sir."

He was gone.

Inspector Blunt was silent and thoughtful a moment, while the fire in his eye cooled down and faded out. Then he turned to me and said in a placid voice:

"I am not given to boasting, it is not my habit; but— we shall find the elephant."

I shook him warmly by the hand and thanked him; and I *felt* my thanks, too. The more I had seen of the man the more I liked him, and the more I admired him and marveled over the mysterious wonders of his profession. Then we parted for the night, and I went home with a far happier heart than I had carried with me to his office.

II.

NEXT morning it was all in the newspapers, in the minutest detail. It even had additions—consisting of Detective This, Detective That, and Detective The Other's "Theory" as to how the robbery was done, who the robbers were, and whither they had flown with their booty. There were eleven of these theories, and they covered all the possibilities; and this single fact shows what independent thinkers detectives are. No two theories were alike, or even much resembled each other, save in one striking particular, and in that one all the eleven theories were absolutely agreed. That was, that although the rear of my building was torn out and the only door remained locked, the elephant had not been removed through the rent, but by some other (undiscovered) outlet. All agreed that the robbers had made that rent only to mislead the detectives. That never would have occurred to me or to any other layman, perhaps, but it had not deceived the detectives for a moment. Thus, what I had supposed was the only thing that had no mystery about it was in fact the very thing I had gone furthest astray in. The eleven theories all named the supposed robbers, but no two named the same robbers; the total number of suspected persons was thirty-seven. The various newspaper accounts all closed with the most important opinion of all —that of Chief Inspector Blunt. A portion of this statement read as follows:

"The chief knows who the two principals are, namely, 'Brick' Duffy and 'Red' McFadden. Ten days before the robbery was achieved he was already aware that it was to be attempted, and had quietly proceeded to shadow these two noted villains; but unfortunately on the night in question their track was lost, and before it could be found again the bird was flown—that is, the elephant.

"Duffy and McFadden are the boldest scoundrels in the profession; the chief has reasons for believing that they are the men who stole the stove out of the detective headquarters on a bitter night last winter—in consequence of which the chief and every detective present were in the hands of the physicians before morning, some with frozen feet, others with frozen fingers, ears, and other members."

When I read the first half of that I was more astonished than ever at the wonderful sagacity of this strange man. He not only saw everything in the present with a clear eye, but even the future could not be hidden from him. I was soon at his office, and said I could not help wishing he had had those men arrested, and so prevented the trouble and loss; but his reply was simple and unanswerable.

"It is not our province to prevent crime, but to punish it. We cannot punish it until it is committed."

I remarked that the secrecy with which we had begun had been marred by the newspapers; not only all our facts but all our plans and purposes had been revealed; even all the suspected persons had been named; these would doubtless disguise themselves now, or go into hiding.

"Let them. They will find that when I am ready for them my hand will descend upon them, in their secret places, as unerringly as the hand of fate. As to the newspapers, we *must* keep in with them. Fame, reputation, constant public mention—these are the detective's bread and butter. He must publish his facts, else he will be supposed to have none; he must publish his theory, for nothing is so strange or striking as a detective's theory, or brings him so much wondering respect; we must publish our plans, for these the journals insist upon having, and we could not deny them without offending. We must constantly show the public what we are doing, or they will believe we are doing nothing. It is much pleasanter to have a newspaper say, 'Inspector Blunt's ingenious and extraordinary theory is as follows,' than to have it say some harsh thing, or, worse still, some sarcastic one."

"I see the force of what you say. But I noticed that in one part of your remarks in the papers this morning you refused to reveal your opinion upon a certain minor point."

"Yes, we always do that; it has a good effect. Besides, I had not formed any opinion on that point, anyway."

I deposited a considerable sum of money with the inspector, to meet current expenses, and sat down to wait for news. We were expecting the telegrams to begin to arrive at any moment now. Meantime I reread the newspapers and also our descriptive circular, and observed that our $25,000 reward seemed to be offered only to detectives. I said I thought it ought to be offered to anybody who would catch the elephant. The inspector said:

"It is the detectives who will find the elephant, hence the reward will go to the right place. If other people found the animal, it would only be by watching the detectives and taking advantage of clews and indications stolen from them, and that would entitle the detectives to the reward, after all. The proper office of a reward is to stimulate the men who deliver up their time and their trained sagacities to this sort of work, and not to confer benefits upon chance citizens who stumble upon a capture without having earned the benefits by their own merits and labors."

This was reasonable enough, certainly. Now the telegraphic machine in the corner began to click, and the following despatch was the result:

FLOWER STATION, N. Y., 7:30 A.M.
Have got a clew. Found a succession of deep tracks across a farm near here. Followed them two miles east without result; think elephant went west. Shall now shadow him in that direction.

DARLEY, *Detective.*

"Darley's one of the best men on the force," said the inspector. "We shall hear from him again before long."
Telegram No. 2 came:

BARKER'S, N. J., 7:40 A.M.

Just arrived. Glass factory broken open here during night, and eight hundred bottles taken. Only water in large quantity near here is five miles distant. Shall strike for there. Elephant will be thirsty. Bottles were empty.

BAKER, *Detective.*

"That promises well, too," said the inspector. "I told you the creature's appetites would not be bad clews." Telegram No. 3:

TAYLORVILLE, L. I., 8:15 A.M.

A haystack near here disappeared during night. Probably eaten. Have got a clew, and am off.

HUBBARD, *Detective.*

"How he does move around!" said the inspector. "I knew we had a difficult job on hand, but we shall catch him yet."

FLOWER STATION, N.Y., 9 A.M.

Shadowed the tracks three miles westward. Large, deep, and ragged. Have just met a farmer who says they are not elephant tracks. Says they are holes where he dug up saplings for shade trees when ground was frozen last winter. Give me orders how to proceed.

DARLEY, *Detective.*

"Aha! a confederate of the thieves! The thing grows warm," said the inspector.

He dictated the following telegram to Darley:

Arrest the man and force him to name his pals. Continue to follow the tracks—to the Pacific, if necessary.

Chief BLUNT.

Next telegram:

CONEY POINT, PA. 8:45 A.M.

Gas office broken open here during night and three months' unpaid gas bills taken. Have got a clew and am away.

MURPHY, *Detective.*

"Heavens!" said the inspector; "would he eat gas bills?"

"Through ignorance, yes; but they cannot support life. At least, unassisted."

Now came this exciting telegram:

IRONVILLE, N. Y., 9:30 A.M.

Just arrived. This village in consternation. Elephant passed through here at five this morning. Some say he went east, some say west, some north, some south—but all say they did not wait to notice particularly. He killed a horse; have secured a piece of it for a clew. Killed it with his trunk; from style of blow, think he struck it left-handed. From position in which horse lies, think elephant traveled northward along line of Berkley railway. Has four and half hours' start, but I move on his track at once.

HAWES, *Detective.*

I uttered exclamations of joy. The inspector was as self-contained as a graven image. He calmly touched his bell.

"Alaric, send Captain Burns here."

Burns appeared.

"How many men are ready for instant orders?"

"Ninety-six, sir."

"Send them north at once. Let them concentrate along the line of the Berkley road north of Ironville."

"Yes, sir."

"Let them conduct their movements with the utmost secrecy. As fast as others are at liberty, hold them for orders."

"Yes, sir."

"Go!"

"Yes, sir."

Presently came another telegram:

SAGE CORNERS, N. Y., 10:30.

Just arrived. Elephant passed through here at 8:15. All escaped from the town but a policeman. Apparently elephant did not strike at policeman, but at the lamppost. Got both. I have secured a portion of the policeman as clew.

STUMM, *Detective.*

"So the elephant has turned westward," said the inspector. "However, he will not escape, for my men are scattered all over that region."

The next telegram said:

GLOVER'S, 11:15

Just arrived. Village deserted, except sick and aged. Elephant passed through three quarters of an hour ago. The anti-temperance mass meeting was in session; he put his trunk in at a window and washed it out with water from cistern. Some swallowed it—since dead; several drowned. Detectives Cross and O'Shaughnessy were passing through town, but going south—so missed elephant. Whole region for many miles around in terror—people flying from their homes. Wherever they turn they meet elephant, and many are killed.

BRANT, *Detective.*

I could have shed tears, this havoc so distressed me. But the inspector only said:

"You see—we are closing in on him. He feels our presence; he has turned eastward again."

Yet further troublous news was in store for us. The telegraph brought this:

HOGANPORT, 12:19.

Just arrived. Elephant passed through half an hour ago, creating wildest fright and excitement. Elephant raged around streets; two plumbers going by, killed one—other escaped. Regret general.

O'FLAHERTY, *Detective.*

"Now he is right in the midst of my men," said the inspector. "Nothing can save him."

A succession of telegrams came from detectives who were scattered through New Jersey and Pennsylvania, and who were following clews consisting of ravaged barns, factories, and Sunday school libraries, with high hopes—hopes amounting to certainties, indeed. The inspector said:

"I wish I could communicate with them and order them north, but that is impossible. A detective only visits a telegraph office to send his report; then he is off again, and you don't know where to put your hand on him."

Now came this despatch:

BRIDGEPORT, CT., 12:15.
Barnum offers rate of $4,000 a year for exclusive privilege of using elephant as traveling advertising medium from now till detectives find him. Wants to paste circus posters on him. Desires immediate answer.

BOGGS, *Detective*.

"That is perfectly absurd!" I exclaimed.

"Of course it is," said the inspector. "Evidently Mr. Barnum, who thinks he is so sharp, does not know me—but I know him."

Then he dictated this answer to the despatch:

Mr. Barnum's offer declined. Make it $7,000 or nothing.

Chief BLUNT.

"There. We shall not have to wait long for an answer. Mr. Barnum is not at home; he is in the telegraph office —it is his way when he has business on hand. Inside of three—"

DONE.—P. T. BARNUM.

So interrupted the clicking telegraphic instrument. Before I could make a comment upon this extraordinary episode, the following despatch carried my thoughts into another and very distressing channel:

BOLIVIA, N. Y., 12:50.
Elephant arrived here from the south and passed through toward the forest at 11:50, dispersing a funeral on the way, and diminishing the mourners by two. Citizens fired some small cannon balls into him, and then fled. Detective Burke and I arrived ten minutes later, from the north, but mistook some excavations for footprints, and so lost a good deal of time; but at last we struck the right trail and followed it to the woods. We then got down on our hands and knees and continued to keep a sharp eye on the track, and so shadowed it into the brush. Burke was in advance. Unfortunately the animal had stopped to rest; therefore, Burke having his head down, intent upon

the track, butted up against the elephant's hind legs before he was aware of his vicinity. Burke instantly rose to his feet, seized the tail, and exclaimed joyfully, "I claim the re—" but got no further, for a single blow of the huge trunk laid the brave fellow's fragments low in death. I fled rearward, and the elephant turned and shadowed me to the edge of the wood, making tremendous speed, and I should inevitably have been lost, but that the remains of the funeral providentially intervened again and diverted his attention. I have just learned that nothing of that funeral is now left; but this is no loss, for there is an abundance of material for another. Meantime, the elephant has disappeared again.

MULROONEY, *Detective.*

We heard no news except from the diligent and confident detectives scattered about New Jersey, Pennsylvania, Delaware, and Virginia—who were all following fresh and encouraging clews—until shortly after 2 P.M., when this telegram came:

BAXTER CENTER, 2:15.

Elephant been here, plastered over with circus bills, and broke up a revival, striking down and damaging many who were on the point of entering upon a better life. Citizens penned him up, and established a guard. When Detective Brown and I arrived, some time after, we entered enclosure and proceeded to identify elephant by photograph and description. All marks tallied exactly except one, which we could not see—the boil-scar under armpit. To make sure, Brown crept under to look, and was immediately brained —that is, head crushed and destroyed, though nothing issued from debris. All fled; so did elephant, striking right and left with much effect. Has escaped, but left bold blood track from cannon-wounds. Rediscovery certain. He broke southward, through a dense forest.

BRENT, *Detective.*

That was the last telegram. At nightfall a fog shut down which was so dense that objects but three feet away could not be discerned. This lasted all night. The ferry boats and even the omnibuses had to stop running.

III.

NEXT morning the papers were as full of detective theories as before; they had all our tragic facts in detail also, and a great many more which they had received from their telegraphic correspondents. Column after column was occupied, a third of its way down, with glaring headlines, which it made my heart sick to read. Their general tone was like this:

"THE WHITE ELEPHANT AT LARGE! HE MOVES UPON HIS FATAL MARCH! WHOLE VILLAGES DESERTED BY THEIR FRIGHT-STRICKEN OCCUPANTS! PALE TERROR GOES BEFORE HIM, DEATH AND DEVASTATION FOLLOW AFTER! AFTER THESE, THE DETECTIVES. BARNS DESTROYED, FACTORIES GUTTED, HARVESTS DEVOURED, PUBLIC ASSEMBLAGES DISPERSED, ACCOMPANIED BY SCENES OF CARNAGE IMPOSSIBLE TO DESCRIBE! THEORIES OF THIRTY-FOUR OF THE MOST DISTINGUISHED DETECTIVES ON THE FORCE! THEORY OF CHIEF BLUNT!"

"There!" said Inspector Blunt, almost betrayed into excitement, "this is magnificent! This is the greatest windfall that any detective organization ever had. The fame of it will travel to the ends of the earth, and endure to the end of time, and my name with it."

But there was no joy for me. I felt as if I had committed all those red crimes, and that the elephant was only my irresponsible agent. And how the list had grown! In one place he had "interfered with an election and killed five repeaters." He had followed this act with the destruction of two poor fellows, named O'Donohue and Mc-Flannigan, who had "found a refuge in the home of the oppressed of all lands only the day before, and were in the act of exercising for the first time the noble right of American citizens at the polls, when stricken down by the relentless hand of the Scourge of Siam." In another, he had "found a crazy sensation-preacher preparing his next season's heroic attacks on the dance, the theater, and other things which can't strike back, and had stepped on him." And in still another place he had "killed a lightning-rod agent." And so the list went on, growing redder and redder, and more and more heartbreaking. Sixty persons had been killed, and two hundred and forty wounded. All the accounts bore just testimony to the activity and devotion of the detectives, and all closed with the remark that "three hundred thousand citizens and four detectives saw the dread creature, and two of the latter he destroyed."

I dreaded to hear the telegraphic instrument begin to click again. By and by the messages began to pour in, but I was happily disappointed in their nature. It was soon apparent that all trace of the elephant was lost. The fog had enabled him to search out a good hiding place unobserved. Telegrams from the most absurdly distant points reported that a dim vast mass had been glimpsed there through the fog at such and such an hour, and was "undoubtedly the elephant." This dim vast mass had been glimpsed in New Haven, in New Jersey, in Pennsylvania, in interior New York, in Brooklyn, and even in the city of New York itself! But in all cases the dim vast mass had vanished quickly and left no trace. Every detective of the large force scattered over this huge extent of country sent his hourly report, and each and every one of them had a clew, and was shadowing something, and was hot upon the heels of it.

But the day passed without other result.

The next day the same.

The next just the same.

The newspaper reports began to grow monotonous with facts that amounted to nothing, clews which led to nothing, and theories which had nearly exhausted the elements which surprise and delight and dazzle.

By advice of the inspector I doubled the reward.

Four more dull days followed. Then came a bitter blow to the poor, hard-working detectives—the journalists declined to print their theories, and coldly said, "Give us a rest."

Two weeks after the elephant's disappearance I raised the reward to $75,000 by the inspector's advice. It was a great sum, but I felt that I would rather sacrifice my whole private fortune than lose my credit with my government. Now that the detectives were in adversity, the newspapers turned upon them, and began to fling the most stinging sarcasms at them. This gave the minstrels an idea, and they dressed themselves as detectives and hunted the elephant on the stage in the most extravagant way. The caricaturists made pictures of detectives scanning the country with spyglasses, while the elephant, at their backs, stole apples out of their pockets. And they made all sorts of ridiculous pictures of the detective badge—you have seen that badge printed in gold on the back of detective novels, no doubt—it is a wide-staring eye, with the legend, "WE NEVER SLEEP." When detectives called for a drink, the would-be facetious barkeeper resurrected an obsolete form of expression and said, "Will you have an eye-opener?" All the air was thick with sarcasms.

But there was one man who moved calm, untouched, unaffected, through it all. It was that heart of oak, the Chief Inspector. His brave eye never drooped, his serene confidence never wavered. He always said:

"Let them rail on; he laughs best who laughs last."

My admiration for the man grew into a species of worship. I was at his side always. His office had become an unpleasant place to me, and now became daily more and more so. Yet if he could endure it I meant to do so also; at least, as long as I could. So I came regularly, and stayed—the only outsider who seemed to be capable of it. Everybody wondered how I could; and often it seemed to me that I must desert, but at such times I looked into that calm and apparently unconscious face, and held my ground.

About three weeks after the elephant's disappearance I was about to say, one morning, that I should *have* to strike my colors and retire, when the great detective arrested the thought by proposing one more superb and masterly move.

This was to compromise with the robbers. The fertility of this man's invention exceeded anything I have ever seen, and I have had a wide intercourse with the world's finest minds. He said he was confident he could compromise for $100,000 and recover the elephant. I said I believed I could scrape the amount together, but what would become of the poor detectives who had worked so faithfully? He said:

"In compromises they always get half."

This removed my only objection. So the inspector wrote two notes, in this form:

> DEAR MADAM—Your husband can make a large sum of money (and be entirely protected from the law) by making an immediate appointment with me.
> *Chief* BLUNT.

He sent one of these by his confidential messenger to the "reputed wife" of Brick Duffy, and the other to the reputed wife of Red McFadden.

Within the hour these offensive answers came:

> YE OWLD FOOL: brick McDuffey's bin ded 2 yere.
> BRIDGET MAHONEY.

> CHIEF BAT—Red McFadden is hung and in heving 18 month. Any Ass but a detective knose that.
> MARY O'HOOLIGAN.

"I had long suspected these facts," said the inspector; "this testimony proves the unerring accuracy of my instinct."

The moment one resource failed him he was ready with another. He immediately wrote an advertisement for the morning papers, and I kept a copy of it.

> A.—xwblv. 242 N. Tjnd—fz328wmlg. Ozpo—; 2 mo. ogw. Mum.

He said that if the thief was alive this would bring him to the usual rendezvous. He further explained that the usual rendezvous was a place where all business affairs between detectives and criminals were conducted. This meeting would take place at twelve the next night.

We could do nothing till then, and I lost no time in getting out of the office, and was grateful indeed for the privilege.

At 11 the next night I brought $100,000 in banknotes and put them into the chief's hands, and shortly afterward he took his leave, with the brave old undimmed confidence in his eye. An almost intolerable hour dragged to a close; then I heard his welcome tread, and rose gasping and tottered to meet him. How his fine eyes flamed with triumph! He said:

"We've compromised! The jokers will sing a different tune tomorrow! Follow me!"

He took a lighted candle and strode down into the vast vaulted basement where sixty detectives always slept, and where a score were now playing cards to while the time. I followed close after him. He walked swiftly down to the dim remote end of the place, and just as I succumbed to the pangs of suffocation and was swooning away he stumbled and fell over the outlying members of a mighty object, and I heard him exclaim as he went down:

"Our noble profession is vindicated. Here is your elephant!"

I was carried to the office above and restored with carbolic acid. The whole detective force swarmed in, and such another season of triumphant rejoicing ensued as I had never witnessed before. The reporters were called, baskets of champagne were opened, toasts were drunk, the handshakings and congratulations were continuous and enthusiastic. Naturally the chief was the hero of the hour, and his happiness was so complete and had been so patiently and worthily and bravely won that it made me happy to see it, though I stood there a homeless beggar, my priceless charge dead, and my position in my country's service lost to me through what would always seem my fatally careless execution of a great trust. Many an eloquent eye testified its deep admiration for the chief, and many a detective's voice murmured, "Look at him— just the king of the profession—only give him a clew, it's all he wants, and there ain't anything hid that he can't find." The dividing of the $50,000 made great pleasure; when it was finished the chief made a little speech while he put his share in his pocket, in which he said, "Enjoy it, boys, for you've earned it; and more than that you've earned for the detective profession undying fame."

A telegram arrived, which read:

MONROE, MICH., 10 P.M.
First time I've struck a telegraph office in over three weeks. Have followed those footprints, horseback, through the woods, a thousand miles to here, and they get stronger

and bigger and fresher every day. Don't worry—inside of another week I'll have the elephant. This is dead sure.

DARLEY, *Detective.*

The chief ordered three cheers for "Darley, one of the finest minds on the force," and then commanded that he be telegraphed to come home and receive his share of the reward.

So ended that marvelous episode of the stolen elephant. The newspapers were pleasant with praises once more, the next day, with one contemptible exception. This sheet said, "Great is the detective! He may be a little slow in finding a little thing like a mislaid elephant—he may hunt him all day and sleep with his rotting carcass all night for three weeks, but he will find him at last—if he can get the man who mislaid him to show him the place!"

Poor Hassan was lost to me forever. The cannon shots had wounded him fatally, he had crept to that unfriendly place in the fog, and there, surrounded by his enemies and in constant danger of detection, he had wasted away with hunger and suffering till death gave him peace.

The compromise cost me $100,000; my detective expenses were $42,000 more; I never applied for a place again under my government; I am a ruined man and a wanderer in the earth—but my admiration for that man, whom I believe to be the greatest detective the world has ever produced, remains undimmed to this day, and will so remain unto the end.

Luck

[NOTE—This is not a fancy sketch. I got it from a clergyman who was an instructor at Woolwich forty years ago, and who vouched for its truth.—M. T.]

IT was at a banquet in London in honor of one of the two or three conspicuously illustrious English military names of this generation. For reasons which will presently appear, I will withhold his real name and titles, and call him Lieutenant General Lord Arthur Scoresby, V.C., K.C.B., etc., etc., etc. What a fascination there is in a renowned name! There sat the man, in actual flesh, whom I had heard of so many thousands of times since that day, thirty years before, when his name shot suddenly to the zenith from a Crimean battlefield, to remain forever celebrated. It was food and drink to me to look, and look, and look at that demigod; scanning, searching, noting: the quietness, the reserve, the noble gravity of his countenance; the simple honesty that expressed itself all over him; the sweet unconsciousness of his greatness— unconsciousness of the hundreds of admiring eyes fastened upon him, unconsciousness of the deep, loving, sincere worship welling out of the breasts of those people and flowing toward him.

The clergyman at my left was an old acquaintance of mine—clergyman now, but had spent the first half of his life in the camp and field, and as an instructor in the military school at Woolwich. Just at the moment I have been talking about, a veiled and singular light glimmered in his eyes, and he leaned down and muttered confidentially to me—indicating the hero of the banquet with a gesture:

"Privately—he's an absolute fool."

This verdict was a great surprise to me. If its subject had been Napoleon, or Socrates, or Solomon, my astonishment could not have been greater. Two things I was well aware of: that the Reverend was a man of strict veracity, and that his judgment of men was good. Therefore I knew, beyond doubt or question, that the world was mistaken about this hero: he *was* a fool. So I meant to find out, at a convenient moment, how the Reverend, all solitary and alone, had discovered the secret.

Some days later the opportunity came, and this is what the Reverend told me.

About forty years ago I was an instructor in the military academy at Woolwich. I was present in one of the sections when young Scoresby underwent his preliminary examination. I was touched to the quick with pity; for the rest of the class answered up brightly and handsomely, while he—why, dear me, he didn't know *anything,* so to speak. He was evidently good, and sweet, and lovable, and guileless; and so it was exceedingly painful to see him stand there, as serene as a graven image, and deliver himself of answers which were veritably miraculous for stupidity and ignorance. All the compassion in me was aroused in his behalf. I said to myself, when he comes to be examined again, he will be flung over, of course; so it will be simply a harmless act of charity to ease his fall as much as I can. I took him aside, and found that he knew a little of Cæsar's history; and as he didn't know anything else, I went to work and drilled him like a galley slave on a certain line of stock questions concerning Cæsar which I knew would be used. If you'll believe me, he went through with flying colors on examination day! He went through on that purely superficial "cram," and got compliments too, while others, who knew a thousand times more than he, got plucked. By some strangely lucky accident—an accident not likely to happen twice in a century—he was asked no question outside of the narrow limits of his drill.

It was stupefying. Well, all through his course I stood by him, with something of the sentiment which a mother feels for a crippled child; and he always saved himself—just by miracle, apparently.

Now of course the thing that would expose him and kill him at last was mathematics. I resolved to make his death as easy as I could; so I drilled him and crammed him, and crammed him and drilled him, just on the line of questions which the examiners would be most likely to use, and then launching him on his fate. Well, sir, try to conceive of the result: to my consternation, he took the first prize! And with it he got a perfect ovation in the way of compliments.

Sleep? There was no more sleep for me for a week. My conscience tortured me day and night. What I had done I had done purely through charity, and only to ease the poor youth's fall—I never had dreamed of any such preposterous result as the thing that had happened. I felt as guilty and miserable as the creator of Frankenstein. Here was a woodenhead whom I had put in the way of glittering promotions and prodigious responsibilities, and but one thing could happen: he and his responsibilities would all go to ruin together at the first opportunity.

The Crimean war had just broken out. Of course there had to be a war, I said to myself: we couldn't have peace and give this donkey a chance to die before he is found out. I waited for the earthquake. It came. And it made me reel when it did come. He was actually gazetted to a captaincy in a marching regiment! Better men grow old and gray in the service before they climb to a sublimity like that. And who could ever have foreseen that they would go and put such a load of responsibility on such green and inadequate shoulders? I could just barely have stood it if they had made him a cornet; but a captain—think of it! I thought my hair would turn white.

Consider what I did—I who so loved repose and inaction. I said to myself, I am responsible to the country for this, and I must go along with him and protect the country against him as far as I can. So I took my poor little capital that I had saved up through years of work and grinding economy, and went with a sigh and bought a cornetcy in his regiment, and away we went to the field.

And there—oh dear, it was awful. Blunders? Why, he never did anything *but* blunder. But, you see, nobody was in the fellow's secret—everybody had him focused wrong, and necessarily misinterpreted his performance every time—consequently they took his idiotic blunders for inspirations of genius; they did, honestly! His mildest blunders were enough to make a man in his right mind cry; and they did make me cry—and rage and rave too, privately. And the thing that kept me always in a sweat of apprehension was the fact that every fresh blunder he made increased the luster of his reputation! I kept saying to myself, he'll get so high, that when discovery does finally come, it will be like the sun falling out of the sky.

He went right along up, from grade to grade, over the dead bodies of his superiors, until at last, in the hottest moment of the battle of —— down went our colonel, and my heart jumped into my mouth, for Scoresby was next in rank! Now for it, said I; we'll all land in Sheol in ten minutes, sure.

The battle was awfully hot; the allies were steadily giving way all over the field. Our regiment occupied a position that was vital; a blunder now must be destruction. At this crucial moment, what does this immortal fool do but detach the regiment from its place and order a charge over a neighboring hill where there wasn't a suggestion of an enemy! "There you go!" I said to myself; "this *is* the end at last."

And away we did go, and were over the shoulder of the hill before the insane movement could be discovered and stopped. And what did we find? An entire and un-suspected Russian army in reserve! And what happened? We were eaten up? That is necessarily what would have happened in ninety-nine cases out of a hundred. But no, those Russians argued that no single regiment would come browsing around there at such a time. It must be the entire English army, and that the sly Russian game was detected and blocked; so they turned tail, and away they went, pell-mell, over the hill and down into the field, in wild confusion, and we after them; they themselves broke the solid Russian center in the field, and tore through, and in no time there was the most tremendous rout you ever saw, and the defeat of the allies was turned into a sweeping and splendid victory! Marshal Canrobert looked on, dizzy with astonishment, admiration, and delight; and sent right off for Scoresby, and hugged him, and decorated him on the field, in presence of all the armies!

And what was Scoresby's blunder that time? Merely the mistaking his right hand for his left—that was all. An order had come to him to fall back and support our right; and instead, he fell *forward* and went over the hill to the left. But the name he won that day as a marvelous military genius filled the world with his glory, and that glory will never fade while history books last.

He is just as good and sweet and lovable and unpretending as a man can be, but he doesn't know enough to come in when it rains. Now that is absolutely true. He is the supremest ass in the universe; and until half an hour ago nobody knew it but himself and me. He has been pursued, day by day and year by year, by a most phenomenal and astonishing luckiness. He has been a shining soldier in all our wars for a generation; he has littered his whole military life with blunders, and yet has never committed one that didn't make him a knight or a baronet or a lord or something. Look at his breast; why, he is just clothed in domestic and foreign decorations. Well, sir, every one of them is the record of some shouting stupidity or other; and taken together, they are proof that the very best thing in all this world that can befall a man is to be born lucky. I say again, as I said at the banquet, Scoresby's an absolute fool.

The £1,000,000 Bank-Note

WHEN I was twenty-seven years old, I was a mining broker's clerk in San Francisco, and an expert in all the details of stock traffic. I was alone in the world, and had nothing to depend upon but my wits and a clean reputation; but these were setting my feet in the road to eventual fortune, and I was content with the prospect.

My time was my own after the afternoon board, Saturdays, and I was accustomed to put it in on a little sailboat on the bay. One day I ventured too far, and was carried out to sea. Just at nightfall, when hope was about gone, I was picked up by a small brig which was bound for London. It was a long and stormy voyage, and they made me work my passage without pay, as a common sailor. When I stepped ashore in London my clothes were ragged and shabby, and I had only a dollar in my pocket. This money fed and sheltered me twenty-four hours. During the next twenty-four I went without food and shelter.

About ten o'clock on the following morning, seedy and hungry, I was dragging myself along Portland Place, when a child that was passing, towed by a nursemaid, tossed a luscious big pear—minus one bite—into the gutter. I stopped, of course, and fastened my desiring eye on that muddy treasure. My mouth watered for it, my stomach craved it, my whole being begged for it. But every time I made a move to get it some passing eye detected my purpose, and of course I straightened up, then, and looked indifferent, and pretended that I hadn't been thinking about the pear at all. This same thing kept happening and happening, and I couldn't get the pear. I was just getting desperate enough to brave all the shame, and to seize it, when a window behind me was raised, and a gentleman spoke out of it, saying:

"Step in here, please."

I was admitted by a gorgeous flunky, and shown into a sumptuous room where a couple of elderly gentlemen were sitting. They sent away the servant, and made me sit down. They had just finished their breakfast, and the sight of the remains of it almost overpowered me. I could hardly keep my wits together in the presence of that food, but as I was not asked to sample it, I had to bear my trouble as best I could.

Now, something had been happening there a little before, which I did not know anything about until a good many days afterward, but I will tell you about it now. Those two old brothers had been having a pretty hot argument a couple of days before, and had ended by agreeing to decide it by a bet, which is the English way of settling everything.

You will remember that the Bank of England once issued two notes of a million pounds each, to be used for a special purpose connected with some public transaction with a foreign country. For some reason or other only one of these had been used and canceled; the other still lay in the vaults of the Bank. Well, the brothers, chatting along, happened to get to wondering what might be the fate of a perfectly honest and intelligent stranger who should be turned adrift in London without a friend, and with no money but that million-pound bank-note, and no way to account for his being in possession of it. Brother A said he would starve to death; Brother B said he wouldn't. Brother A said he couldn't offer it at a bank or anywhere else, because he would be arrested on the spot. So they went on disputing till Brother B said he would bet twenty thousand pounds that the man would live thirty days, *anyway*, on that million, and keep out of jail, too. Brother A took him up. Brother B went down to the Bank and bought that note. Just like an Englishman, you see; pluck to the backbone. Then he dictated a letter, which one of his clerks wrote out in a beautiful round hand, and then the two brothers sat at the window a whole day watching for the right man to give it to.

They saw many honest faces go by that were not intelligent enough; many that were intelligent, but not honest enough; many that were both, but the possessors were not poor enough, or, if poor enough, were not strangers. There was always a defect, until I came along; but they agreed that I filled the bill all around; so they elected me unanimously, and there I was, now, waiting to know why I was called in. They began to ask me questions about myself, and pretty soon they had my story. Finally they told me I would answer their purpose. I said I was sincerely glad, and asked what it was. Then one of them handed me an envelope, and said I would find the explanation inside. I was going to open it, but he said no; take it to my lodgings, and look it over carefully, and not be hasty or rash. I was puzzled, and wanted to discuss the matter a little further, but they didn't; so I took my leave, feeling hurt and insulted to be made the butt of what was apparently some kind of a practical joke, and yet obliged to put up with it, not being in circumstances to resent affronts from rich and strong folk.

I would have picked up the pear, now, and eaten it before all the world, but it was gone; so I had lost that by this unlucky business, and the thought of it did not soften my feeling toward those men. As soon as I was out of sight of that house I opened my envelope, and saw that it contained money! My opinion of those people changed, I can tell you! I lost not a moment, but shoved note and money into my vest-pocket, and broke for the nearest cheap eating house. Well, how I did eat! When at last I couldn't hold any more, I took out my money and unfolded it, took one glimpse and nearly fainted. Five millions of dollars! Why, it made my head swim.

I must have sat there stunned and blinking at the note as much as a minute before I came rightly to myself again. The first thing I noticed, then, was the landlord. His eye was on the note, and he was petrified. He was worshiping, with all his body and soul, but he looked as if he couldn't stir hand or foot. I took my cue in a

moment, and did the only rational thing there was to do.
I reached the note toward him, and said carelessly:

"Give me the change, please."

Then he was restored to his normal condition, and
made a thousand apologies for not being able to break
the bill, and I couldn't get him to touch it. He wanted
to look at it, and keep on looking at it; he couldn't seem
to get enough of it to quench the thirst of his eye, but he
shrank from touching it as if it had been something
too sacred for poor common clay to handle. I said:

"I am sorry if it is an inconvenience, but I must insist.
Please change it; I haven't anything else."

But he said that wasn't any matter; he was quite willing
to let the trifle stand over till another time. I said I might
not be in his neighborhood again for a good while; but
he said it was of no consequence, he could wait, and,
moreover, I could have anything I wanted, any time I
chose, and let the account run as long as I pleased. He
said he hoped he wasn't afraid to trust as rich a gentleman as I was, merely because I was of a merry disposition, and chose to play larks on the public in the matter
of dress. By this time another customer was entering, and
the landlord hinted to me to put the monster out of sight;
then he bowed me all the way to the door, and I started
straight for that house and those brothers, to correct the
mistake which had been made before the police should
hunt me up, and help me do it. I was pretty nervous, in
fact pretty badly frightened, though, of course, I was no
way in fault; but I knew men well enough to know that
when they find they've given a tramp a million-pound
bill when they thought it was a one-pounder, they are in
a frantic rage against *him* instead of quarreling with their
own nearsightedness, as they ought. As I approached
the house my excitement began to abate, for all was
quiet there, which made me feel pretty sure the blunder
was not discovered yet. I rang. The same servant appeared. I asked for those gentlemen.

"They are gone." This in the lofty, cold way of that
fellow's tribe.

"Gone? Gone where?"

"On a journey."

"But whereabouts?"

"To the Continent, I think."

"The Continent?"

"Yes, sir."

"Which way—by what route?"

"I can't say, sir."

"When will they be back?"

"In a month, they said."

"A month! Oh, this is awful! Give me *some* sort of idea of how to get a word to them. It's of the last importance."

"I can't, indeed. I've no idea where they've gone, sir."

"Then I must see some member of the family."

"Family's away too; been abroad months—in Egypt and India, I think."

"Man, there's been an immense mistake made. They'll be back before night. Will you tell them I've been here, and that I will keep coming till it's all made right, and they needn't be afraid?"

"I'll tell them, if they come back, but I am not expecting them. They said you would be here in an hour to make inquiries, but I must tell you it's all right, they'll be here on time and expect you."

So I had to give it up and go away. What a riddle it all was! I was like to lose my mind. They would be here "on time." What could that mean? Oh, the letter would explain, maybe. I had forgotten the letter; I got it out and read it. This is what it said:

You are an intelligent and honest man, as one may see by your face. We conceive you to be poor and a stranger. Enclosed you will find a sum of money. It is lent to you for thirty days, without interest. Report at this house at the end of that time. I have a bet on you. If I win it you shall have any situation that is in my gift—any, that is, that you shall be able to prove yourself familiar with and competent to fill.

No signature, no address, no date.

Well, here was a coil to be in! You are posted on what had preceded all this, but I was not. It was just a deep, dark puzzle to me. I hadn't the least idea what the game was, nor whether harm was meant me or a kindness. I went into a park, and sat down to try to think it out, and to consider what I had best do.

At the end of an hour, my reasonings had crystallized into this verdict.

Maybe those men mean me well, maybe they mean me ill; no way to decide that—let it go. They've got a game, or a scheme, or an experiment, of some kind on hand; no way to determine what it is—let it go. There's a bet on me; no way to find out what it is—let it go. That disposes of the indeterminable quantities; the remainder of the matter is tangible, solid, and may be classed and labeled with certainty. If I ask the Bank of England to place this bill to the credit of the man it belongs to, they'll do it, for they know him, although I don't; but they will ask me how I came in possession of it, and if I tell the truth, they'll put me in the asylum, naturally, and a lie will land me in jail. The same result would follow if I tried to bank the bill anywhere or to borrow money on it. I have got to carry this immense burden around until those men come back, whether I want to or not. It is useless to me, as useless as a handful of ashes, and yet I must take care of it, and watch over it, while I beg my living. I couldn't *give* it away, if I should try, for neither honest citizen nor highwayman would accept it or meddle with it for anything. Those brothers are safe. Even if I lose their bill, or burn it, they are still safe, because they can stop payment, and the Bank will make them whole; but meantime, I've got to do a month's suffering without wages or profit—unless I help win that bet, whatever it may be, and get that situation that I am promised. I *should* like to get that; men of their sort have situations in their gift that are worth having.

I got to thinking a good deal about that situation. My hopes began to rise high. Without doubt the salary would be large. It would begin in a month; after that I should be all right. Pretty soon I was feeling first rate. By this time I was tramping the streets again. The sight of a tailor shop gave me a sharp longing to shed my rags, and to clothe myself decently once more. Could I afford it? No; I had nothing in the world but a million pounds. So I forced myself to go on by. But soon I was drifting back again. The temptation persecuted me cruelly. I must have passed that shop back and forth six times during that manful struggle. At last I gave in; I had to. I asked if they had a misfit suit that had been thrown on their hands. The fellow I spoke to nodded his head toward another fellow, and gave me no answer. I went to the indicated fellow, and he indicated another fellow with *his* head, and no words. I went to him, and he said:

" 'Tend to you presently."

I waited till he was done with what he was at, then he took me into a back room, and overhauled a pile of rejected suits, and selected the rattiest one for me. I put it on. It didn't fit, and wasn't in any way attractive, but it was new, and I was anxious to have it; so I didn't find any fault, but said with some diffidence:

"It would be an accommodation to me if you could wait some days for the money. I haven't any small change about me."

The fellow worked up a most sarcastic expression of countenance, and said:

"Oh, you haven't? Well, of course, I didn't expect it. I'd only expect gentlemen like you to carry large change."

I was nettled, and said:

"My friend, you shouldn't judge a stranger always by the clothes he wears. I am quite able to pay for this suit; I simply didn't wish to put you to the trouble of changing a large note."

He modified his style a little at that, and said, though still with something of an air:

"I didn't mean any particular harm, but as long as rebukes are going, I might say it wasn't quite your affair to jump to the conclusion that we couldn't change any note that you might happen to be carrying around. On the contrary, we *can*."

I handed the note to him, and said:

"Oh, very well; I apologize."

He received it with a smile, one of those large smiles which goes all around over, and has folds in it, and wrinkles, and spirals, and looks like the place where you have thrown a brick in a pond; and then in the act of his taking a glimpse of the bill this smile froze solid, and turned yellow, and looked like those wavy, wormy spreads of lava which you find hardened on little levels on the side of Vesuvius. I never before saw a smile caught like that, and perpetuated. The man stood there holding the bill, and looking like that, and the proprietor hustled up to see what was the matter, and said briskly:

"Well, what's up? what's the trouble? what's wanting?"

I said: "There isn't any trouble. I'm waiting for my change."

"Come, come; get him his change, Tod; get him his change."

Tod retorted: "Get him his change! It's easy to say, sir; but look at the bill yourself."

The proprietor took a look, gave a low, eloquent whistle, then made a dive for the pile of rejected clothing, and began to snatch it this way and that, talking all the time excitedly, and as if to himself:

"Sell an eccentric millionaire such an unspeakable suit as that! Tod's a fool—a born fool. Always doing something like this. Drives every millionaire away from this place, because he can't tell a millionaire from a tramp, and never could. Ah, here's the thing I'm after. Please get those things off, sir, and throw them in the fire. Do me the favor to put on this shirt and this suit; it's just the thing, the very thing—plain, rich, modest, and just ducally nobby; made to order for a foreign prince—you may know him, sir, his Serene Highness the Hospodar of Halifax; had to leave it with us and take a mourning suit because his mother was going to die—which she didn't. But that's all right; we can't always have things the way we—that is, the way they—there! trousers all right, they fit you to a charm, sir; now the waistcoat; aha, right again! now the coat—Lord! look at that, now! Perfect—the whole thing! I never saw such a triumph in all my experience."

I expressed my satisfaction.

"Quite right, sir, quite right; it'll do for a makeshift, I'm bound to say. But wait till you see what we'll get up for you on your own measure. Come, Tod, book and pen; get at it. Length of leg, 32"—and so on. Before I could get in a word he had measured me, and was giving orders for dress suits, morning suits, shirts, and all sorts of things. When I got a chance I said:

"But, my dear sir, I *can't* give these orders, unless you can wait indefinitely, or change the bill."

"Indefinitely! It's a weak word, sir, a weak word. Eternally—*that's* the word, sir. Tod, rush these things through, and send them to the gentleman's address without any waste of time. Let the minor customers wait. Set down the gentleman's address and—"

"I'm changing my quarters. I will drop in and leave the new address."

"Quite right, sir, quite right. One moment—let me show you out, sir. There—good day, sir, good day."

Well, don't you see what was bound to happen? I drifted naturally into buying whatever I wanted, and asking for change. Within a week I was sumptuously equipped with all needful comforts and luxuries, and was housed in an expensive private hotel in Hanover Square. I took my dinners there, but for breakfast I stuck by Harris's humble feeding house, where I had got my first meal on my million-pound bill. I was the making of Harris. The fact had gone all abroad that the foreign crank who carried million-pound bills in his vest-pocket was the patron saint of the place. That was enough. From being a poor, struggling, little hand-to-mouth enterprise, it had become celebrated, and overcrowded with customers. Harris was so grateful that he forced loans upon me, and would not be denied; and so, pauper as I was, I had money to spend, and was living like the rich and the great. I judged that there was going to be a crash by and by, but I was in, now, and must swim across or drown. You see there was just that element of impending disaster to give a serious side, a sober side, yes, a tragic side, to a state of things which would otherwise have been purely ridiculous. In the night, in the dark, the tragedy part was always to the front, and always warning, always threatening; and so I moaned and tossed, and sleep was hard to find. But in the cheerful daylight the tragedy element faded out and disappeared, and I walked on air, and was happy to giddiness, to intoxication, you may say.

And it was natural; for I had become one of the notorieties of the metropolis of the world, and it turned my head, not just a little, but a good deal. You could not take up a newspaper, English, Scotch, or Irish, without finding in it one or more references to the "vest-pocket million-pounder" and his latest doings and sayings. At first, in these mentions, I was at the bottom of the personal gossip column; next, I was listed above the knights; next, above the baronets; next, above the barons, and so on, and so on, climbing steadily as my notoriety augmented, until I reached the highest altitude possible, and there I remained, taking precedence of all dukes not royal, and of all ecclesiastics except the primate of all England. But mind, this was not fame; as yet I had achieved only notoriety. Then came the climaxing stroke —the accolade, so to speak—which in a single instant transmuted the perishable dross of notoriety into the enduring gold of fame: *Punch* caricatured me! Yes, I was a made man, now; my place was established. I might be joked about still, but reverently, not hilariously, not rudely; I could be smiled at, but not laughed at. The time for that had gone by. *Punch* pictured me all a-flutter with rags, dickering with a beefeater for the Tower of London. Well, you can imagine how it was with a young fellow who had never been taken notice of before, and now all of a sudden couldn't say a thing that wasn't taken up and repeated everywhere; couldn't stir abroad without constantly overhearing the remark flying from lip to lip, "There he goes; that's him!" couldn't take his breakfast without a crowd to look on; couldn't appear in an opera box without concentrating there the fire of a thousand lorgnettes. Why, I just swam in glory all day long—that is the amount of it.

You know, I even kept my old suit of rags, and every now and then appeared in them, so as to have the old pleasure of buying trifles, and being insulted, and then shooting the scoffer dead with the million-pound bill. But I couldn't keep that up. The illustrated papers made the outfit so familiar that when I went out in it I was at once recognized and followed by a crowd, and if I attempted to purchase the man would offer me his whole shop on credit before I could pull my note on him.

About the tenth day of my fame I went to fulfill my duty to my flag by paying my respects to the American minister. He received me with the enthusiasm proper in my case, upbraided me for being so tardy in my duty, and said that there was only one way to get his forgiveness, and that was to take the seat at his dinner party that night made vacant by the illness of one of his guests. I said I would, and we got to talking. It turned out that he and my father had been schoolmates in boyhood, Yale students together later, and always warm friends up to my father's death. So then he required me to put in at his house all the odd time I might have to spare, and I was very willing, of course.

In fact I was more than willing; I was glad. When the crash should come, he might somehow be able to save me from total destruction; I didn't know how, but he might think of a way, maybe. I couldn't venture to unbosom myself to him at this late date, a thing which I would have been quick to do in the beginning of this awful career of mine in London. No, I couldn't venture it now; I was in too deep; that is, too deep for me to be risking revelations to so new a friend, though not yet clear beyond my depth, as *I* looked at it. Because, you see, with all my borrowing, I was carefully keeping within my means—I mean within my salary. Of course I couldn't *know* what my salary was going to be, but I had a good enough basis for an estimate in the fact that, if I won the bet, I was to have *choice* of any situation in that rich old gentleman's gift provided I was competent—and I should certainly prove competent; I hadn't any doubt about that. And as to the bet, I wasn't worrying about that; I had always been lucky. Now my estimate of the salary was six hundred to a thousand a year; say, six hundred for the first year, and so on up year by year, till I struck the upper figure by proved merit. At present I was only in debt for my first year's salary. Everybody had been trying to lend me money, but I had fought off the most of them on one pretext or another; so this indebtedness represented only £300 borrowed money, the other £300 represented my keep and my purchases. I believed my second year's salary would carry me through the rest of the month if I went on being cautious and economical, and I intended to look sharply out for that. My month ended, my employer back from his journey, I should be all right once more, for I should at once divide the two years' salary among my creditors by assignment, and get right down to my work.

It was a lovely dinner party of fourteen. The Duke and Duchess of Shoreditch, and their daughter the Lady Anne-Grace-Eleanor-Celeste-and-so-forth-and-so-forth-de-Bohun, the Earl and Countess of Newgate, Viscount Cheapside, Lord and Lady Blatherskite, some untitled people of both sexes, the minister and his wife and daughter, and this daughter's visiting friend, an English girl of twenty-two, named Portia Langham, whom I fell in love with in two minutes, and she with me—I could see it without glasses. There was still another guest, an American—but I am a little ahead of my story. While the people were still in the drawing room, whetting up for dinner, and coldly inspecting the late-comers, the servant announced:

"Mr. Lloyd Hastings."

The moment the usual civilities were over, Hastings caught sight of me, and came straight with cordially outstretched hand; then stopped short when about to shake; and said with an embarrassed look:

"I beg your pardon, sir, I thought I knew you."

"Why, you do know me, old fellow."

"No! Are *you* the—the—"

"Vest-pocket monster? I am, indeed. Don't be afraid to call me by my nickname; I'm used to it."

"Well, well, well, this is a surprise. Once or twice I've seen your own name coupled with the nickname, but it never occurred to me that *you* could be the Henry Adams referred to. Why, it isn't six months since you were clerking away for Blake Hopkins in Frisco on a salary, and sitting up nights on an extra allowance, helping me arrange and verify the Gould and Curry Extension papers and statistics. The idea of your being in London, and a vast millionaire, and a colossal celebrity! Why, it's the Arabian Nights come again. Man, I can't take it in at all; can't realize it; give me time to settle the whirl in my head."

"The fact is, Lloyd, you are no worse off than I am. I can't realize it myself."

"Dear me, it *is* stunning, now isn't it? Why, it's just three months today since we went to the Miners' restaurant—"

"No; the What Cheer."

"Right, it *was* the What Cheer; went there at two in the morning, and had a chop and coffee after a hard six hours' grind over those Extension papers, and I tried to persuade you to come to London with me, and offered to get leave of absence for you and pay all your expenses, and give you something over if I succeeded in making the sale; and you would not listen to me, said I wouldn't succeed, and you couldn't afford to lose the run of business and be no end of time getting the hang of things again when you got back home. And yet here you are. How odd it all is! How did you happen to come, and whatever *did* give you this incredible start?"

"Oh, just an accident. It's a long story—a romance, a body may say. I'll tell you all about it, but not now."

"When?"

"The end of this month."

"That's more than a fortnight yet. It's too much of a strain on a person's curiosity. Make it a week."

"I can't. You'll know why, by and by. But how's the trade getting along?"

His cheerfulness vanished like a breath, and he said with a sigh:

"You were a true prophet, Hal, a true prophet. I wish I hadn't come. I don't want to talk about it."

"But you must. You must come and stop with me to-night, when we leave here, and tell me all about it."

"Oh, may I? Are you in earnest?" and the water showed in his eyes.

"Yes; I want to hear the whole story, every word."

"I'm so grateful! Just to find a human interest once more, in some voice and in some eye, in me and affairs of mine, after what I've been through here—Lord! I could go down on my knees for it!"

He gripped my hand hard, and braced up, and was all right and lively after that for the dinner—which didn't come off. No; the usual thing happened, the thing that is always happening under that vicious and aggravating English system—the matter of precedence couldn't be settled, and so there was no dinner. Englishmen always eat dinner before they go out to dinner, because *they* know the risks they are running; but nobody ever warns the stranger, and so he walks placidly into the trap. Of course nobody was hurt this time, because we had all been to dinner, none of us being novices except Hastings, and he having been informed by the minister at the time that he invited him that in deference to the English custom he had not provided any dinner. Everybody took a lady and processioned down to the dining room, because it is usual to go through the motions; but there the dispute began. The Duke of Shoreditch wanted to take precedence, and sit at the head of the table, holding that he outranked a minister who represented merely a nation and not a monarch; but I stood for my rights, and refused to yield. In the gossip column I ranked all dukes not royal, and said so, and claimed precedence of this one. It couldn't be settled, of course, struggle as we might and did, he finally (and injudiciously) trying to play birth and antiquity, and I "seeing" his Conqueror and "raising" him with Adam, whose direct posterity I was, as shown by my name, while *he* was of a collateral branch, as shown by *his*, and by his recent Norman origin; so we all processioned back to the drawing room again and had a perpendicular lunch—plate of sardines and a strawberry, and you group yourself and stand up and eat it. Here the religion of precedence is not so strenuous; the two persons of highest rank chuck up a shilling, the one that wins has first go at his strawberry, and the loser gets the shilling. The next two chuck up, then the next two, and so on. After refreshment, tables were brought, and we all played cribbage, sixpence a game. The English never play any game for amusement. If they can't make something or lose something—they don't care which—they won't play.

We had a lovely time; certainly two of us had, Miss Langham and I. I was so bewitched with her that I couldn't count my hands if they went above a double sequence; and when I struck home I never discovered it, and started up the outside row again, and would have lost the game every time, only the girl did the same, she being in just my condition, you see; and consequently neither of us ever got out, or cared to wonder why we didn't; we only just knew we were happy, and didn't wish to know anything else, and didn't want to be interrupted. And I *told* her—I did indeed—told her I loved her; and

she—well, she blushed till her hair turned red, but she
liked it; she *said* she did. Oh, there was never such an
evening! Every time I pegged I put on a postscript;
every time she pegged she acknowledged receipt of it,
counting the hands the same. Why, I couldn't even say
"Two for his heels" without adding, "*My,* how sweet you
do look!" and she would say, "Fifteen two, fifteen four,
fifteen six, and a pair are eight, and eight are sixteen—
do you think so?"—peeping out aslant from under her
lashes, you know, so sweet and cunning. Oh, it was just
too-too!

Well, I was perfectly honest and square with her; told
her I hadn't a cent in the world but just the million-pound
note she'd heard so much talk about, and *it* didn't belong
to me; and that started her curiosity, and then I talked
low, and told her the whole history right from the start,
and it nearly killed her, laughing. What in the nation she
could find to laugh about, I couldn't see, but there it
was; every half minute some new detail would fetch her,
and I would have to stop as much as a minute and a half
to give her a chance to settle down again. Why, she
laughed herself lame, she did indeed; I never saw anything like it. I mean I never saw a painful story—a story
of a person's troubles and worries and fears—produce
just *that* kind of effect before. So I loved her all the more,
seeing she could be so cheerful when there wasn't anything to be cheerful about; for I might soon need that
kind of wife, you know, the way things looked. Of course
I told her we should have to wait a couple of years, till
I could catch up on my salary; but she didn't mind that,
only she hoped I would be as careful as possible in the
matter of expenses, and not let them run the least risk
of trenching on our third year's pay. Then she began to
get a little worried, and wondered if we were making any
mistake, and starting the salary on a higher figure for
the first year than I would get. This was good sense, and
it made me feel a little less confident than I had been
feeling before; but it gave me a good business idea, and
I brought it frankly out.

"Portia, dear, would you mind going with me that day,
when I confront those old gentlemen?"

She shrank a little, but said:

"N-o; if my being with you would help hearten you. But—would it be quite proper, do you think?"

"No, I don't know that it would; in fact I'm afraid it wouldn't: but you see, there's so *much* dependent upon it that—"

"Then I'll go anyway, proper or improper," she said, with a beautiful and generous enthusiasm. "Oh, I shall be so happy to think I'm helping."

"Helping, dear? Why, you'll be doing it all. You're so beautiful and so lovely and so winning, that with you there I can pile our salary up till I break those good old fellows, and they'll never have the heart to struggle."

Sho! you should have seen the rich blood mount, and her happy eyes shine!

"You wicked flatterer! There isn't a word of truth in what you say, but still I'll go with you. Maybe it will teach you not to expect other people to look with your eyes."

Were my doubts dissipated? Was my confidence restored? You may judge by this fact: privately I raised my salary to twelve hundred the first year on the spot. But I didn't tell her; I saved it for a surprise.

All the way home I was in the clouds, Hastings talking, I not hearing a word. When he and I entered my parlor, he brought me to myself with his fervent appreciations of my manifold comforts and luxuries.

"Let me just stand here a little and look my fill! Dear me, it's a palace; it's just a palace! And in it everything a body *could* desire, including cozy coal fire and supper standing ready. Henry, it doesn't merely make me realize how rich you are; it makes me realize, to the bone, to the marrow, how poor I am—how poor I am, and how miserable, how defeated, routed, annihilated!"

Plague take it! this language gave me the cold shudders. It scared me broad awake, and made me comprehend that I was standing on a half-inch crust, with a crater underneath. *I* didn't know I had been dreaming—that is, I hadn't been allowing myself to know it for a while back; but *now*—oh, dear! Deep in debt, not a cent in the world, a lovely girl's happiness or woe in my hands, and nothing in front of me but a salary which might never—oh, *would* never—materialize! Oh, oh, oh, I am ruined past hope; nothing can save me!

"Henry, the mere unconsidered drippings of your daily income would—"

"Oh, my daily income! Here, down with this hot Scotch, and cheer up your soul. Here's with you! Or, no—you're hungry; sit down and—"

"Not a bite for me; I'm past it. I can't eat, these days; but I'll drink with you till I drop. Come!"

"Barrel for barrel, I'm with you! Ready? Here we go! Now, then, Lloyd, unreel your story while I brew."

"Unreel it? What, again?"

"Again? What do you mean by that?"

"Why, I mean do you want to hear it *over* again?"

"Do I want to hear it *over* again? This *is* a puzzler. Wait; don't take any more of that liquid. You don't need it."

"Look here, Henry, you alarm me. Didn't I tell you the whole story on the way here?"

"You?"

"Yes, I."

"I'll be hanged if I heard a word of it."

"Henry, this is a serious thing. It troubles me. What did you take up yonder at the minister's?"

Then it all flashed on me, and I owned up, like a man.

"I took the dearest girl in this world—prisoner!"

So then he came with a rush, and we shook, and shook, and shook till our hands ached; and he didn't blame me for not having heard a word of a story which had lasted while we walked three miles. He just sat down then, like the patient, good fellow he was, and told it all over again. Synopsized, it amounted to this: He had come to England with what he thought was a grand opportunity; he had an "option" to sell the Gould and Curry Extension for the "locators" of it, and keep all he could get over a million dollars. He had worked hard, had pulled every wire he knew of, had left no honest expedient untried, had spent nearly all the money he had in the world, had not been able to get a solitary capitalist to listen to him, and his option would run out at the end of the month. In a word, he was ruined. Then he jumped up and cried out:

"Henry, you can save me! You can save me, and you're

the only man in the universe that can. Will you do it? *Won't* you do it?"

"Tell me how. Speak out, my boy."

"Give me a million and my passage home for my 'option'! Don't, *don't* refuse!"

I was in a kind of agony. I was right on the point of coming out with the words, "Loyd, I'm a pauper myself— absolutely penniless, and in *debt!*" But a white-hot idea came flaming through my head, and I gripped my jaws together, and calmed myself down till I was as cold as a capitalist. Then I said, in a commercial and self-pos- sessed way:

"I will save you, Lloyd—"

"Then I'm already saved! God be merciful to you for- ever! If ever I—"

"Let me finish, Lloyd. I will save you, but not in that way; for that would not be fair to you, after your hard work, and the risks you've run. I don't need to buy mines; I can keep my capital moving, in a commercial center like London without that; it's what I'm at, all the time; but here is what I'll do. I know all about that mine, of course; I know its immense value, and can swear to it if anybody wishes it. You shall sell out inside of the fortnight for three millions cash, using my name freely, and we'll divide, share and share alike."

Do you know, he would have danced the furniture to kindling wood in his insane joy, and broken everything on the place, if I hadn't tripped him up and tied him.

Then he lay there, perfectly happy, saying:

"I may use your name! Your name—think of it! Man, they'll flock in droves, these rich Londoners; they'll *fight* for that stock! I'm a made man, I'm a made man forever, and I'll never forget you as long as I live!"

In less than twenty-four hours London was abuzz! I hadn't anything to do, day after day, but sit at home, and say to all comers:

"Yes; I told him to refer to me. I know the man, and I know the mine. His character is above reproach, and the mine is worth far more than he asks for it."

Meantime I spent all my evenings at the minister's with Portia. I didn't say a word to her about the mine; I saved it for a surprise. We talked salary; never anything but

salary and love; sometimes love, sometimes salary, sometimes love and salary together. And my! the interest the
minister's wife and daughter took in our little affair, and
the endless ingenuities they invented to save us from interruption, and to keep the minister in the dark and
unsuspicious—well, it was just lovely of them!

When the month was up, at last, I had a million dollars
to my credit in the London and County Bank, and Hastings was fixed in the same way. Dressed at my level best,
I drove by the house in Portland Place, judged by the
look of things that my birds were home again, went on
toward the minister's and got my precious, and we started
back, talking salary with all our might. She was so excited
and anxious that it made her just intolerably beautiful. I
said:

"Dearie, the way you're looking it's a crime to strike
for a salary a single penny under three thousand a year."

"Henry, Henry, you'll ruin us!"

"Don't you be afraid. Just keep up those looks, and
trust to me. It'll all come out right."

So as it turned out, I had to keep bolstering up *her*
courage all the way. She kept pleading with me, and saying:

"Oh, please remember that if we ask for too much
we may get no salary at all; and then what will become
of us, with no way in the world to earn our living?"

We were ushered in by that same servant, and there
they were, the two old gentlemen. Of course they were
surprised to see that wonderful creature with me, but I
said:

"It's all right, gentlemen; she is my future stay and
helpmate."

And I introduced them to her, and called them by
name. It didn't surprise them; they knew I would know
enough to consult the directory. They seated us, and were
very polite to me, and very solicitous to relieve her from
embarrassment, and put her as much at her ease as they
could. Then I said:

"Gentlemen, I am ready to report."

"We are glad to hear it," said *my* man, "for now we
can decide the bet which my brother Abel and I made.

If you have won for me, you shall have any situation in my gift. Have you the million-pound note?"

"Here it is, sir," and I handed it to him.

"I've won!" he shouted, and slapped Abel on the back. "*Now* what do you say, brother?"

"I say he *did* survive, and I've lost twenty thousand pounds. I never would have believed it."

"I've a further report to make," I said, "and a pretty long one. I want you to let me come soon, and detail my whole month's history; and I promise you it's worth hearing. Meantime, take a look at that."

"What, man! Certificate of deposit for £200,000? Is it yours?"

"Mine. I earned it by thirty days' judicious use of that little loan you let me have. And the only use I made of it was to buy trifles and offer the bill in change."

"Come, this is astonishing! It's incredible, man!"

"Never mind, I'll prove it. Don't take my word unsupported."

But now Portia's turn was come to be surprised. Her eyes were spread wide, and she said:

"Henry, is that really your money? Have you been fibbing to me?"

"I have indeed, dearie. But you'll forgive me, *I* know."

She put up an arch pout, and said:

"Don't you be so sure. You are a naughty thing to deceive me so!"

"Oh, you'll get over it, sweetheart, you'll get over it; it was only fun, you know. Come, let's be going."

"But wait, wait! The situation, you know. I want to give you the situation," said my man.

"Well," I said, "I'm just as grateful as I can be, but really I don't want one."

"But you can have the very choicest one in my gift."

"Thanks again, with all my heart; but I don't even want *that* one."

"Henry, I'm ashamed of you. You don't half thank the good gentleman. May I do it for you?"

"Indeed you shall, dear, if you can improve it. Let us see you try."

She walked to my man, got up in his lap, put her arm round his neck, and kissed him right on the mouth. Then the two old gentlemen shouted with laughter, but I was dumfounded, just petrified, as you may say. Portia said:

"Papa, he has said you haven't a situation in your gift that he'd take; and I feel just as hurt as—"

"My darling!—Is that your papa?"

"Yes; he's my steppapa, and the dearest one that ever was. You understand now, don't you, why I was able to laugh when you told me at the minister's, not knowing my relationships, what trouble and worry papa's and Uncle Abel's scheme was giving you?"

Of course I spoke right up, now, without any fooling, and went straight to the point.

"Oh, my dearest dear sir, I want to take back what I said. You *have* got a situation open that I want."

"Name it."

"Son-in-law."

"Well, well, well! But you know, if you haven't ever served in that capacity, you of course can't furnish recommendations of a sort to satisfy the conditions of the contract, and so—"

"Try me—oh, do, I beg of you! Only just try me thirty or forty years, and if—"

"Oh, well, all right; it's but a little thing to ask. Take her along."

Happy, we two? There're not words enough in the unabridged to describe it. And when London got the whole history, a day or two later, of my month's adventures with that bank-note, and how they ended, did London talk, and have a good time? Yes.

My Portia's papa took that friendly and hospitable bill back to the Bank of England and cashed it; then the Bank canceled it and made him a present of it, and he gave it to us at our wedding, and it has always hung in its frame in the sacredest place in our home, ever since. For it gave me my Portia. But for it I could not have remained in London, would not have appeared at the minister's, never should have met her. And so I always say, "Yes, it's a million-pounder, as you see; but it never made but one purchase in its life, and *then* got the article for only about a tenth part of its value."

The Man That Corrupted

Hadleyburg

I

IT was many years ago. Hadleyburg was the most honest and upright town in all the region round about. It had kept that reputation unsmirched during three generations, and was prouder of it than of any other of its possessions. It was so proud of it, and so anxious to insure its perpetuation, that it began to teach the principles of honest dealing to its babies in the cradle, and made the like teachings the staple of their culture thenceforward through all the years devoted to their education. Also, throughout the formative years temptations were kept out of the way of the young people, so that their honesty could have every chance to harden and solidify, and become a part of their very bone. The neighboring towns were jealous of this honorable supremacy, and affected to sneer at Hadleyburg's pride in it and call it vanity; but all the same they were obliged to acknowledge that Hadleyburg was in reality an incorruptible town; and if pressed they would also acknowledge that the mere fact that a young man hailed from Hadleyburg was all the recommendation he needed when he went forth from his natal town to seek for responsible employment.

But at last, in the drift of time, Hadleyburg had the ill luck to offend a passing stranger—possibly without knowing it, certainly without caring, for Hadleyburg was sufficient unto itself, and cared not a rap for strangers or their opinions. Still, it would have been well to make an exception in this one's case, for he was a bitter man and revengeful. All through his wanderings during a whole year he kept his injury in mind, and gave all his leisure moments to trying to invent a compensating satisfaction for it. He contrived many plans, and all of them were good, but none of them was quite sweeping enough; the poorest of them would hurt a great many individuals, but what he wanted was a plan which would comprehend the entire town, and not let so much as one person escape unhurt. At last he had a fortunate idea, and when it fell into his brain it lit up his whole head with an evil joy. He began to form a plan at once, saying to himself, "That is the thing to do—I will corrupt the town."

Six months later he went to Hadleyburg, and arrived in a buggy at the house of the old cashier of the bank about ten at night. He got a sack out of the buggy, shouldered it, and staggered with it through the cottage yard, and knocked at the door. A woman's voice said "Come in," and he entered, and set his sack behind the stove in the parlor, saying politely to the old lady who sat reading the *Missionary Herald* by the lamp:

"Pray keep your seat, madam, I will not disturb you. There—now it is pretty well concealed; one would hardly know it was there. Can I see your husband a moment, madam?"

No, he was gone to Brixton, and might not return before morning.

"Very well, madam, it is no matter. I merely wanted to leave that sack in his care, to be delivered to the rightful owner when he shall be found. I am a stranger; he does not know me; I am merely passing through the town to-night to discharge a matter which has been long in my mind. My errand is now completed, and I go pleased and a little proud, and you will never see me again. There is a paper attached to the sack which will explain everything. Good night, madam."

The old lady was afraid of the mysterious big stranger, and was glad to see him go. But her curiosity was roused, and she went straight to the sack and brought away the paper. It began as follows:

TO BE PUBLISHED: or, the right man sought out by

private inquiry—either will answer. This sack contains gold coin weighing a hundred and sixty pounds four ounces—

"Mercy on us, and the door not locked!"

Mrs. Richards flew to it all in a tremble and locked it, then pulled down the window shades and stood frightened, worried, and wondering if there was anything else she could do toward making herself and the money more safe. She listened awhile for burglars, then surrendered to curiosity and went back to the lamp and finished reading the paper:

I am a foreigner, and am presently going back to my own country, to remain there permanently. I am grateful to America for what I have received at her hands during my long stay under her flag; and to one of her citizens— a citizen of Hadleyburg—I am especially grateful for a great kindness done me a year or two ago. Two great kindnesses, in fact. I will explain. I was a gambler. I say I WAS. I was a ruined gambler. I arrived in this village at night, hungry and without a penny. I asked for help—in the dark; I was ashamed to beg in the light. I begged of the right man. He gave me twenty dollars—that is to say, he gave me life, as I considered it. He also gave me fortune; for out of that money I have made myself rich at the gaming table. And finally, a remark which he made to me has remained with me to this day, and has at last conquered me; and in conquering has saved the remnant of my morals: I shall gamble no more. Now I have no idea who that man was, but I want him found, and I want him to have this money, to give away, throw away, or keep, as he pleases. It is merely my way of testifying my gratitude to him. If I could stay, I would find him myself; but no matter, he will be found. This is an honest town, an incorruptible town, and I know I can trust it without fear. This man can be identified by the remark which he made to me; I feel persuaded that he will remember it.

And now my plan is this: If you prefer to conduct the inquiry privately, do so. Tell the contents of this present writing to anyone who is likely to be the right man. If he shall answer, "I am the man; the remark I made was so-and-so," apply the test—to wit: open the sack, and in it you will find a sealed envelope containing that remark. If the remark mentioned by the candidate tallies with it, give him the money, and ask no further questions, for he is certainly the right man.

But if you shall prefer a public inquiry, then publish this present writing in the local paper—with these instructions added, to wit: Thirty days from now, let the candidate appear at the town hall at eight in the evening (Friday), and hand his remark, in a sealed envelope, to the Rev. Mr. Burgess (if he will be kind enough to act); and let Mr. Burgess there and then destroy the seals of the sack, open it, and see if the remark is correct: if correct, let the money be delivered, with my sincere gratitude, to my benefactor thus identified.

Mrs. Richards sat down, gently quivering with excitement, and was soon lost in thinkings—after this pattern: "What a strange thing it is! . . . And what a fortune for that kind man who set his bread afloat upon the waters! . . . If it had only been my husband that did it!—for we are so poor, so old and poor! . . ." Then, with a sigh—"But it was not my Edward; no, it was not he that gave a stranger twenty dollars. It is a pity, too; I see it now. . . ." Then, with a shudder—"But it is *gambler's* money! the wages of sin: we couldn't take it; we couldn't touch it. I don't like to be near it; it seems a defilement." She moved to a farther chair. . . . "I wish Edward would come, and take it to the bank; a burglar might come at any moment; it is dreadful to be here all alone with it."

At eleven Mr. Richards arrived, and while his wife was saying, "I am *so* glad you've come!" he was saying, "I'm so tired—tired clear out; it is dreadful to be poor, and have to make these dismal journeys at my time of life. Always at the grind, grind, grind, on a salary—another man's slave, and he sitting at home in his slippers, rich and comfortable."

"I am so sorry for you, Edward, you know that; but be comforted: we have our livelihood; we have our good name—"

"Yes, Mary, and that is everything. Don't mind my talk—it's just a moment's irritation and doesn't mean anything. Kiss me—there, it's all gone now, and I am not complaining any more. What have you been getting? What's in the sack?"

Then his wife told him the great secret. It dazed him for a moment; then he said:

"It weighs a hundred and sixty pounds? Why, Mary, it's for-ty thou-sand dollars—think of it—a whole fortune! Not ten men in this village are worth that much. Give me the paper."

He skimmed through it and said:

"Isn't it an adventure! Why, it's a romance; it's like the impossible things one reads about in books, and never sees in life." He was well stirred up now; cheerful, even gleeful. He tapped his old wife on the cheek, and said, humorously, "Why, we're rich, Mary, rich; all we've got to do is to bury the money and burn the papers. If the gambler ever comes to inquire, we'll merely look coldly upon him and say: 'What is this nonsense you are talk-ing? We have never heard of you and your sack of gold before'; and then he would look foolish, and—"

"And in the meantime, while you are running on with your jokes, the money is still here, and it is fast getting along toward burglar-time."

"True. Very well, what shall we do—make the inquiry private? No, not that: it would spoil the romance. The public method is better. Think what a noise it will make! And it will make all the other towns jealous; for no stranger would trust such a thing to any town but Hadley-burg, and they know it. It's a great card for us. I must get to the printing office now, or I shall be too late."

"But stop—stop—don't leave me here alone with it, Edward!"

But he was gone. For only a little while, however. Not far from his own house he met the editor-proprietor of the paper, and gave him the document, and said, "Here is a good thing for you, Cox—put it in."

"It may be too late, Mr. Richards, but I'll see."

At home again he and his wife sat down to talk the charming mystery over; they were in no condition for sleep. The first question was, Who could the citizen have been who gave the stranger the twenty dollars? It seemed a simple one; both answered it in the same breath.

"Barclay Goodson."

"Yes," said Richards, "he could have done it, and it would have been like him, but there's not another in the town."

"Everybody will grant that, Edward—grant it privately,

anyway. For six months, now, the village has been its own proper self once more—honest, narrow, self-righteous, and stingy."

"It is what he always called it, to the day of his death —said it right out publicly, too."

"Yes, and he was hated for it."

"Oh, of course; but he didn't care. I reckon he was the best-hated man among us, except the Reverend Burgess."

"Well, Burgess deserves it—he will never get another congregation here. Mean as the town is, it knows how to estimate *him*. Edward, doesn't it seem odd that the stranger should appoint Burgess to deliver the money?"

"Well, yes—it does. That is—that is—".

"Why so much that-*is*-ing? Would *you* select him?"

"Mary, maybe the stranger knows him better than this village does."

"Much *that* would help Burgess!"

The husband seemed perplexed for an answer; the wife kept a steady eye upon him, and waited. Finally Richards said, with the hesitancy of one who is making a statement which is likely to encounter doubt:

"Mary, Burgess is not a bad man."

His wife was certainly surprised.

"Nonsense!" she exclaimed.

"He is not a bad man. I know. The whole of his unpopularity had its foundation in that one thing—the thing that made so much noise."

"That 'one thing,' indeed! As if that 'one thing' wasn't enough, all by itself."

"Plenty. Plenty. Only he wasn't guilty of it."

"How you talk! Not guilty of it! Everybody knows he *was* guilty."

"Mary, I give you my word—he was innocent."

"I can't believe it, and I don't. How do you know?"

"It is a confession. I am ashamed, but I will make it. I was the only man who knew he was innocent. I could have saved him, and—and—well, you know how the town was wrought up—I hadn't the pluck to do it. It would have turned everybody against me. I felt mean, ever so mean; but I didn't dare; I hadn't the manliness to face that."

Mary looked troubled, and for a while was silent. Then she said, stammeringly:

"I—I don't think it would have done for you to—to— One mustn't—er—public opinion—one has to be so careful—so—" It was a difficult road, and she got mired; but after a little she got started again. "It was a great pity, but— Why, we couldn't afford it, Edward—we couldn't indeed. Oh, I wouldn't have had you do it for anything!"

"It would have lost us the good will of so many people, Mary; and then—and then—"

"What troubles me now is, what *he* thinks of us, Edward."

"He? *He* doesn't suspect that I could have saved him."

"Oh," exclaimed the wife, in a tone of relief, "I am glad of that. As long as he doesn't know that you could have saved him, he—he—well, that makes it a great deal better. Why, I might have known he didn't know, because he is always trying to be friendly with us, as little encouragement as we give him. More than once people have twitted me with it. There's the Wilsons, and the Wilcoxes, and the Harknesses, they take a mean pleasure in saying, '*Your friend* Burgess,' because they know it pesters me. I wish he wouldn't persist in liking us so; I can't think why he keeps it up."

"I can explain it. It's another confession. When the thing was new and hot, and the town made a plan to ride him on a rail, my conscience hurt me so that I couldn't stand it, and I went privately and gave him notice, and he got out of the town and stayed out till it was safe to come back."

"Edward! If the town had found it out—"

"*Don't!* It scares me yet, to think of it. I repented of it the minute it was done; and I was even afraid to tell you, lest your face might betray it to somebody. I didn't sleep any that night, for worrying. But after a few days I saw that no one was going to suspect me, and after that I got to feeling glad I did it. And I feel glad yet, Mary— glad through and through."

"So do I, now, for it would have been a dreadful way to treat him. Yes, I'm glad; for really you did owe him that, you know. But, Edward, suppose it should come out yet, some day!"

"It won't."

"Why?"

"Because everybody thinks it was Goodson."

"Of course they would!"

"Certainly. And of course *he* didn't care. They persuaded poor old Sawlsberry to go and charge it on him, and he went blustering over there and did it. Goodson looked him over, like as if he was hunting for a place on him that he could despise the most, then he says, 'So you are the Committee of Inquiry, are you?' Sawlsberry said that was about what he was. 'Hm. Do they require particulars, or do you reckon a kind of a *general* answer will do?' 'If they require particulars, I will come back. Mr. Goodson; I will take the general answer first.' 'Very well, then, tell them to go to hell—I reckon that's general enough. And I'll give you some advice, Sawlsberry; when you come back for the particulars, fetch a basket to carry the relics of yourself home in.' "

"Just like Goodson; it's got all the marks. He had only one vanity: he thought he could give advice better than any other person."

"It settled the business, and saved us, Mary. The subject was dropped."

"Bless you, I'm not doubting *that*."

Then they took up the gold-sack mystery again, with strong interest. Soon the conversation began to suffer breaks—interruptions caused by absorbed thinkings. The breaks grew more and more frequent. At last Richards lost himself wholly in thought. He sat long, gazing vacantly at the floor, and by and by he began to punctuate his thoughts with little nervous movements of his hands that seemed to indicate vexation. Meantime his wife too had relapsed into a thoughtful silence, and her movements were beginning to show a troubled discomfort. Finally Richards got up and strode aimlessly about the room, plowing his hands through his hair, much as a somnambulist might do who was having a bad dream. Then he seemed to arrive at a definite purpose; and without a word he put on his hat and passed quickly out of the house. His wife sat brooding, with a drawn face, and did not seem to be aware that she was alone. Now and then she murmured, "Lead us not into t— . . . but—

but—we are so poor, so poor! . . . Lead us not into.
. . . Ah, who would be hurt by it?—and no one would
ever know. . . . Lead us. . . ." The voice died out in
mumblings. After a little she glanced up and muttered
in a half-frightened, half-glad way:

"He is gone! But, oh dear, he may be too late—too
late. . . . Maybe not—maybe there is still time." She rose
and stood thinking, nervously clasping and unclasping
her hands. A slight shudder shook her frame, and she
said, out of a dry throat, "God forgive me—it's awful
to think such things—but . . . Lord, how we are made—
how strangely we are made!"

She turned the light low, and slipped stealthily over
and kneeled down by the sack and felt of its ridgy sides
with her hands, and fondled them lovingly; and there
was a gloating light in her poor old eyes. She fell into fits
of absence; and came half out of them at times to mutter, "If we had only waited!—oh, if we had only waited
a little, and not been in such a hurry!"

Meantime Cox had gone home from his office and told
his wife all about the strange thing that had happened,
and they had talked it over eagerly, and guessed that the
late Goodson was the only man in the town who could
have helped a suffering stranger with so noble a sum as
twenty dollars. Then there was a pause, and the two became thoughtful and silent. And by and by nervous and
fidgety. At last the wife said, as if to herself:

"Nobody knows this secret but the Richardses . . . and
us . . . nobody."

The husband came out of his thinkings with a slight
start, and gazed wistfully at his wife, whose face was become very pale; then he hesitatingly rose, and glanced
furtively at his hat, then at his wife—a sort of mute inquiry. Mrs. Cox swallowed once or twice, with her hand
at her throat, then in place of speech she nodded her
head. In a moment she was alone, and mumbling to herself.

And now Richards and Cox were hurrying through the
deserted streets, from opposite directions. They met,
panting, at the foot of the printing office stairs; by the
night light there they read each other's face. Cox whispered:

"Nobody knows about this but us?"

The whispered answer was:

"Not a soul—on honor, not a soul!"

"If it isn't too late to—"

The men were starting upstairs; at this moment they were overtaken by a boy, and Cox asked:

"Is that you, Johnny?"

"Yes, sir."

"You needn't ship the early mail—nor *any* mail; wait till I tell you."

"It's already gone, sir."

"*Gone?*" It had the sound of an unspeakable disappointment in it.

"Yes, sir. Timetable for Brixton and all the towns beyond changed today, sir—had to get the papers in twenty minutes earlier than common. I had to rush; if I had been two minutes later—"

The men turned and walked slowly away, not waiting to hear the rest. Neither of them spoke during ten minutes; then Cox said, in a vexed tone:

"What possessed you to be in such a hurry, *I* can't make out."

The answer was humble enough:

"I see it now, but somehow I never thought, you know, until it was too late. But the next time—"

"Next time be hanged! It won't come in a thousand years."

Then the friends separated without a good night, and dragged themselves home with the gait of mortally stricken men. At their homes their wives sprang up with an eager "Well?" —then saw the answer with their eyes and sank down sorrowing, without waiting for it to come in words. In both houses a discussion followed of a heated sort— a new thing; there had been discussions before, but not heated ones, not ungentle ones. The discussions tonight were a sort of seeming plagiarisms of each other. Mrs. Richards said:

"If you had only waited, Edward—if you had only stopped to think; but no, you must run straight to the printing office and spread it all over the world."

"It *said* publish it."

"That is nothing; it also said do it privately, if you liked. There, now—is that true, or not?"

"Why, yes—yes, it is true; but when I thought what a stir it would make, and what a compliment it was to Hadleyburg that a stranger should trust it so—"

"Oh, certainly, I know all that; but if you had only stopped to think, you would have seen that you *couldn't* find the right man, because he is in his grave, and hasn't left chick nor child nor relation behind him; and as long as the money went to somebody that awfully needed it, and nobody would be hurt by it, and—and—"

She broke down, crying. Her husband tried to think of some comforting thing to say, and presently came out with this:

"But after all, Mary, it must be for the best—it *must* be; we know that. And we must remember that it was so ordered—"

"Ordered! Oh, everything's *ordered*, when a person has to find some way out when he has been stupid. Just the same, it was *ordered* that the money should come to us in this special way, and it was you that must take it on yourself to go meddling with the designs of Providence—and who gave you the right? It was wicked, that is what it was—just blasphemous presumption, and no more becoming to a meek and humble professor of—"

"But, Mary, you know how we have been trained all our lives long, like the whole village, till it is absolutely second nature to us to stop not a single moment to think when there's an honest thing to be done—"

"Oh, I know it, I know it—it's been one everlasting training and training and training in honesty—honesty shielded, from the very cradle, against every possible temptation, and so it's *artificial* honesty, and weak as water when temptation comes, as we have seen this night. God knows I never had shade nor shadow of a doubt of my petrified and indestructible honesty until now—and now, under the very first big and real temptation, I—Edward, it is my belief that this town's honesty is as rotten as mine is; as rotten as yours is. It is a mean town, a hard, stingy town, and hasn't a virtue in the world but this honesty it is so celebrated for and so conceited about; and so help me, I do believe that if ever the day comes that its honesty falls under great temptation, its grand reputation will go to ruin like a house of cards. There, now, I've made confession, and I feel better; I am a humbug, and I've been one all my life, without knowing it. Let no man call me honest again—I will not have it."

"I—well, Mary, I feel a good deal as you do; I certainly do. It seems strange, too, so strange. I never could have believed it—never."

A long silence followed; both were sunk in thought. At last the wife looked up and said:

"I know what you are thinking, Edward."

Richards had the embarrassed look of a person who is caught.

"I am ashamed to confess it, Mary, but—"

"It's no matter, Edward, I was thinking the same question myself."

"I hope so. State it."

"You were thinking, if a body could only guess out *what the remark was* that Goodson made to the stranger."

"It's perfectly true. I feel guilty and ashamed. And you?"

"I'm past it. Let us make a pallet here; we've got to stand watch till the bank vault opens in the morning and admits the sack. . . . Oh dear, oh dear—if we hadn't made the mistake!"

The pallet was made, and Mary said:

"The open sesame—what could it have been? I do wonder what that remark could have been? But come; we will get to bed now."

"And sleep?"

"No: think."

"Yes, think."

By this time the Coxes too had completed their spat and their reconciliation, and were turning in—to think, to think, and toss, and fret, and worry over what the remark could possibly have been which Goodson made to the stranded derelict; that golden remark; that remark worth forty thousand dollars, cash.

The reason that the village telegraph office was open later than usual that night was this: The foreman of Cox's paper was the local representative of the Associated Press. One might say its honorary representative, for it wasn't

four times a year that he could furnish thirty words that
would be accepted. But this time it was different. His
dispatch stating what he had caught got an instant answer:

> Send the whole thing—all the details—twelve hundred
> words.

A colossal order! The foreman filled the bill; and he
was the proudest man in the state. By breakfast time the
next morning the name of Hadleyburg the Incorruptible
was on every lip in America, from Montreal to the Gulf,
from the glaciers of Alaska to the orange groves of
Florida; and millions and millions of people were dis-
cussing the stranger and his money sack, and wondering
if the right man would be found, and hoping some more
news about the matter would come soon—right away.

II

Hadleyburg village woke up world-celebrated—astonished—happy—vain. Vain beyond imagination. Its nineteen principal citizens and their wives went about shaking
hands with each other, and beaming, and smiling, and
congratulating, and saying *this* thing adds a new word to
the dictionary—*Hadleyburg*, synonym for *incorruptible*—
destined to live in dictionaries forever! And the minor
and unimportant citizens and their wives went around
acting in much the same way. Everybody ran to the bank
to see the gold sack; and before noon grieved and envious
crowds began to flock in from Brixton and all neighboring towns; and that afternoon and next day reporters began
to arrive from everywhere to verify the sack and its
history and write the whole thing up anew, and make
dashing freehand pictures of the sack, and of Richards's
house, and the bank, and the Presbyterian church, and
the Baptist church, and the public square, and the town
hall where the test would be applied and the money delivered; and damnable portraits of the Richardses, and
Pinkerton the banker, and Cox, and the foreman, and
Reverend Burgess, and the postmaster—and even of
Jack Halliday, who was the loafing, good-natured, no-
account, irreverent fisherman, hunter, boys' friend, stray-

dogs' friend, typical "Sam Lawson" of the town. The little mean, smirking, oily Pinkerton showed the sack to all comers, and rubbed his sleek palms together pleasantly, and enlarged upon the town's fine old reputation for honesty and upon this wonderful endorsement of it, and hoped and believed that the example would now spread far and wide over the American world, and be epoch-making in the matter of moral regeneration. And so on, and so on.

By the end of a week things had quieted down again; the wild intoxication of pride and joy had sobered to a soft, sweet, silent delight—a sort of deep, nameless, unutterable content. All faces bore a look of peaceful, holy happiness.

Then a change came. It was a gradual change: so gradual that its beginnings were hardly noticed; maybe were not noticed at all, except by Jack Halliday, who always noticed everything; and always made fun of it, too, no matter what it was. He began to throw out chaffing remarks about people not looking quite so happy as they did a day or two ago; and next he claimed that the new aspect was deepening to positive sadness; next, that it was taking on a sick look; and finally he said that everybody was become so moody, thoughtful, and absent-minded that he could rob the meanest man in town of a cent out of the bottom of his breeches pocket and not disturb his revery.

At this stage—or at about this stage—a saying like this was dropped at bedtime—with a sigh, usually—by the head of each of the nineteen principal households: "Ah, what *could* have been the remark that Goodson made?"

And straightway—with a shudder—came this, from the man's wife:

"Oh, *don't!* What horrible thing are you mulling in your mind? Put it away from you, for God's sake!"

But that question was wrung from those men again the next night—and got the same retort. But weaker.

And the third night the men uttered the question yet again—with anguish, and absently. This time—and the following night—the wives fidgeted feebly, and tried to say something. But didn't.

And the night after that they found their tongues and responded—longingly:

"Oh, if we *could* only guess!"

Halliday's comments grew daily more and more sparklingly disagreeable and disparaging. He went diligently about, laughing at the town, individually and in mass. But his laugh was the only one left in the village: it fell upon a hollow and mournful vacancy and emptiness. Not even a smile was findable anywhere. Halliday carried a cigar box around on a tripod, playing that it was a camera, and halted all passers and aimed the thing and said, "Ready!—now look pleasant, please," but not even this capital joke could surprise the dreary faces into any softening.

So three weeks passed—one week was left. It was Saturday evening—after supper. Instead of the aforetime Saturday evening flutter and bustle and shopping and larking, the streets were empty and desolate. Richards and his old wife sat apart in their little parlor—miserable and thinking. This was become their evening habit now: the lifelong habit which had preceded it, of reading, knitting, and contented chat, or receiving or paying neighborly calls, was dead and gone and forgotten, ages ago—two or three weeks ago; nobody talked now, nobody read, nobody visited—the whole village sat at home, sighing, worrying, silent. Trying to guess out that remark.

The postman left a letter. Richards glanced listlessly at the superscription and the postmark—unfamiliar, both —and tossed the letter on the table and resumed his might-have-beens and his hopeless dull miseries where he had left them off. Two or three hours later his wife got wearily up and was going away to bed without a goodnight—custom now—but she stopped near the letter and eyed it awhile with a dead interest, then broke it open, and began to skim it over. Richards, sitting there with his chair tilted back against the wall and his chin between his knees, heard something fall. It was his wife. He sprang to her side, but she cried out:

"Leave me alone, I am too happy. Read the letter— read it!"

He did. He devoured it, his brain reeling. The letter was from a distant state, and it said:

I am a stranger to you, but no matter: I have something to tell. I have just arrived home from Mexico, and learned about that episode. Of course you do not know who made that remark, but I know, and I am the only person living who does know. It was GOODSON. I knew him well, many years ago. I passed through your village that very night, and was his guest till the midnight train came along. I overheard him make that remark to the stranger in the dark—it was in Hale Alley. He and I talked of it the rest of the way home, and while smoking in his house. He mentioned many of your villagers in the course of his talk—most of them in a very uncomplimentary way, but two or three favorably; among these latter yourself. I say "favorably"—nothing stronger. I remember his saying he did not actually LIKE any person in the town—not one; but that you—I THINK he said you—am almost sure—had done him a very great service once, possibly without knowing the full value of it, and he wished he had a fortune, he would leave it to you when he died, and a curse apiece for the rest of the citizens. Now, then, if it was you that did him that service, you are his legitimate heir, and entitled to the sack of gold. I know that I can trust to your honor and honesty, for in a citizen of Hadleyburg these virtues are an unfailing inheritance, and so I am going to reveal to you the remark, well satisfied that if you are not the right man you will seek and find the right one and see that poor Goodson's debt of gratitude for the service referred to is paid. This is the remark: "YOU ARE FAR FROM BEING A BAD MAN: GO, AND REFORM."
HOWARD L. STEPHENSON.

"Oh, Edward, the money is ours, and I am so grateful, *oh,* so grateful—kiss me, dear, it's forever since we kissed—and we needed it so—the money—and now you are free of Pinkerton and his bank, and nobody's slave any more; it seems to me I could fly for joy."

It was a happy half-hour that the couple spent there on the settee caressing each other; it was the old days come again—days that had begun with their courtship and lasted without a break till the stranger brought the deadly money. By and by the wife said:

"Oh, Edward, how lucky it was you did him that grand service, poor Goodson! I never liked him, but I love him now. And it was fine and beautiful of you never to mention it or brag about it." Then, with a touch of reproach,

"But you ought to have told *me,* Edward, you ought to have told your wife, you know."

"Well, I—er—well, Mary, you see—"

"Now stop hemming and hawing, and tell me about it, Edward. I always loved you, and now I'm proud of you. Everybody believes there was only one good generous soul in this village, and now it turns out that you— Edward, why don't you tell me?"

"Well—er—er— Why, Mary, I can't!"

"You *can't? Why* can't you?"

"You see, he—well, he—he made me promise I wouldn't."

The wife looked him over, and said, very slowly.

"Made—you—promise? Edward, what do you tell me that for?"

"Mary, do you think I would lie?"

She was troubled and silent for a moment, then she laid her hand within his and said:

"No . . . no. We have wandered far enough from our bearings—God spare us that! In all your life you have never uttered a lie. But now—now that the foundations of things seem to be crumbling from under us, we— we—" She lost her voice for a moment, then said, brokenly, "Lead us not into temptation. . . . I think you made the promise, Edward. Let it rest so. Let us keep away from that ground. Now—that is all gone by; let us be happy again; it is no time for clouds."

Edward found it something of an effort to comply, for his mind kept wandering—trying to remember what the service was that he had done Goodson.

The couple lay awake the most of the night, Mary happy and busy, Edward busy but not so happy. Mary was planning what she would do with the money. Edward was trying to recall that service. At first his conscience was sore on account of the lie he had told Mary—if it was a lie. After much reflection—suppose it *was* a lie? What then? Was it such a great matter? Aren't we always *acting* lies? Then why not *tell* them? Look at Mary —look what she had done. While he was hurrying off on his honest errand, what was she doing? Lamenting because the papers hadn't been destroyed and the money kept! Is theft better than lying?

That point lost its sting—the lie dropped into the background and left comfort behind it. The next point came to the front: *Had* he rendered that service? Well, here was Goodson's own evidence as reported in Stephenson's letter; there could be no better evidence than that—it was even *proof* that he had rendered it. Of course. So that point was settled. . . . No, not quite. He recalled with a wince that this unknown Mr. Stephenson was just a trifle unsure as to whether the performer of it was Richards or some other—and, oh dear, he had put Richards on his honor! He must himself decide whither that money must go—and Mr. Stephenson was not doubting that if he was the wrong man he would go honorably and find the right one. Oh, it was odious to put a man in such a situation—ah, why couldn't Stephenson have left out that doubt! What did he want to intrude that for?

Further reflection. How did it happen that *Richards'* name remained in Stephenson's mind as indicating the right man, and not some other man's name? That looked good. Yes, that looked very good. In fact, it went on looking better and better, straight along—until by and by it grew into positive *proof*. And then Richards put the matter at once out of his mind, for he had a private instinct that a proof once established is better left so.

He was feeling reasonably comfortable now, but there was still one other detail that kept pushing itself on his notice: of course he had done that service—that was settled; but what *was* that service? He must recall it—he would not go to sleep till he had recalled it; it would make his peace of mind perfect. And so he thought and thought. He thought of a dozen things—possible services, even probable services—but none of them seemed adequate, none of them seemed large enough, none of them seemed worth the money—worth the fortune Goodson had wished he could leave in his will. And besides, he couldn't remember having done them, anyway. Now, then —now, then—what *kind* of a service would it be that would make a man so inordinately grateful? Ah—the saving of his soul! That must be it. Yes, he could remember, now, how he once set himself the task of converting Goodson, and labored at it as much as—he was going to say three months; but upon closer examination it shrunk to a month, then to a week, then to a day, then to nothing. Yes, he remembered now, and with unwelcome vividness, that Goodson had told him to go to thunder and mind his own business—*he* wasn't hankering to follow Hadleyburg to heaven!

So that solution was a failure—he hadn't saved Goodson's soul. Richards was discouraged. Then after a little came another idea: had he saved Goodson's property? No, that wouldn't do—he hadn't any. His life? That is it! Of course. Why, he might have thought of it before. This time he was on the right track, sure. His imagination mill was hard at work in a minute, now.

Thereafter during a stretch of two exhausting hours he was busy saving Goodson's life. He saved it in all kinds of difficult and perilous ways. In every case he got it saved satisfactorily up to a certain point; then, just as he was beginning to get well persuaded that it had really happened, a troublesome detail would turn up which made the whole thing impossible. As in the matter of drowning, for instance. In that case he had swum out and tugged Goodson ashore in an unconscious state with a great crowd looking on and applauding, but when he had got it all thought out and was just beginning to remember all about it, a whole swarm of disqualifying details arrived on the ground: the town would have known of the circumstance, Mary would have known of it, it would glare like a limelight in his own memory instead of being an inconspicuous service which he had possibly rendered "without knowing its full value." And at this point he remembered that he couldn't swim, anyway.

Ah—*there* was a point which he had been overlooking from the start: it had to be a service which he had rendered "possibly without knowing the full value of it." Why, really, that ought to be an easy hunt—much easier than those others. And sure enough, by and by he found it. Goodson, years and years ago, came near marrying a very sweet and pretty girl, named Nancy Hewitt, but in some way or other the match had been broken off; the girl died, Goodson remained a bachelor, and by and by became a soured one and a frank despiser of the human species. Soon after the girl's death the village found out, or thought it had found out, that she carried a spoonful of Negro blood in her veins. Richards worked at these details a good while, and in the end he thought he remembered things concerning them which must have gotten mislaid in his memory through long neglect. He seemed to dimly remember that it was *he* that found out about the Negro blood; that it was he that told the village; that the village told Goodson where they got it; that he thus saved Goodson from marrying the tainted girl; that he had done him this great service "without knowing the full value of it," in fact without knowing that he *was* doing it; but that Goodson knew the value of it, and what a narrow escape he had had, and so went to his grave grateful to his benefactor and wishing he had a fortune to leave him. It was all clear and simple now, and the more he went over it the more luminous and certain it grew; and at last, when he nestled to sleep satisfied and happy, he remembered the whole thing just as if it had been yesterday. In fact, he dimly remembered Goodson's *telling* him his gratitude once. Meantime Mary had spent six thousand dollars on a new house for herself and a pair of slippers for her pastor, and then had fallen peacefully to rest.

That same Saturday evening the postman had delivered a letter to each of the other principal citizens—nineteen letters in all. No two of the envelopes were alike, and no two of the superscriptions were in the same hand, but the letters inside were just like each other in every detail but one. They were exact copies of the letter received by Richards—handwriting and all—and were all signed by Stephenson, but in place of Richards' name each receiver's own name appeared.

All night long eighteen principal citizens did what their caste-brother Richards was doing at the same time—they put in their energies trying to remember what notable service it was that they had unconsciously done Barclay Goodson. In no case was it a holiday job; still they succeeded.

And while they were at this work, which was difficult, their wives put in the night spending the money, which was easy. During that one night the nineteen wives spent an average of seven thousand dollars each out of the forty-thousand in the sack—a hundred and thirty-three thousand altogether.

Next day there was a surprise for Jack Halliday. He noticed that the faces of the nineteen chief citizens and their wives bore that expression of peaceful and holy happiness again. He could not understand it, neither was he able to invent any remarks about it that could damage it or disturb it. And so it was his turn to be dissatisfied with life. His private guesses at the reasons for the happiness failed in all instances, upon examination. When he met Mrs. Wilcox and noticed the placid ecstasy in her face, he said to himself, "Her cat has had kittens"—and went and asked the cook: it was not so; the cook had detected the happiness, but did not know the cause. When Halliday found the duplicate ecstasy in the face of "Shadbelly" Billson (village nickname), he was sure some neighbor of Billson's had broken his leg, but inquiry showed that this had not happened. The subdued ecstasy in Gregory Yates's face could mean but one thing—he was a mother-in-law short: it was another mistake. "And Pinkerton—Pinkerton—he has collected ten cents that he thought he was going to lose." And so on, and so on. In some cases the guesses had to remain in doubt, in the others they proved distinct errors. In the end Halliday said to himself, "Anyway it foots up that there's nineteen Hadleyburg families temporarily in heaven: I don't know how it happened; I only know Providence is off duty today."

An architect and builder from the next state had lately ventured to set up a small business in this unpromising village, and his sign had now been hanging out a week. Not a customer yet; he was a discouraged man, and sorry he had come. But his weather changed suddenly now. First one and then another chief citizen's wife said to him privately:

"Come to my house Monday week—but say nothing about it for the present. We think of building."

He got eleven invitations that day. That night he wrote his daughter and broke off her match with her student. He said she could marry a mile higher than that.

Pinkerton the banker and two or three other well-to-

do men planned country-seats—but waited. That kind
don't count their chickens until they are hatched.

The Wilsons devised a grand new thing—a fancy-dress
ball. They made no actual promises, but told all their
acquaintanceship in confidence that they were thinking
the matter over and thought they should give it—"and
if we do, you will be invited, of course." People were
surprised, and said, one to another, "Why, they are crazy,
those poor Wilsons, they can't afford it." Several among
the nineteen said privately to their husbands, "It is a
good idea: we will keep still till their cheap thing is
over, then *we* will give one that will make it sick."

The days drifted along, and the bill of future squan-
derings rose higher and higher, wilder and wilder, more
and more foolish and reckless. It began to look as if
every member of the nineteen would not only spend his
whole forty thousand dollars before receiving day, but
be actually in debt by the time he got the money. In some
cases lightheaded people did not stop with planning to
spend, they really spent—on credit. They bought land,
mortgages, farms, speculative stocks, fine clothes, horses,
and various other things, paid down the bonus, and
made themselves liable for the rest—at ten days. Presently the sober second thought came, and Halliday noticed that a ghastly anxiety was beginning to show up in
a good many faces. Again he was puzzled, and didn't
know what to make of it. "The Wilcox kittens aren't
dead, for they weren't born; nobody's broken a leg; there's
no shrinkage in mother-in-laws; *nothing* has happened—
it is an unsolvable mystery."

There was another puzzled man, too—the Rev. Mr.
Burgess. For days, wherever he went, people seemed to
follow him or to be watching out for him; and if he ever
found himself in a retired spot, a member of the nineteen
would be sure to appear, thrust an envelope privately into
his hand, whisper "To be opened at the town hall Friday
evening," then vanish away like a guilty thing. He was
expecting that there might be one claimant for the sack,
—doubtful, however, Goodson being dead—but it never
occurred to him that all this crowd might be claimants.
When the great Friday came at last, he found that he had
nineteen envelopes.

III

The town hall had never looked finer. The platform at the end of it was backed by a showy draping of flags; at intervals along the walls were festoons of flags; the gallery fronts were clothed in flags; the supporting columns were swathed in flags; all this was to impress the stranger, for he would be there in considerable force, and in a large degree he would be connected with the press. The house was full. The 412 fixed seats were occupied; also the 68 extra chairs which had been packed into the aisles; the steps of the platform were occupied; some distinguished strangers were given seats on the platform; at the horseshoe of tables which fenced the front and sides of the platform sat a strong force of special correspondents who had come from everywhere. It was the best-dressed house the town had ever produced. There were some tolerably expensive toilets there, and in several cases the ladies who wore them had the look of being unfamiliar with that kind of clothes. At least the town thought they had that look, but the notion could have arisen from the town's knowledge of the fact that these ladies had never inhabited such clothes before.

The gold sack stood on a little table at the front of the platform where all the house could see it. The bulk of the house gazed at it with a burning interest, a mouth-watering interest, a wistful and pathetic interest; a minority of nineteen couples gazed at it tenderly, lovingly, proprietarily, and the male half of this minority kept saying over to themselves the moving little impromptu speeches of thankfulness for the audience's applause and congratulations which they were presently going to get up and deliver. Every now and then one of these got a piece of paper out of his vest-pocket and privately glanced at it to refresh his memory.

Of course there was a buzz of conversation going on—there always is; but at last when the Rev. Mr. Burgess rose and laid his hand on the sack he could hear the microbes gnaw, the place was so still. He related the curious history of the sack, then went on to speak in warm tones of Hadleyburg's old and well-earned repu-

tation for spotless honesty, and of the town's just pride
in this reputation. He said that this reputation was a
treasure of priceless value; that under Providence its
value had now become inestimably enhanced, for the recent episode had spread this fame far and wide, and thus
had focused the eyes of the American world upon this
village, and made its name for all time, as he hoped and
believed, a synonym for commercial incorruptibility.
[*Applause.*] "And who is to be the guardian of this
noble treasure—the community as a whole? No! The responsibility is individual, not communal. From this day
forth each and every one of you is in his own person its
special guardian, and individually responsible that no
harm shall come to it. Do you—does each of you—accept
this great trust? [*Tumultuous assent.*] Then all is well.
Transmit it to your children and to your children's children. Today your purity is beyond reproach—see to it
that it shall remain so. Today there is not a person in
your community who could be beguiled to touch a penny
not his own—see to it that you abide in this grace. [*"We
will! we will!"*] This is not the place to make compari-
sons between ourselves and other communities—some of
them ungracious toward us; they have their ways, we
have ours; let us be content. [*Applause.*] I am done.
Under my hand, my friends, rests a stranger's eloquent
recognition of what we are; through him the world will
always henceforth know what we are. We do not know
who he is, but in your name I utter your gratitude, and
ask you to raise your voices in endorsement."

The house rose in a body and made the walls quake
with the thunders of its thankfulness for the space of a
long minute. Then it sat down, and Mr. Burgess took an
envelope out of his pocket. The house held its breath
while he slit the envelope open and took from it a slip of
paper. He read its contents—slowly and impressively—
the audience listening with tranced attention to this magic
document, each of whose words stood for an ingot of
gold.

" 'The remark which I made to the distressed stranger
was this: "You are very far from being a bad man: go,
and reform." ' " Then he continued:

"We shall know in a moment now whether the remark

here quoted corresponds with the one concealed in the sack; and if that shall prove to be so—and it undoubtedly will—this sack of gold belongs to a fellow citizen who will henceforth stand before the nation as the symbol of the special virtue which has made our town famous throughout the land—Mr. Billson!"

The house had gotten itself all ready to burst into the proper tornado of applause; but instead of doing it, it seemed stricken with a paralysis; there was a deep hush for a moment or two, then a wave of whispered murmurs swept the place—of about this tenor: "*Billson!* oh, come, this is *too* thin! Twenty dollars to a stranger—or *anybody—Billson!* Tell it to the marines!" And now at this point the house caught its breath all of a sudden in a new access of astonishment, for it discovered that whereas in one part of the hall Deacon Billson was standing up with his head meekly bowed, in another part of it Lawyer Wilson was doing the same. There was a wondering silence now for a while.

Everybody was puzzled, and nineteen couples were surprised and indignant.

Billson and Wilson turned and stared at each other. Billson asked, bitingly:

"Why do *you* rise, Mr. Wilson?"

"Because I have a right to. Perhaps you will be good enough to explain to the house why *you* rise?"

"With great pleasure. Because I wrote that paper."

"It is an impudent falsity! I wrote it myself."

It was Burgess's turn to be paralyzed. He stood looking vacantly at first one of the men and then the other, and did not seem to know what to do. The house was stupefied. Lawyer Wilson spoke up, now, and said:

"I ask the Chair to read the name signed to that paper."

That brought the Chair to itself, and it read out the name:

" 'John Wharton *Billson.*' "

"There!" shouted Billson. "What have you got to say for yourself, now? And what kind of apology are you going to make to me and to this insulted house for the imposture which you have attempted to play here?"

"No apologies are due, sir; and as for the rest of it,

I publicly charge you with pilfering my note from Mr. Burgess and substituting a copy of it signed with your own name. There is no other way by which you could have gotten hold of the test-remark; I alone, of living men, possessed the secret of its wording."

There was likely to be a scandalous state of things if this went on; everybody noticed with distress that the shorthand scribes were scribbling like mad; many people were crying "Chair, Chair! Order! Order!" Burgess rapped with his gavel, and said:

"Let us not forget the proprieties due. There has evidently been a mistake somewhere, but surely that is all. If Mr. Wilson gave me an envelope—and I remember now that he did—I still have it."

He took one out of his pocket, opened it, glanced at it, looked surprised and worried, and stood silent a few moments. Then he waved his hand in a wandering and mechanical way, and made an effort or two to say something, then gave it up, despondently. Several voices cried out:

"Read it! Read it! What is it?"

So he began in a dazed and sleepwalker fashion:

" *'The remark which I made to the unhappy stranger was this: "You are far from being a bad man.* [The house gazed at him, marveling.] *Go, and reform."* ' [*Murmurs:* "Amazing! what can this mean?"] This one," said the Chair, "is signed Thurlow G. Wilson."

"There!" cried Wilson, "I reckon that settles it! I knew perfectly well my note was purloined."

"Purloined!" retorted Billson. "I'll let you know that neither you nor any man of your kidney must venture to—"

The Chair. "Order, gentlemen, order! Take your seats, both of you, please."

They obeyed, shaking their heads and grumbling angrily. The house was profoundly puzzled; it did not know what to do with this curious emergency. Presently Thompson got up. Thompson was the hatter. He would have liked to be a Nineteener; but such was not for him: his stock of hats was not considerable enough for the position. He said:

"Mr. Chairman, if I may be permitted to make a suggestion, can both of these gentlemen be right? I put it to you, sir, can both have happened to say the very same words to the stranger? It seems to me—"

The tanner got up and interrupted him. The tanner was a disgruntled man; he believed himself entitled to be a Nineteener, but he couldn't get recognition. It made him a little unpleasant in his ways and speech. Said he:

"Sho, *that's* not the point! *That* could happen—twice in a hundred years—but not the other thing. *Neither* of them gave the twenty dollars!"

[*A ripple of applause.*]

Billson. "*I* did!"

Wilson. "*I* did!"

Then each accused the other of pilfering.

The Chair. "Order! Sit down, if you please—both of you. Neither of the notes has been out of my possession at any moment."

A Voice. "Good—that settles *that!*"

The Tanner. "Mr. Chairman, one thing is now plain: one of these men has been eavesdropping under the other one's bed, and filching family secrets. If it is not unparliamentary to suggest it, I will remark that both are equal to it. [*The Chair.* "Order! Order!"] I withdraw the remark, sir, and will confine myself to suggesting that *if* one of them has overheard the other reveal the test-remark to his wife, we shall catch him now."

A Voice. "How?"

The Tanner. "Easily. The two have not quoted the remark in exactly the same words. You would have noticed that, if there hadn't been a considerable stretch of time and an exciting quarrel inserted between the two readings."

A Voice. "Name the difference."

The Tanner. "The word *very* is in Billson's note, and not in the other."

Many Voices. "That's so—he's right!"

The Tanner. "And so, if the Chair will examine the test-remark in the sack, we shall know which of these two frauds— [*The Chair.* "Order!"]—which of these two adventurers— [*The Chair.* "Order! Order!"]— which of these two gentlemen—[*Laughter and applause*]—is entitled to wear the belt as being the first dishonest blatherskite ever bred in this town—which he has dishonored, and which will be a sultry place for him from now out!" [*Vigorous applause.*]

Many Voices. "Open it!—open the sack!"

Mr. Burgess made a slit in the sack, slid his hand in and brought out an envelope. In it were a couple of folded notes. He said:

"One of these is marked, 'Not to be examined until all written communications which have been addressed to the Chair—if any—shall have been read.' The other is marked *'The Test.'* Allow me. It is worded—to wit:

" 'I do not require that the first half of the remark which was made to me by my benefactor shall be quoted with exactness, for it was not striking, and could be forgotten; but its closing fifteen words are quite striking, and I think easily rememberable; unless *these* shall be accurately reproduced, let the applicant be regarded as an impostor. My benefactor began by saying he seldom gave advice to anyone, but that it always bore the hallmark of high value when he did give it. Then he said this —and it has never faded from my memory: *"You are far from being a bad man—"* ' "

Fifty Voices. "That settles it—the money's Wilson's! Wilson! Wilson! Speech! Speech!"

People jumped up and crowded around Wilson, wringing his hand and congratulating fervently—meantime the Chair was hammering with the gavel and shouting:

"Order, gentlemen! Order! Order! Let me finish reading, please." When quiet was restored, the reading was resumed, as follows:

" '*Go, and reform—or, mark my words—some day, for your sins, you will die and go to hell or Hadleyburg—* TRY AND MAKE IT THE FORMER.' "

A ghastly silence followed. First an angry cloud began to settle darkly upon the faces of the citizenship; after a pause the cloud began to rise, and a tickled expression tried to take its place; tried so hard that it was only kept under with great and painful difficulty; the reporters, the Brixtonites, and other strangers bent their heads down and shielded their faces with their hands, and managed to hold in by main strength and heroic courtesy. At this most inopportune time burst upon the stillness the roar of a solitary voice—Jack Halliday's:

"That's got the hallmark on it!"

Then the house let go, strangers and all. Even Mr. Burgess' gravity broke down presently, then the audience considered itself officially absolved from all restraint, and it made the most of its privilege. It was a good long laugh, and a tempestuously wholehearted one, but it ceased at last—long enough for Mr. Burgess to try to resume, and for the people to get their eyes partially wiped; then it broke out again; and afterward yet again; then at last Burgess was able to get out these serious words:

"It is useless to try to disguise the fact—we find ourselves in the presence of a matter of grave import. It involves the honor of your town, it strikes at the town's good name. The difference of a single word between the test-remarks offered by Mr. Wilson and Mr. Billson was itself a serious thing, since it indicated that one or the other of these gentlemen had committed a theft—"

The two men were sitting limp, nerveless, crushed; but at these words both were electrified into movement, and started to get up.

"Sit down!" said the Chair, sharply, and they obeyed. "That, as I have said, was a serious thing. And it was—but for only one of them. But the matter has become graver; for the honor of *both* is now in formidable peril. Shall I go even further, and say in inextricable peril? *Both* left out the crucial fifteen words." He paused. During several moments he allowed the pervading stillness to gather and deepen its impressive effects, then added: "There would seem to be but one way whereby this could happen. I ask these gentlemen—Was there *collusion?—agreement?*"

A low murmur sifted through the house; its import was, "He's got them both."

Billson was not used to emergencies; he sat in a helpless collapse. But Wilson was a lawyer. He struggled to his feet, pale and worried, and said:

"I ask the indulgence of the house while I explain this most painful matter. I am sorry to say what I am about to say, since it must inflict irreparable injury upon Mr. Billson, whom I have always esteemed and respected until now, and in whose invulnerability to temptation I entirely believed—as did you all. But for the preservation of my own honor I must speak—and with frankness. I confess with shame—and I now beseech your pardon for it—that I said to the ruined stranger all of the words contained in the test-remark, including the disparaging fifteen. [*Sensation.*] When the late publication was made I recalled them, and I resolved to claim the sack of coin, for by every right I was entitled to it. Now I will ask you to consider this point, and weigh it well: that stranger's gratitude to me that night knew no bounds; he said himself that he could find no words for it that were adequate, and that if he should ever be able he would repay me a thousandfold. Now, then, I ask you this: Could I expect—could I believe—could I even remotely imagine—that, feeling as he did, he would do so ungrateful a thing as to add those quite unnecessary fifteen words to his test?—set a trap for me?—expose me as a slanderer of my own town before my own people assembled in a public hall? It was preposterous; it was impossible. His test would contain only the kindly opening clause of my remark. Of that I had no shadow of doubt. You would have thought as I did. You would not have expected a base betrayal from one whom you had befriended and against whom you had committed no offense. And so, with perfect confidence, perfect trust, I wrote on a piece of paper the opening words—ending with 'Go, and reform'—and signed it. When I was about to put it in an envelope I was called into my back office, and without thinking I left the paper lying open on my desk." He stopped, turned his head slowly toward Billson, waited a moment, then added: "I ask you to note this: when I returned, a little later, Mr. Billson was retiring by my street door." [*Sensation.*]

In a moment Billson was on his feet and shouting:

"It's a lie! It's an infamous lie!"

The Chair. "Be seated, sir! Mr. Wilson has the floor."

Billson's friends pulled him into his seat and quieted him, and Wilson went on:

"Those are the simple facts. My note was now lying in a different place on the table from where I had left it. I noticed that, but attached no importance to it, thinking a draft had blown it there. That Mr. Billson would read a private paper was a thing which could not occur to me; he was an honorable man, and he would be above that. If you will allow me to say it, I think his extra word '*very*' stands explained; it is attributable to a defect of memory. I was the only man in the world who could furnish here any detail of the test-remark—by *honorable* means. I have finished."

There is nothing in the world like a persuasive speech to fuddle the mental apparatus and upset the convictions and debauch the emotions of an audience not practiced in the tricks and delusions of oratory. Wilson sat down victorious. The house submerged him in tides of approving applause; friends swarmed to him and shook him by the hand and congratulated him, and Billson was shouted down and not allowed to say a word. The Chair hammered and hammered with its gavel, and kept shouting:

"But let us proceed, gentlemen, let us proceed!"

At last there was a measurable degree of quiet, and the hatter said:

"But what is there to proceed with, sir, but to deliver the money?"

Voices. "That's it! That's it! Come forward, Wilson!"

The Hatter. "I move three cheers for Mr. Wilson, Symbol of the special virtue which—"

The cheers burst forth before he could finish; and in the midst of them—and in the midst of the clamor of the gavel also—some enthusiasts mounted Wilson on a big friend's shoulder and were going to fetch him in triumph to the platform. The Chair's voice now rose above the noise:

"Order! To your places! You forget that there is still a document to be read." When quiet had been restored he took up the document, and was going to read it, but laid it down again, saying, "I forgot; this is not to be read until all written communications received by me have first been read." He took an envelope out of his pocket, removed its enclosure, glanced at it—seemed astonished —held it out and gazed at it—stared at it.

Twenty or thirty voices cried out:

"What is it? Read it! Read it!"

And he did—slowly, and wondering:

" 'The remark which I made to the stranger—
[*Voices.* "Hello! how's this?"]—was this: "You are
far from being a bad man. [*Voices.* "Great Scott!"] Go,
and reform." ' [*Voice.* "Oh, saw my leg off!"] Signed
by Mr. Pinkerton the banker."

The pandemonium of delight which turned itself loose
now was of a sort to make the judicious weep. Those
whose withers were unwrung laughed till the tears ran
down; the reporters, in throes of laughter, set down dis-
ordered pothooks which would never in the world be de-
cipherable; and a sleeping dog jumped up, scared out of
its wits, and barked itself crazy at the turmoil. All manner of cries were scattered through the din: "We're getting rich—*two* Symbols of Incorruptibility!—without
counting Billson!" "*Three!*—count Shadbelly in—we
can't have too many!" "All right—Billson's elected!"
"Alas, poor Wilson—victim of *two* thieves!"

A Powerful Voice. "Silence! The Chair's fished up
something more out of its pocket."

Voices. "Hurrah! Is it something fresh? Read it! Read!
Read!"

The Chair [*reading.*] " 'The remark which I made,'
etc.: "You are far from being a bad man. Go," etc.
Signed, Gregory Yates.' "

Tornado of Voices. "Four Symbols!" " 'Rah for Yates!"
"Fish again!"

The house was in a roaring humor now, and ready to
get all the fun out of the occasion that might be in it.
Several Nineteeners, looking pale and distressed, got up
and began to work their way toward the aisles, but a
score of shouts went up:

"The doors, the doors—close the doors; no Incorruptible shall leave this place! Sit down, everybody!"

The mandate was obeyed.

"Fish again! Read! Read!"

The Chair fished again, and once more the familiar
words began to fall from its lips— " 'You are far from
being a bad man—' "

"Name! name! What's his name?"

"L. Ingoldsby Sargent."

"Five elected! Pile up the Symbols! Go on, go on!"

" 'You are far from being a bad—' "

"Name! name!"

"Nicholas Whitworth."

"Hooray! hooray! It's a symbolical day!"

Somebody wailed in, and began to sing this rhyme (leaving out "it's") to the lovely "Mikado" tune of "When a man's afraid, a beautiful maid—"; the audience joined in, with joy; then, just in time, somebody contributed another line:

"And don't you this forget—"

The house roared it out. A third line was at once furnished:

"Corruptibles far from Hadleyburg are—"

The house roared that one too. As the last note died, Jack Halliday's voice rose high and clear, freighted with a final line:

"But the Symbols are here, you bet!"

That was sung, with booming enthusiasm. Then the happy house started in at the beginning and sang the four lines through twice, with immense swing and dash, and finished up with a crashing three-times-three and a tiger for "Hadleyburg the Incorruptible and all Symbols of it which we shall find worthy to receive the hallmark tonight."

Then the shoutings at the Chair began again, all over the place:

"Go on! Go on! Read! Read some more! Read all you've got!"

"That's it—go on! We are winning eternal celebrity!"

A dozen men got up now and began to protest. They said that this farce was the work of some abandoned joker, and was an insult to the whole community. Without a doubt these signatures were all forgeries—

"Sit down! Sit down! Shut up! You are confessing. We'll find *your* names in the lot."

"Mr. Chairman, how many of those envelopes have you got?"

The Chair counted.

"Together with those that have been already examined, there are nineteen."

A storm of derisive applause broke out.

"Perhaps they all contain the secret. I move that you open them all and read every signature that is attached to a note of that sort—and read also the first eight words of the note."

"Second the motion!"

It was put and carried—uproariously. Then poor old Richards got up, and his wife rose and stood at his side. Her head was bent down, so that none might see that she was crying. Her husband gave her his arm, and so supporting her, he began to speak in a quavering voice:

"My friends, you have known us two—Mary and me —all our lives, and I think you have liked us and respected us—"

The Chair interrupted him:

"Allow me. It is quite true—that which you are saying, Mr. Richards: this town *does* know you two; it *does* like you; it *does* respect you; more—it honors you and *loves* you—"

Halliday's voice rang out:

"That's the hallmarked truth, too! If the Chair is right, let the house speak up and say it. Rise! Now, then—hip! hip! hip!—all together!"

The house rose in mass, faced toward the old couple eagerly, filled the air with a snowstorm of waving handkerchiefs, and delivered the cheers with all its affectionate heart.

The Chair then continued:

"What I was going to say is this: We know your good heart, Mr. Richards, but this is not a time for the exercise of charity toward offenders. [*Shouts of "Right! right!"*] I see your generous purpose in your face, but I cannot allow you to plead for these men—"

"But I was going to—"

"Please take your seat, Mr. Richards. We must examine the rest of these notes—simple fairness to the men who have already been exposed requires this. As soon as that has been done—I give you my word for this—you shall be heard."

Many Voices. "Right!—the Chair is right—no interruption can be permitted at this stage! Go on!—the names! the names!—according to the terms of the motion!"

The old couple sat reluctantly down, and the husband whispered to the wife, "It is pitifully hard to have to wait; the shame will be greater than ever when they find we were only going to plead for *ourselves.*"

Straightway the jollity broke loose again with the reading of the names.

" 'You are far from being a bad man—' Signature, Robert J. Titmarsh.

" 'You are far from being a bad man—' Signature, Eliphalet Weeks.

" 'You are far from being a bad man—' Signature, Oscar B. Wilder."

At this point the house lit upon the idea of taking the eight words out of the Chairman's hands. He was not unthankful for that. Thenceforward he held up each note in its turn, and waited. The house droned out the eight words in a massed and measured and musical deep volume of sound (with a daringly close resemblance to a well-known church chant)— " 'You are f-a-r from being a b-a-a-a-d man.' " Then the Chair said, "Signature, Archibald Wilcox." And so on, and so on, name after name, and everybody had an increasingly and gloriously good time except the wretched Nineteen. Now and then, when a particularly shining name was called, the house made the Chair wait while it chanted the whole of the test-remark from the beginning to the closing words, "And go to hell or Hadleyburg—try and make it the for-or-m-e-r!" and in these special cases they added a grand and agonized and imposing "A-a-a-a-*men!*"

The list dwindled, dwindled, dwindled, poor old Richards keeping tally of the count, wincing when a name resembling his own was pronounced, and waiting in miserable suspense for the time to come when it would be his humiliating privilege to rise with Mary and finish his plea, which he was intending to word thus: ". . . for until now we have never done any wrong thing, but have gone our humble way unreproached. We are very poor, we are old, and have no chick nor child to help us; we were sorely tempted, and we fell. It was my purpose when I got up before to make confession and beg that my name might not be read out in this public place, for it seemed to us that we could not bear it; but I was prevented. It was just; it was our place to suffer with the rest. It has been hard for us. It is the first time we have ever heard our name fall from anyone's lips—sullied. Be merciful—for the sake of the better days; make our shame as light to bear as in your charity you can." At this point in his reverie Mary nudged him, perceiving that his mind was absent. The house was chanting, "You are f-a-r," etc.

"Be ready," Mary whispered. "Your name comes now; he has read eighteen."

The chant ended.

"Next! next! next!" came volleying from all over the house.

Burgess put his hand into his pocket. The old couple, trembling, began to rise. Burgess fumbled a moment, then said:

"I find I have read them all."

Faint with joy and surprise, the couple sank into their seats, and Mary whispered:

"Oh, bless God, we are saved! He has lost ours—I wouldn't give this for a hundred of those sacks!"

The house burst out with its "Mikado" travesty, and sang it three times with ever-increasing enthusiasm, rising to its feet when it reached for the third time the closing line:

"But the Symbols are here, you bet!"

and finishing up with cheers and a tiger for "Hadleyburg purity and our eighteen immortal representatives of it."

Then Wingate, the saddler, got up and proposed cheers "for the cleanest man in town, the one solitary important citizen in it who didn't try to steal that money—Edward Richards."

They were given with great and moving heartiness; then somebody proposed that Richards be elected sole guardian and Symbol of the now Sacred Hadleyburg Tradition, with power and right to stand up and look the whole sarcastic world in the face.

Passed, by acclamation. Then they sang the "Mikado" again, and ended it with:

"And there's *one* Symbol left, you bet!"

There was a pause; then:

A Voice. "Now, then, who's to get the sack?"

The Tanner (with bitter sarcasm). "That's easy. The money has to be divided among the eighteen Incorruptibles. They gave the suffering stranger twenty dollars apiece—and that remark—each in his turn—it took twenty-two minutes for the procession to move past. Staked the stranger—total contribution, $360. All they want is just the loan back—and interest—forty thousand dollars altogether."

Many Voices [derisively.] "That's it! Divvy! Divvy! Be kind to the poor—don't keep them waiting!"

The Chair. "Order! I now offer the stranger's remaining document. It says: 'If no claimant shall appear [*grand chorus of groans*], I desire that you open the sack and count out the money to the principal citizens of your town, they to take it in trust [*cries of "Oh! Oh! Oh!"*], and use it in such ways as to them shall seem best for the propagation and preservation of your community's noble reputation for incorruptible honesty [*more cries*]—a reputation to which their names and their efforts will add a new and far-reaching luster.' [*Enthusiastic outburst of sarcastic applause.*] That seems to be all. No—here is a postscript:

" 'P. S.—CITIZENS OF HADLEYBURG: There *is* no test-remark—nobody made one. [*Great sensation.*] There wasn't any pauper stranger, nor any twenty-dollar contribution, nor any accompanying benediction and compliment—these are all inventions. [*General buzz and hum of astonishment and delight.*] Allow me to tell my story —it will take but a word or two. I passed through your town at a certain time, and received a deep offense which I had not earned. Any other man would have been content to kill one or two of you and call it square, but to me that would have been a trivial revenge, and inadequate; for the dead do not *suffer*. Besides, I could not kill you all—and, anyway, made as I am, even that would not have satisfied me. I wanted to damage every man in the place, and every woman—and not in their bodies or in their estate, but in their vanity—the place where feeble

and foolish people are most vulnerable. So I disguised
myself and came back and studied you. You were easy
game. You had an old and lofty reputation for honesty,
and naturally you were proud of it—it was your treasure
of treasures, the very apple of your eye. As soon as I
found out that you carefully and vigilantly kept yourselves and your children *out of temptation,* I knew how
to proceed. Why, you simple creatures, the weakest of
all weak things is a virtue which has not been tested in
the fire. I laid a plan, and gathered a list of names. My
project was to corrupt Hadleyburg the Incorruptible.
My idea was to make liars and thieves of nearly half a
hundred smirchless men and women who had never in
their lives uttered a lie or stolen a penny. I was afraid of
Goodson. He was neither born nor reared in Hadleyburg.
I was afraid that if I started to operate my scheme by
getting my letter laid before you, you would say to yourselves, "Goodson is the only man among us who would
give away twenty dollars to a poor devil"—and then you
might not bite at my bait. But Heaven took Goodson;
then I knew I was safe, and I set my trap and baited it.
It may be that I shall not catch all the men to whom I
mailed the pretended test secret, but I shall catch the
most of them, if I know Hadleyburg nature. [*Voices.*
"Right—he got every last one of them."] I believe they
will even steal ostensible *gamble*-money, rather than miss,
poor, tempted, and mistrained fellows. I am hoping to
eternally and everlastingly squelch your vanity and give
Hadleyburg a new renown—one that will *stick*—and
spread far. If I have succeeded, open the sack and summon the Committee on Propagation and Preservation of
the Hadleyburg Reputation.' "

A Cyclone of Voices. "Open it! Open it! The Eighteen
to the front! Committee on Propagation of the Tradition!
Forward—the Incorruptibles!"

The Chair ripped the sack wide, and gathered up a
handful of bright, broad, yellow coins, shook them together, then examined them.

"Friends, they are only gilded disks of lead!"

There was a crashing outbreak of delight over this
news, and when the noise had subsided, the tanner called
out:

"By right of apparent seniority in this business, Mr. Wilson is Chairman of the Committee on Propagation of the Tradition. I suggest that he step forward on behalf of his pals, and receive in trust the money."

A Hundred Voices. "Wilson! Wilson! Wilson! Speech! Speech!"

Wilson [*in a voice trembling with anger.*] "You will allow me to say, and without apologies for my language, *damn* the money!"

A Voice. "Oh, and him a Baptist!"

A Voice. "Seventeen Symbols left! Step up, gentlemen, and assume your trust!"

There was a pause—no response.

The Saddler. "Mr. Chairman, we've got *one* clean man left, anyway, out of the late aristocracy; and he needs money, and deserves it. I move that you appoint Jack Halliday to get up there and auction off that sack of gilt twenty-dollar pieces, and give the result to the right man— the man whom Hadleyburg delights to honor—Edward Richards."

This was received with great enthusiasm, the dog taking a hand again; the saddler started the bids at a dollar, the Brixton folk and Barnum's representative fought hard for it, the people cheered every jump that the bids made, the excitement climbed moment by moment higher and higher, the bidders got on their mettle and grew steadily more and more daring, more and more determined, the jumps went from a dollar up to five, then to ten, then to twenty, then fifty, then to a hundred, then—

At the beginning of the auction Richards whispered in distress to his wife: "O Mary, can we allow it? It—it —you see, it is an honor reward, a testimonial to purity of character, and—and—can we allow it? Hadn't I better get up and—O Mary, what ought we to do?—what do you think we—" [*Halliday's voice.* "Fifteen I'm bid!— fifteen for the sack!—twenty!—ah, thanks!— thirty—thanks again! Thirty, thirty, thirty!—do I hear forty?—forty it is! Keep the ball rolling, gentlemen, keep it rolling!—fifty!—thanks, noble Roman! going at fifty, fifty, fifty!—seventy!—ninety!—splendid!—a hundred!— pile it up, pile it up!—hundred and twenty—forty!—just in time!—hundred and fifty!—*TWO hundred!*—superb! Do*

I hear two h—thanks!—two hundred and fifty!—"]

"It is another temptation, Edward—I'm all in a tremble —but, oh, we've escaped *one* temptation, and that ought to warn us to— [*"Six did I hear?—thanks!—six fifty, six f—*SEVEN *hundred!"*]   And yet, Edward, when you think—nobody susp— [*"Eight hundred dollars!—hurrah!—make it nine!—Mr. Parsons, did I hear you say— thanks—nine!—this noble sack of virgin lead going at only nine hundred dollars, gilding and all—come! do I hear—a thousand!—gratefully yours!—did someone say eleven?—a sack which is going to be the most celebrated in the whole Uni—"*]   O Edward" (beginning to sob), "we are *so* poor!—but—but—do as you think best—do as you think best."

Edward fell—that is, he sat still; sat with a conscience which was not satisfied, but which was overpowered by circumstances.

Meantime a stranger, who looked like an amateur detective gotten up as an impossible English earl, had been watching the evening's proceedings with manifest interest, and with a contented expression in his face; and he had been privately commenting to himself. He was now soliloquizing somewhat like this: "None of the Eighteen are bidding; that is not satisfactory; I must change that—the dramatic unities require it; they must buy the sack they tried to steal; they must pay a heavy price, too—some of them are rich. And another thing, when I make a mistake in Hadleyburg nature the man that puts that error upon me is entitled to a high honorarium, and someone must pay it. This poor old Richards has brought my judgment to shame; he is an honest man. I don't understand it, but I acknowledge it. Yes, he saw my deuces *and* with a straight flush, and by rights the pot is his. And it shall be a jackpot, too, if I can manage it. He disappointed me, but let that pass."

He was watching the bidding. At a thousand, the market broke; the prices tumbled swiftly. He waited—and still watched. One competitor dropped out; then another, and another. He put in a bid or two, now. When the bids had sunk to ten dollars, he added a five; someone raised him a three; he waited a moment, then flung in a fifty-dollar jump, and the sack was his—at $1,282. The house broke out in cheers—then stopped; for he was on his feet, and had lifted his hand. He began to speak.

"I desire to say a word, and ask a favor. I am a speculator in rarities, and I have dealings with persons interested in numismatics all over the world. I can make a profit on this purchase, just as it stands; but there is a way, if I can get your approval, whereby I can make every one of these leaden twenty-dollar pieces worth its face in gold, and perhaps more. Grant me that approval, and I will give part of my gains to your Mr. Richards, whose invulnerable probity you have so justly and so cordially recognized to-night; his share shall be ten thousand dollars, and I will hand him the money to-morrow. [*Great applause from the house.* But the "invulnerable probity" made the Richardses blush prettily; however, it went for modesty, and did no harm.] If you will pass my proposition by a good majority—I would like a two-thirds vote—I will regard that as the town's consent, and that is all I ask. Rarities are always helped by any device which will rouse curiosity and compel remark. Now if I may have your permission to stamp upon the faces of each of these ostensible coins the names of the eighteen gentlemen who—"

Nine-tenths of the audience were on their feet in a moment—dog and all—and the proposition was carried with a whirlwind of approving applause and laughter.

They sat down, and all the Symbols except "Dr." Clay Harkness got up, violently protesting against the proposed outrage, and threatening to—

"I beg you not to threaten me," said the stranger, calmly. "I know my legal rights, and am not accustomed to being frightened at bluster." [*Applause.*] He sat down. "Dr." Harkness saw an opportunity here. He was one of the two very rich men of the place, and Pinkerton was the other. Harkness was proprietor of a mint; that is to say, a popular patent medicine. He was running for the Legislature on one ticket, and Pinkerton on the other. It was a close race and a hot one, and getting hotter every day. Both had strong appetites for money; each had bought a great tract of land, with a purpose; there was going to be a new railway, and each wanted to be in the Legislature and help locate the route to his own advantage; a single vote might make the decision, and with it two or three fortunes. The stake was large, and Harkness was a daring speculator. He was sitting close to the stranger. He leaned over while one or another of the other Symbols was entertaining the house with protests and appeals, and asked, in a whisper:

"What is your price for the sack?"

"Forty thousand dollars."

"I'll give you twenty."

"No."

"Twenty-five."

"No."

"Say thirty."

"The price is forty thousand dollars; not a penny less."

"All right, I'll give it. I will come to the hotel at ten in the morning. I don't want it known; will see you privately."

"Very good." Then the stranger got up and said to the house:

"I find it late. The speeches of these gentlemen are not without merit, not without interest, not without grace; yet if I may be excused I will take my leave. I thank you for the great favor which you have shown me in granting my petition. I ask the Chair to keep the sack for me until tomorrow, and to hand these three five-hundred-dollar notes to Mr. Richards." They were passed up to the Chair. "At nine I will call for the sack, and at eleven will deliver the rest of the ten thousand to Mr. Richards in person, at his home. Good night."

Then he slipped out, and left the audience making a vast noise, which was composed of a mixture of cheers, the "Mikado" song, dog-disapproval, and the chant, "You are f-a-r from being a b-a-a-d man—a-a-a a-men!"

IV

At home the Richardses had to endure congratulations and compliments until midnight. Then they were left to themselves. They looked a little sad, and they sat silent and thinking. Finally Mary sighed and said:

"Do you think we are to blame, Edward—*much* to blame?" And her eyes wandered to the accusing triplet of big banknotes lying on the table, where the congratulators had been gloating over them and reverently fingering them. Edward did not answer at once; then he brought out a sigh and said, hesitatingly:

"We—we couldn't help it, Mary. It—well, it was ordered. *All* things are."

Mary glanced up and looked at him steadily, but he didn't return the look. Presently she said:

"I thought congratulations and praises always tasted good. But—it seems to me, now—Edward?"

"Well?"

"Are you going to stay in the bank?"

"N-no."

"Resign?"

"In the morning—by note."

"It does seem best."

Richards bowed his head in his hands and muttered:

"Before, I was not afraid to let oceans of people's money pour through my hands, but—Mary, I am so tired, so tired—"

"We will go to bed."

At nine in the morning the stranger called for the sack and took it to the hotel in a cab. At ten Harkness had a talk with him privately. The stranger asked for and got five checks on a metropolitan bank—drawn to "Bearer" —four for $1,500 each, and one for $34,000. He put one of the former in his pocketbook, and the remainder, representing $38,500, he put in an envelope, and with these he added a note, which he wrote after Harkness was gone. At eleven he called at the Richards house and knocked. Mrs. Richards peeped through the shutters, then went and received the envelope, and the stranger disappeared without a word. She came back flushed and a little unsteady on her legs, and gasped out:

"I am sure I recognized him! Last night it seemed to me that maybe I had seen him somewhere before."

"He is the man that brought the sack here?"

"I am almost sure of it."

"Then he is the ostensible Stephenson, too, and sold every important citizen in this town with his bogus secret. Now if he has sent checks instead of money, we are sold, too, after we thought we had escaped. I was beginning to feel fairly comfortable once more, after my night's rest, but the look of that envelope makes me sick. It isn't fat enough; $8,500 in even the largest banknotes makes more bulk than that."

"Edward, why do you object to checks?"

"Checks signed by Stephenson! I am resigned to take the $8,500 if it could come in banknotes—for it does seem that it was so ordered, Mary—but I have never had much courage, and I have not the pluck to try to market a check signed with that disastrous name. It would be a trap. That man tried to catch me; we escaped somehow or other; and now he is trying a new way. If it is checks—"

"Oh, Edward, it is *too* bad!" And she held up the checks and began to cry.

"Put them in the fire! Quick! We mustn't be tempted. It is a trick to make the world laugh at *us,* along with the rest, and— Give them to *me,* since you can't do it!" He snatched them and tried to hold his grip till he could get to the stove; but he was human, he was a cashier, and he stopped a moment to make sure of the signature. Then he came near to fainting.

"Fan me, Mary, fan me! They are the same as gold!"

"Oh, how lovely, Edward! Why?"

"Signed by Harkness. What can the mystery of that be, Mary?"

"Edward, do you think—"

"Look here—look at this! Fifteen—fifteen—fifteen—thirty-four. Thirty-eight thousand five hundred! Mary, the sack isn't worth twelve dollars, and Harkness—apparently —has paid about par for it."

"And does it all come to us, do you think—instead of the ten thousand?"

"Why, it looks like it. And the checks are made to 'Bearer,' too."

"Is that good, Edward? What is it for?"

"A hint to collect them at some distant bank, I reckon. Perhaps Harkness doesn't want the matter known. What is that—a note?"

"Yes. It was with the checks."

It was in the "Stephenson" handwriting, but there was no signature. It said:

I am a disappointed man. Your honesty is beyond the reach of temptation. I had a different idea about it, but I wronged you in that, and I beg pardon, and do it sincerely. I honor you—and that is sincere too. This town is not worthy to kiss the hem of your garment. Dear sir, I made a square bet with myself that there were nineteen debauchable men in your self-righteous community. I have lost. Take the whole pot, you are entitled to it.

Richards drew a deep sigh, and said:

"It seems written with fire—it burns so. Mary—I am miserable again."

"I, too. Ah, dear, I wish—"

"To think, Mary—he *believes* in me."

"Oh, don't, Edward—I can't bear it."

"If those beautiful words were deserved, Mary—and God knows I believed I deserved them once—I think I could give the forty thousand dollars for them. And I would put that paper away, as representing more than gold and jewels, and keep it always. But now— We could not live in the shadow of its accusing presence, Mary."

He put it in the fire.

A messenger arrived and delivered an envelope.

Richards took from it a note and read it; it was from Burgess.

You saved me, in a difficult time. I saved you last night. It was at cost of a lie, but I made the sacrifice freely, and out of a grateful heart. None in this village knows so well as I know how brave and good and noble you are. At bottom you cannot respect me, knowing as you do of that matter of which I am accused, and by the general voice condemned; but I beg that you will at least believe that I am a grateful man; it will help me to bear my burden.

[Signed]   BURGESS.

"Saved, once more. And on such terms!" He put the note in the fire. "I—I wish I were dead, Mary, I wish I were out of it all."

"Oh, these are bitter, bitter days, Edward. The stabs, through their very generosity, are so deep—and they come so fast!"

Three days before the election each of two thousand voters suddenly found himself in possession of a prized

memento—one of the renowned bogus double eagles.
Around one of its faces was stamped these words:
"THE REMARK I MADE TO THE POOR STRANGER WAS—"
Around the other face was stamped these: "GO, AND RE-
FORM. [SIGNED] PINKERTON." Thus the entire remaining refuse of the renowned joke was emptied upon a
single head, and with calamitous effect. It revived the
recent vast laugh and concentrated it upon Pinkerton;
and Harkness's election was a walkover.

Within twenty-four hours after the Richardses had received their checks their consciences were quieting down,
discouraged; the old couple were learning to reconcile
themselves to the sin which they had committed. But they
were to learn, now, that a sin takes on new and real
terrors when there seems a chance that it is going to be
found out. This gives it a fresh and most substantial and
important aspect. At church the morning sermon was of
the usual pattern; it was the same old things said in the
same old way; they had heard them a thousand times
and found them innocuous, next to meaningless, and easy
to sleep under; but now it was different: the sermon
seemed to bristle with accusations; it seemed aimed
straight and specially at people who were concealing
deadly sins. After church they got away from the mob of
congratulators as soon as they could, and hurried homeward, chilled to the bone at they did not know what—
vague, shadowy, indefinite fears. And by chance they
caught a glimpse of Mr. Burgess as he turned a corner.
He paid no attention to their nod of recognition! He hadn't
seen it; but they did not know that. What could his conduct mean? It might mean—it might mean—oh, a dozen
dreadful things. Was it possible that he knew that
Richards could have cleared him of guilt in that bygone
time, and had been silently waiting for a chance to even
up accounts? At home, in their distress they got to
imagining that their servant might have been in the next
room listening when Richards revealed the secret to his
wife that he knew of Burgess's innocence; next, Richards
began to imagine that he had heard the swish of a gown
in there at that time; next, he was sure he *had* heard it.
They would call Sarah in, on a pretext, and watch her
face: if she had been betraying them to Mr. Burgess, it

would show in her manner. They asked her some questions—questions which were so random and incoherent and seemingly purposeless that the girl felt sure that the old people's minds had been affected by their sudden good fortune; the sharp and watchful gaze which they bent upon her frightened her, and that completed the business. She blushed, she became nervous and confused, and to the old people these were plain signs of guilt—guilt of some fearful sort or other—without doubt she was a spy and a traitor. When they were alone again they began to piece many unrelated things together and get horrible results out of the combination. When things had got about to the worst, Richards was delivered of a sudden gasp, and his wife asked:

"Oh what is it?—What is it?"

"The note—Burgess's note! Its language was sarcastic, I see it now." He quoted: "'At bottom you cannot respect me, *knowing,* as you do, of *that matter* of which I am accused'—oh, it is perfectly plain, now, God help me! He knows that I know! You see the ingenuity of the phrasing. It was a trap—and like a fool, I walked into it. And Mary—?"

"Oh, it is dreadful—I know what you are going to say—he didn't return your transcript of the pretended test-remark."

"No—kept it to destroy us with. Mary, he has exposed us to some already. I know it—I know it well. I saw it in a dozen faces after church. Ah, he wouldn't answer our nod of recognition—*he* knew what he had been doing!"

In the night the doctor was called. The news went around in the morning that the old couple were rather seriously ill—prostrated by the exhausting excitement growing out of their great windfall, the congratulations, and the late hours, the doctor said. The town was sincerely distressed; for these old people were about all it had left to be proud of, now.

Two days later the news was worse. The old couple were delirious, and were doing strange things. By witness of the nurses, Richards had exhibited checks—for $8,500? No—for an amazing sum—$38,500! What could be the explanation of this gigantic piece of luck?

The following day the nurses had more news—and wonderful. They had concluded to hide the checks, lest harm come to them; but when they searched they were gone from under the patient's pillow—vanished away. The patient said:

"Let the pillow alone; what do you want?"

"We thought it best that the checks—"

"You will never see them again—they are destroyed. They came from Satan. I saw the hell-brand on them, and I knew they were sent to betray me to sin." Then he fell to gabbling strange and dreadful things which were not clearly understandable, and which the doctor admonished them to keep to themselves.

Richards was right; the checks were never seen again.

A nurse must have talked in her sleep, for within two days the forbidden gabblings were the property of the town; and they were of a surprising sort. They seemed to indicate that Richards had been a claimant for the sack himself, and that Burgess had concealed that fact and then maliciously betrayed it.

Burgess was taxed with this and stoutly denied it. And he said it was not fair to attach weight to the chatter of a sick old man who was out of his mind. Still, suspicion was in the air, and there was much talk.

After a day or two it was reported that Mrs. Richards' delirious deliveries were getting to be duplicates of her husband's. Suspicion flamed up into conviction, now, and the town's pride in the purity of its one undiscredited important citizen began to dim down and flicker toward extinction.

Six days passed, then came more news. The old couple were dying. Richards' mind cleared in his latest hour, and he sent for Burgess. Burgess said:

"Let the room be cleared. I think he wishes to say something in privacy."

"No!" said Richards: "I want witnesses. I want you all to hear my confession, so that I may die a man, and not a dog. I was clean—artificially—like the rest; and like the rest I fell when temptation came. I signed a lie, and claimed the miserable sack. Mr. Burgess remembered that I had done him a service, and in gratitude (and ignorance) he suppressed my claim and saved me.

You know the thing that was charged against Burgess years ago. My testimony, and mine alone, could have cleared him, and I was a coward, and left him to suffer disgrace—"

"No—no—Mr. Richards, you—"

"My servant betrayed my secret to him—"

"No one has betrayed anything to me—"

—"and then he did a natural and justifiable thing, he repented of the saving kindness which he had done me, and he *exposed* me—as I deserved—"

"Never!—I make oath—"

"Out of my heart I forgive him."

Burgess's impassioned protestations fell upon deaf ears; the dying man passed away without knowing that once more he had done poor Burgess a wrong. The old wife died that night.

The last of the sacred Nineteen had fallen a prey to the fiendish sack; the town was stripped of the last rag of its ancient glory. Its mourning was not showy, but it was deep.

By act of the Legislature—upon prayer and petition—Hadleyburg was allowed to change its name to (never mind what—I will not give it away), and leave one word out of the motto that for many generations had graced the town's official seal.

It is an honest town once more, and the man will have to rise early that catches it napping again.

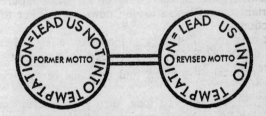

FORMER MOTTO — LEAD US NOT INTO TEMPTATION

REVISED MOTTO — LEAD US INTO TEMPTATION

The Five Boons of Life

I

IN the morning of life came the good fairy with her basket, and said: "Here are gifts. Take one, leave the others. And be wary, choose wisely! oh, choose wisely! for only one of them is valuable."

The gifts were five: Fame, Love, Riches, Pleasure, Death. The youth said eagerly:

"There is no need to consider": and he chose Pleasure.

He went out into the world and sought out the pleasures that youth delights in. But each in its turn was short-lived and disappointing, vain and empty; and each, departing, mocked him. In the end he said: "Those years I have wasted. If I could but choose again, I would choose wisely."

II

The fairy appeared, and said:

"Four of the gifts remain. Choose once more; and oh remember—time is flying, and only one of them is precious."

The man considered long, then chose Love; and did not mark the tears that rose in the fairy's eyes.

After many, many years the man sat by a coffin, in an empty home. And he communed with himself, saying: "One by one they have gone away and left me; and now she lies here, the dearest and the last. Desolation after

138

desolation has swept over me; for each hour of happiness the treacherous trader, Love, has sold me I have paid a thousand hours of grief. Out of my heart of hearts I curse him."

III

"Choose again." It was the fairy speaking. "The years have taught you wisdom—surely it must be so. Three gifts remain. Only one of them has any worth—remember it, and choose warily."

The man reflected long, and then chose Fame; and the fairy, sighing, went her way.

Years went by and she came again, and stood behind the man where he sat solitary in the fading day, thinking. And she knew his thought:

"My name filled the world, and its praises were on every tongue, and it seemed well with me for a little while. How little a while it was! Then came envy; then detraction; then calumny; then hate; then persecution. Then derision, which is the beginning of the end. And last of all came pity, which is the funeral of fame. Oh, the bitterness and misery of renown! Target for mud in its prime, for contempt and compassion in its decay."

IV

"Choose yet again." It was the fairy's voice. "Two gifts remain. And do not despair. In the beginning there was but one that was precious, and it is still here."

"Wealth—which is power! How blind I was!" said the man. "Now, at last, life will be worth the living. I will spend, squander, dazzle. These mockers and despisers will crawl in the dirt before me, and I will feed my hungry heart with their envy. I will have all luxuries, all joys, all enchantments of the spirit, all contentments of the body that man holds dear. I will buy, buy, buy! deference, respect, esteem, worship—every pinchbeck grace of life the market of a trivial world can furnish forth. I have lost much time, and chosen badly heretofore, but let that pass; I was ignorant then, and could but take for best what seemed so."

Three short years went by, and a day came when the man sat shivering in a mean garret; and he was gaunt and wan and hollow-eyed, and clothed in rags; and he was gnawing a dry crust and mumbling:

"Curse all the world's gifts, for mockeries and gilded lies! And miscalled, every one. They are not gifts but merely lendings. Pleasure, Love, Fame, Riches, they are but temporary disguises for lasting realities—Pain, Grief, Shame, Poverty. The fairy said true: in all her store there was but one gift which was precious, only one that was not valueless. How poor and cheap and mean I know those others now to be, compared with that inestimable one, that dear and sweet and kindly one, that steeps in dreamless and enduring sleep the pains that persecute the body, and the shames and griefs that eat the mind and heart. Bring it! I am weary, I would rest."

V

The fairy came, bringing again four of the gifts, but Death was wanting. She said:

"I gave it to a mother's pet, a little child. It was ignorant, but trusted me, asking me to choose for it. You did not ask me to choose."

"Oh, miserable me! What is there left for me?"

"What not even you have deserved: the wanton insult of Old Age."

Was It Heaven? Or Hell?

I

Y ou told a *lie?*"

"You confess it—you actually confess it—you told a lie!"

II

The family consisted of four persons: Margaret Lester, widow, aged thirty-six; Helen Lester, her daughter, aged sixteen; Mrs. Lester's maiden aunts, Hannah and Hester Gray, twins, aged sixty-seven. Waking and sleeping, the three women spent their days and nights in adoring the young girl; in watching the movements of her sweet spirit in the mirror of her face; in refreshing their souls with the vision of her bloom and beauty; in listening to the music of her voice; in gratefully recognizing how rich and fair for them was the world with this presence in it; in shuddering to think how desolate it would be with this light gone out of it.

By nature—and inside—the aged aunts were utterly dear and lovable and good, but in the matter of morals and conduct their training had been so uncompromisingly strict that it had made them exteriorly austere, not to say stern. Their influence was effective in the house; so effective that the mother and the daughter conformed to its moral and religious requirements cheerfully, contentedly, happily, unquestioningly. To do this was become second nature to them. And so in this peaceful heaven there were no clashings, no irritations, no faultfindings, no heartburnings.

In it a lie had no place. In it a lie was unthinkable. In it speech was restricted to absolute truth, iron-bound truth, implacable and uncompromising truth, let the resulting consequences be what they might. At last, one day, under stress of circumstances, the darling of the house sullied her lips with a lie—and confessed it, with tears and self-upbraidings. There are not any words that can paint the consternation of the aunts. It was as if the sky had crumpled up and collapsed and the earth had tumbled to ruin with a crash. They sat side by side, white and stern, gazing speechless upon the culprit, who was on her knees before them with her face buried first in one lap and then the other, moaning and sobbing, and appealing for sympathy and forgiveness and getting no response, humbly kissing the hand of the one, then of the other, only to see it withdrawn as suffering defilement by those soiled lips.

Twice, at intervals, Aunt Hester said, in frozen amazement:

"You told a *lie?*"

Twice, at intervals, Aunt Hannah followed with the muttered and amazed ejaculation:

"You confess it—you actually confess it—you told a lie!"

It was all they could say. The situation was new, unheard-of, incredible; they could not understand it, they did not know how to take hold of it, it approximately paralyzed speech.

At length it was decided that the erring child must be taken to her mother, who was ill, and who ought to know what had happened. Helen begged, besought, implored that she might be spared this further disgrace, and that her mother might be spared the grief and pain of it; but this could not be: duty required this sacrifice, duty takes precedence of all things, nothing can absolve one from a duty, with a duty no compromise is possible.

Helen still begged, and said the sin was her own, her mother had had no hand in it—why must she be made to suffer for it?

But the aunts were obdurate in their righteousness, and said the law that visited the sins of the parent upon the child was by all right and reason reversible; and therefore it was but just that the innocent mother of a sinning child should suffer her rightful share of the grief and pain and shame which were the allotted wages of the sin.

The three moved toward the sickroom.

At this time the doctor was approaching the house. He was still a good distance away, however. He was a good doctor and a good man, and he had a good heart, but one had to know him a year to get over hating him, two years to learn to endure him, three to learn to like him, and four or five to learn to love him. It was a slow and trying education, but it paid. He was of great stature; he had a leonine head, a leonine face, a rough voice, and an eye which was sometimes a pirate's and sometimes a woman's, according to the mood. He knew nothing about etiquette, and cared nothing about it; in speech, manner, carriage, and conduct he was the reverse of conventional. He was frank, to the limit; he had opinions on all subjects; they were always on tap and ready for delivery, and he cared not a farthing whether his listener liked them or didn't. Whom he loved he loved, and manifested it; whom he didn't love he hated, and published it from the housetops. In his young days he had been a sailor, and the salt airs of all the seas blew from him yet. He was a sturdy and loyal Christian, and believed he was the best one in the land, and the only one whose Christianity was perfectly sound, healthy, full-charged with common sense, and had no decayed places in it. People who had an ax to grind, or people who for any reason wanted to get on the soft side of him, called him The Christian—a phrase whose delicate flattery was music to his ears, and whose capital T was such an enchanting and vivid object to him that he could *see* it when it fell out of a person's mouth even in the dark. Many who were fond of him stood on their consciences with both feet and brazenly called him by that large title habitually, because it was a pleasure to them to do anything that would please him; and with eager and cordial malice his extensive and diligently cultivated crop of enemies gilded it, beflowered it, expanded it to "The *only* Christian." Of these two titles, the latter had the wider currency; the enemy, being greatly in the majority, attended to that. Whatever the doctor believed, he believed with all his heart, and would fight for it whenever he got the chance; and if the intervals between chances grew to be irksomely wide, he would invent ways of shortening them himself. He was severely conscientious, according to his rather independent lights, and whatever he took to be a duty he performed, no matter whether the judgment of the professional moralists agreed with his own or not. At sea, in his young days, he had used profanity freely, but as soon as he was converted he made a rule, which he rigidly stuck to ever afterward, never to use it except on the rarest occasions, and then only when duty commanded. He had been a hard drinker at sea, but after his conversion he became a firm and outspoken teetotaler, in order to be an example to the young, and from that time forth he seldom drank; never, indeed, except when it seemed to him to be a duty—a condition which sometimes occurred a couple of times a year, but never as many as five times.

Necessarily such a man is impressionable, impulsive, emotional. This one was, and had no gift at hiding his feelings; or if he had it he took no trouble to exercise it. He carried his soul's prevailing weather in his face, and when he entered a room the parasols or the umbrellas went up—figuratively speaking—according to the indications. When the soft light was in his eye it meant approval, and delivered a benediction; when he came with a frown he lowered the temperature ten degrees. He was a well-beloved man in the house of his friends, but sometimes a dreaded one.

He had a deep affection for the Lester household, and its several members returned this feeling with interest. They mourned over his kind of Christianity, and he frankly scoffed at theirs; but both parties went on loving each other just the same.

He was approaching the house—out of the distance; the aunts and the culprit were moving toward the sick-chamber.

III

The three last named stood by the bed; the aunts austere, the transgressor softly sobbing. The mother turned her head on the pillow; her tired eyes flamed up instantly with sympathy and passionate mother love when they fell upon her child, and she opened the refuge and shelter of her arms.

"Wait!" said Aunt Hannah, and put out her hand and stayed the girl from leaping into them.

"Helen," said the other aunt, impressively, "tell your mother all. Purge your soul; leave nothing unconfessed."

Standing stricken and forlorn before her judges, the young girl mourned her sorrowful tale through to the end, then in a passion of appeal cried out:

"Oh, mother, can't you forgive me? Won't you forgive me?—I am so desolate!"

"Forgive you, my darling? Oh, come to my arms!— There, lay your head upon my breast, and be at peace. If you had told a thousand lies—"

There was a sound—a warning—the clearing of a throat. The aunts glanced up, and withered in their clothes—there stood the doctor, his face a thundercloud. Mother and child knew nothing of his presence; they lay locked together, heart to heart, steeped in immeasurable content, dead to all things else. The physician stood many moments glaring and glooming upon the scene before him; studying it, analyzing it, searching out its genesis; then he put up his hand and beckoned to the aunts. They came trembling to him and stood humbly before him and waited. He bent down and whispered:

"Didn't I tell you this patient must be protected from all excitement? What the hell have you been doing? Clear out of the place!"

They obeyed. Half an hour later he appeared in the parlor, serene, cheery, clothed in sunshine, conducting Helen, with his arm about her waist, petting her, and saying gentle and playful things to her; and she also was her sunny and happy self again.

"Now, then," he said, "goodbye, dear. Go to your room, and keep away from your mother, and behave yourself. But wait—put out your tongue. There, that will do—you're as sound as a nut!" He patted her cheek and added, "Run along now; I want to talk to these aunts."

She went from the presence. His face clouded over again at once; and as he sat down he said:

"You two have been doing a lot of damage—and maybe some good. Some good, yes—such as it is. That woman's disease is typhoid! You've brought it to a show-up, I think, with your insanities, and that's a service—such as it is. I hadn't been able to determine what it was before."

With one impulse the old ladies sprang to their feet, quaking with terror.

"Sit down! What are you proposing to do?"

"Do? We must fly to her. We—"

"You'll do nothing of the kind; you've done enough harm for one day. Do you want to squander all your capital of crimes and follies on a single deal? Sit down, I tell you. I have arranged for her to sleep; she needs it; if you disturb her without my orders, I'll brain you—if you've got the materials for it."

They sat down, distressed and indignant, but obedient, under compulsion. He proceeded:

"Now, then, I want this case explained. *They* wanted to explain it to me—as if there hadn't been emotion and excitement enough already. You knew my orders; how did you dare to go in there and get up that riot?"

Hester looked appealingly at Hannah; Hannah returned a beseeching look at Hester—neither wanted to dance to this unsympathetic orchestra. The doctor came to their help. He said:

"Begin, Hester."

Fingering at the fringes of her shawl, and with lowered eyes, Hester said, timidly:

"We should not have disobeyed for any ordinary cause, but this was vital. This was a duty. With a duty one has no choice; one must put all lighter considerations aside and perform it. We were obliged to arraign her before her mother. She had told a lie."

The doctor glowered upon the woman a moment, and seemed to be trying to work up in his mind an understanding of a wholly incomprehensible proposition; then he stormed out:

"She told a lie! *Did* she? God bless my soul! I tell a million a day! And so does every doctor. And so does everybody—including you—for that matter. And *that* was the important thing that authorized you to venture to disobey my orders and imperil that woman's life! Look here, Hester Gray, this is pure lunacy; that girl *couldn't* tell a lie that was intended to injure a person. The thing is impossible—absolutely impossible. You know it yourselves—both of you; you know it perfectly well."

Hannah came to her sister's rescue:

"Hester didn't mean that it was that kind of a lie, and it wasn't. But it was a lie."

"Well, upon my word, I never heard such nonsense! Haven't you got sense enough to discriminate between lies? Don't you know the difference between a lie that helps and a lie that hurts?"

"*All* lies are sinful," said Hannah, setting her lips together like a vise; "all lies are forbidden."

The Only Christian fidgeted impatiently in his chair. He wanted to attack this proposition, but he did not quite know how or where to begin. Finally he made a venture:

"Hester, wouldn't you tell a lie to shield a person from an undeserved injury or shame?"

"No."

"Not even a friend?"

"No."

"Not even your dearest friend?"

"No. I would not."

The doctor struggled in silence a while with this situation; then he asked:

"Not even to save him from bitter pain and misery and grief?"

"No. Not even to save his life."

Another pause. Then:

"Nor his soul?"

There was a hush—a silence which endured a measurable interval—then Hester answered, in a low voice, but with decision:

"Nor his soul."

No one spoke for a while; then the doctor said:

"Is it with you the same, Hannah?"

"Yes," she answered.

"I ask you both——why?"

"Because to tell such a lie, or any lie, is a sin, and could cost us the loss of our own souls—*would*, indeed, if we died without time to repent."

"Strange . . . strange . . . it is past belief." Then he asked, roughly, "Is such a soul as that *worth* saving?" He rose up, mumbling and grumbling, and started for the door, stumping vigorously along. At the threshold he turned and rasped out an admonition: "Reform! Drop this mean and sordid and selfish devotion to the saving of your shabby little souls, and hunt up something to do that's got some dignity to it! *Risk* your souls! risk them in good causes; then if you lose them, why should you care? Reform!"

The good old gentlewomen sat paralyzed, pulverized, outraged, insulted, and brooded in bitterness and indignation over these blasphemies. They were hurt to the heart, poor old ladies, and said they could never forgive these injuries.

"Reform!"

They kept repeating that word resentfully. "Reform—and learn to tell lies!"

Time slipped along, and in due course a change came over their spirits. They had completed the human being's first duty—which is to think about himself until he has exhausted the subject, then he is in a condition to take up minor interests and think of other people. This changes the complexion of his spirits—generally wholesomely. The minds of the two old ladies reverted to their beloved niece and the fearful disease which had smitten her; instantly they forgot the hurts their self-love had received, and a passionate desire rose in their hearts to go to the help of the sufferer and comfort her with their love, and minister to her, and labor for her the best they could with their weak hands, and joyfully and affectionately wear out their poor old bodies in her dear service if only they might have the privilege.

"And we shall have it!" said Hester, with the tears running down her face. "There are no nurses comparable to us, for there are no others that will stand their watch by that bed till they drop and die, and God knows we would do that."

"Amen," said Hannah, smiling approval and endorsement through the mist of moisture that blurred her glasses. "The doctor knows us, and knows we will not disobey again; and he will call no others. He will not dare!"

"He will," said Hester, with temper, and dashing the water from her eyes. "He will dare anything—that Christian devil! But it will do no good for him to try it this time—but, laws! Hannah, after all's said and done, he is gifted and wise and good, and he would not think of such a thing. . . . It is surely time for one of us to go to that room. What is keeping him? Why doesn't he come and say so?"

They caught the sound of his approaching step. He entered, sat down, and began to talk.

"Margaret is a sick woman," he said. "She is still sleeping, but she will wake presently; then one of you must go to her. She will be worse before she is better. Pretty soon a night-and-day watch must be set. How much of it can you two undertake?"

"All of it!" burst from both ladies at once.

The doctor's eyes flashed, and he said, with energy:

"You *do* ring true, you grave old relics! And you *shall* do all of the nursing you can, for there's none to match you in that divine office in this town; but you can't do all of it, and it would be a crime to let you." It was grand praise, golden praise, coming from such a source, and it took nearly all the resentment out of the aged twins' hearts. "Your Tilly and my old Nancy shall do the rest—good nurses both, white souls with black skins, competent liars from the cradle. . . . Look you! keep a little watch on Helen; she is sick, and is going to be sicker."

The ladies looked a little surprised, and not credulous; and Hester said:

"How is that? It isn't an hour since you said she was as sound as a nut."

The doctor answered, tranquilly:

"It was a lie."

The ladies turned upon him indignantly, and Hannah said:

"How can you make an odious confession like that, in so indifferent a tone, when you know how we feel about all forms of—"

"Hush! You are as ignorant as cats, both of you, and you don't know what you are talking about. You are like all the rest of the moral moles: you lie from morning till night, but because you don't do it with your mouths, but only with your lying eyes, your lying inflections, your deceptively misplaced emphasis, and your misleading gestures, you turn up your complacent noses and parade before God and the world as saintly and unsmirched truth-speakers, in whose cold-storage souls a lie would freeze to death if it got there! Why will you humbug yourselves with that foolish notion that no lie is a lie except a spoken one? What is the difference between lying with your eyes and lying with your mouth? There is none; and if you would reflect a moment you would see that it is so. There isn't a human being that doesn't tell a gross of lies every day of his life; and you—why, between you, you tell thirty thousand; yet you flare up here in a lurid hypocritical horror because I tell that child a benevolent and sinless lie to protect her from her imagination, which would get to work and warm up her blood to a fever in an hour, if I were disloyal enough to my duty to let it. Which I should probably do if I were interested in saving my soul by such disreputable means.

"Come, let us reason together. Let us examine details. When you two were in the sickroom raising that riot, what would you have done if you had known I was coming?"

"Well, what?"

"You would have slipped out and carried Helen with you—wouldn't you?"

The ladies were silent.

"What would be your object and intention?"

"Well, what?"

"To keep me from finding out your guilt; to beguile me to infer that Margaret's excitement proceeded from some cause not known to you. In a word, to tell me a lie—a silent lie. Moreover, a possibly harmful one."

The twins colored, but did not speak.

"You not only tell myriads of silent lies, but you tell lies with your mouths—you two."

"*That* is not so!"

"It is so. But only harmless ones. You never dream of uttering a harmful one. Do you know that that is a concession—and a confession?"

"How do you mean?"

"It is an unconscious concession that harmless lies are not criminal; it is a confession that you constantly *make* that discrimination. For instance, you declined old Mrs. Foster's invitation last week to meet those odious Higbies at supper—in a polite note in which you expressed regret and said you were very sorry you could not go. It was a lie. It was as unmitigated a lie as was ever uttered. Deny it, Hester—with another lie."

Hester replied with a toss of her head.

"That will not do. Answer. Was it a lie, or wasn't it?"

The color stole into the cheeks of both women, and with a struggle and an effort they got out their confession:

"It was a lie."

"Good—the reform is beginning; there is hope for you yet; you will not tell a lie to save your dearest friend's soul, but you will spew out one without a scruple to save yourself the discomfort of telling an unpleasant truth."

He rose. Hester, speaking for both, said, coldly:

"We have lied; we perceive it; it will occur no more. To lie is a sin. We shall never tell another one of any kind whatsoever, even lies of courtesy or benevolence, to save anyone a pang or a sorrow decreed for him by God."

"Ah, how soon you will fall! In fact, you have fallen already; for what you have just uttered is a lie. Goodbye. Reform! One of you go to the sick-room now."

IV

Twelve days later.

Mother and child were lingering in the grip of the hideous disease. Of hope for either there was little. The aged sisters looked white and worn, but they would

not give up their posts. Their hearts were breaking, poor
old things, but their grit was steadfast and indestructible.
All the twelve days the mother had pined for the child,
and the child for the mother, but both knew that the
prayer of these longings could not be granted. When the
mother was told—on the first day—that her disease
was typhoid, she was frightened, and asked if there was
danger that Helen could have contracted it the day before, when she was in the sick-chamber on that confession visit. Hester told her the doctor had pooh-poohed
the idea. It troubled Hester to say it, although it was
true, for she had not believed the doctor; but when she
saw the mother's joy in the news, the pain in her conscience lost something of its force—a result which made
her ashamed of the constructive deception which she had
practiced, though not ashamed enough to make her distinctly and definitely wish she had refrained from it.
From that moment the sick woman understood that her
daughter must remain away, and she said she would reconcile herself to the separation the best she could, for
she would rather suffer death than have her child's health
imperiled. That afternoon Helen had to take to her bed,
ill. She grew worse during the night. In the morning her
mother asked after her:

"Is she well?"

Hester turned cold; she opened her lips, but the words
refused to come. The mother lay languidly looking, musing, waiting; suddenly she turned white and gasped out:

"Oh, my God! What is it? Is she sick?"

Then the poor aunt's tortured heart rose in rebellion,
and words came:

"No—be comforted; she is well."

The sick woman put all her happy heart in her gratitude:

"Thank God for those dear words! Kiss me. How I
worship you for saying them."

Hester told this incident to Hannah, who received it
with a rebuking look, and said, coldly:

"Sister, it was a lie."

Hester's lips trembled piteously; she choked down a
sob, and said:

"Oh, Hannah, it was a sin, but I could not help it; I

could not endure the fright and the misery that were in her face."

"No matter. It was a lie. God will hold you to account for it."

"Oh, I know it, I know it," cried Hester, wringing her hands, "but even if it were now, I could not help it. I know I should do it again."

"Then take my place with Helen in the morning. I will make the report myself."

Hester clung to her sister, begging and imploring:

"Don't, Hannah, oh, don't—you will kill her."

"I will at least speak the truth."

In the morning she had a cruel report to bear to the mother, and she braced herself for the trial. When she returned from her mission, Hester was waiting, pale and trembling, in the hall. She whispered:

"Oh, how did she take it—that poor, desolate mother?"

Hannah's eyes were swimming in tears. She said:

"God forgive me, I told her the child was well!"

Hester gathered her to her heart, with a grateful "God bless you, Hannah!" and poured out her thankfulness in an inundation of worshiping praises.

After that, the two knew the limit of their strength, and accepted their fate. They surrendered humbly, and abandoned themselves to the hard requirements of the situation. Daily they told the morning lie, and confessed their sin in prayer; not asking forgiveness, as not being worthy of it, but only wishing to make record that they realized their wickedness and were not desiring to hide it or excuse it.

Daily, as the fair young idol of the house sank lower and lower, the sorrowful old aunts painted her glowing bloom and her fresh young beauty to the wan mother, and winced under the stabs her ecstasies of joy and gratitude gave them.

In the first days, while the child had strength to hold a pencil, she wrote fond little love notes to her mother, in which she concealed her illness; and these the mother read and reread through happy eyes wet with thankful tears, and kissed them over and over again, and treasured them as precious things under her pillow.

Then came a day when the strength was gone from the

hand, and the mind wandered, and the tongue babbled pathetic incoherences. This was a sore dilemma for the poor aunts. There were no love notes for the mother. They did not know what to do. Hester began a carefully studied and plausible explanation, but lost the track of it and grew confused; suspicion began to show in the mother's face, then alarm. Hester saw it, recognized the imminence of the danger, and descended to the emergency, pulling herself resolutely together and plucking victory from the open jaws of defeat. In a placid and convincing voice she said:

"I thought it might distress you to know it, but Helen spent the night at the Sloanes'. There was a little party there, and although she did not want to go, and you so sick, we persuaded her, she being young and needing the innocent pastimes of youth, and we believing you would approve. Be sure she will write the moment she comes."

"How good you are, and how dear and thoughtful for us both! Approve? Why, I thank you with all my heart. My poor little exile! Tell her I want her to have every pleasure she can—I would not rob her of one. Only let her keep her health, that is all I ask. Don't let that suffer; I could not bear it. How thankful I am that she escaped this infection—and what a narrow risk she ran, Aunt Hester! Think of that lovely face all dulled and burnt with fever. I can't bear the thought of it. Keep her health. Keep her bloom! I can see her now, the dainty creature —with the big blue earnest eyes; and sweet, oh, so sweet and gentle and winning! Is she as beautiful as ever, dear Aunt Hester?"

"Oh, more beautiful and bright and charming than ever she was before, if such a thing can be"—and Hester turned away and fumbled with the medicine bottles, to hide her shame and grief.

V

After a little, both aunts were laboring upon a difficult and baffling work in Helen's chamber. Patiently and earnestly, with their stiff old fingers, they were trying to forge the required note. They made failure after failure, but they improved little by little all the time. The pity of it all, the pathetic humor of it, there was none to see; they themselves were unconscious of it. Often their tears fell upon the notes and spoiled them; sometimes a single mis-formed word made a note risky which could have been ventured but for that; but at last Hannah produced one whose script was a good enough imitation of Helen's to pass any but a suspicious eye, and bountifully enriched it with the petting phrases and loving nicknames that had been familiar on the child's lips from her nursery days. She carried it to the mother, who took it with avidity, and kissed it, and fondled it, reading its precious words over and over again, and dwelling with deep contentment upon its closing paragraph:

"Mousie darling, if I could only see you, and kiss your eyes, and feel your arms about me! I am so glad my practicing does not disturb you. Get well soon. Every-body is good to me, but I am so lonesome without you, dear mamma."

"The poor child, I know just how she feels. She can-not be quite happy without me; and I—oh, I live in the light of her eyes! Tell her she must practice all she pleases; and, Aunt Hannah—tell her I can't hear the piano this far, nor her dear voice when she sings: God knows I wish I could. No one knows how sweet that voice is to me; and to think—some day it will be silent! What are you crying for?"

"Only because—because—it was just a memory. When I came away she was singing 'Loch Lomond.' The pathos of it! It always moves me so when she sings that."

"And me, too. How heartbreakingly beautiful it is when some youthful sorrow is brooding in her breast and she sings it for the mystic healing it brings. . . . Aunt Hannah?"

"Dear Margaret?"

"I am very ill. Sometimes it comes over me that I shall never hear that dear voice again."

"Oh, don't—don't, Margaret! I can't bear it!"

Margaret was moved and distressed, and said, gently:

"There—there—let me put my arms around you. Don't cry. There—put your cheek to mine. Be comforted. I wish to live. I will live if I can. Ah, what could she do without me! . . . Does she often speak of me?—but I know she does."

"Oh, all the time—all the time!"

"My sweet child! She wrote the note the moment she came home?"

"Yes—the first moment. She would not wait to take off her things."

"I knew it. It is her dear, impulsive, affectionate way. I knew it without asking, but I wanted to hear you say it. The petted wife knows she is loved, but she makes her husband tell her so, every day, just for the joy of hearing it. . . . She used the pen this time. That is better; the pencil marks could rub out, and I should grieve for that. Did you suggest that she use the pen?"

"Y-no—she—it was her own idea."

The mother looked her pleasure, and said:

"I was hoping you would say that. There was never such a dear and thoughtful child! . . . Aunt Hannah?"

"Dear Margaret?"

"Go and tell her I think of her all the time, and worship her. Why—you are crying again. Don't be so worried about me, dear; I think there is nothing to fear, yet."

The grieving messenger carried her message, and piously delivered it to unheeding ears. The girl babbled on unaware; looking up at her with wondering and startled eyes flaming with fever, eyes in which was no light of recognition:

"Are you—no, you are not my mother. I want her—oh, I want her! She was here a minute ago—I did not see her go. Will she come? will she come quickly? will she come now? . . . There are so many houses . . . and they oppress me so . . . and everything whirls and turns and whirls . . . oh, my head, my head!" And so she wandered on and on, in her pain, flitting from one torturing fancy to another, and tossing her arms about in a weary and ceaseless persecution of unrest.

Poor old Hannah wetted the parched lips and softly stroked the hot brow, murmuring endearing and pitying words, and thanking the Father of all that the mother was happy and did not know.

VI

Daily the child sank lower and steadily lower toward the grave, and daily the sorrowing old watchers carried gilded tidings of her radiant health and loveliness to the happy mother, whose pilgrimage was also now nearing its end. And daily they forged loving and cheery notes in the child's hand, and stood by with remorseful consciences and bleeding hearts, and wept to see the grateful mother devour them and adore them and treasure them away as things beyond price, because of their sweet source, and sacred because her child's hand had touched them.

At last came that kindly friend who brings healing and peace to all. The lights were burning low. In the solemn hush which precedes the dawn vague figures flitted soundless along the dim hall and gathered silent and awed in Helen's chamber, and grouped themselves about her bed, for a warning had gone forth, and they knew. The dying girl lay with closed lids, and unconscious, the drapery upon her breast faintly rising and falling as her wasting life ebbed away. At intervals a sigh or a muffled sob broke upon the stillness. The same haunting thought was in all minds there: the pity of this death, the going out into the great darkness, and the mother not here to help and hearten and bless.

Helen stirred; her hands began to grope wistfully about as if they sought something—she had been blind some hours. The end was come; all knew it. With a great sob Hester gathered her to her breast, crying, "Oh, my child, my darling!" A rapturous light broke in the dying girl's face, for it was mercifully vouchsafed her to mistake those sheltering arms for another's; and she went to her rest murmuring, "Oh, mamma, I am so happy—I so longed for you—now I can die."

Two hours later Hester made her report. The mother asked:

"How is it with the child?"

"She is well."

VII

A sheaf of white crêpe and black was hung upon the door of the house, and there it swayed and rustled in the wind and whispered its tidings. At noon the preparation of the dead was finished, and in the coffin lay the fair young form, beautiful, and in the sweet face a great peace. Two mourners sat by it, grieving and worshiping—Hannah and the black woman Tilly. Hester came, and she was trembling, for a great trouble was upon her spirit. She said:

"She asks for a note."

Hannah's face blanched. She had not thought of this; it had seemed that that pathetic service was ended. But she realized now that that could not be. For a little while the two women stood looking into each other's face, with vacant eyes; then Hannah said:

"There is no way out of it—she must have it; she will suspect, else."

"And she would find out."

"Yes. It would break her heart." She looked at the dead face, and her eyes filled. "I will write it," she said.

Hester carried it. The closing line said:

"Darling Mousie, dear sweet mother, we shall soon be together again. Is not that good news? And it is true; they all say it is true."

The mother mourned, saying:

"Poor child, how will she bear it when she knows? I shall never see her again in life. It is hard, so hard. She does not suspect? You guard her from that?"

"She thinks you will soon be well."

"How good you are, and careful, dear Aunt Hester! None goes near her who could carry the infection?"

"It would be a crime."

"But you *see* her?"

"With a distance between—yes."

"That is so good. Others one could not trust; but you two guardian angels—steel is not so true as you. Others would be unfaithful; and many would deceive, and lie."

Hester's eyes fell, and her poor old lips trembled.

"Let me kiss you for her, Aunt Hester; and when I am

gone, and the danger is past, place the kiss upon her dear lips some day, and say her mother sent it, and all her mother's broken heart is in it."

Within the hour Hester, raining tears upon the dead face, performed her pathetic mission.

VIII

Another day dawned, and grew, and spread its sunshine in the earth. Aunt Hannah brought comforting news to the failing mother, and a happy note, which said again, "We have but little time to wait, darling mother, then we shall be together."

The deep note of a bell came moaning down the wind.

"Aunt Hannah, it is tolling. Some poor soul is at rest. As I shall be soon. You will not let her forget me?"

"Oh, God knows she never will!"

"Do not you hear strange noises, Aunt Hannah? It sounds like the shuffling of many feet."

"We hoped you would not hear it, dear. It is a little company gathering, for—for Helen's sake, poor little prisoner. There will be music—and she loves it so. We thought you would not mind."

"Mind? Oh, no, no—oh, give her everything her dear heart can desire. How good you two are to her, and how good to me. God bless you both, always!"

After a listening pause:

"How lovely! It is her organ. Is she playing it herself, do you think?" Faint and rich and inspiring the chords floated to her ears on the still air. "Yes, it is her touch, dear heart; I recognize it. They are singing. Why—it is a hymn! and the sacredest of all, the most touching, the most consoling. . . . It seems to open the gates of paradise to me. . . . If I could die now. . . ."

Faint and far the words rose out of the stillness:

> Nearer, my God, to Thee,
> Nearer to Thee,
> E'en though it be a cross
> That raiseth me.

With the closing of the hymn another soul passed to

its rest, and they that had been one in life were not sundered in death. The sisters, mourning and rejoicing, said:

"How blessed it was that she never knew."

IX

At midnight they sat together, grieving, and the angel of the Lord appeared in their midst transfigured with a radiance not of earth; and speaking, said:

"For liars a place is appointed. There they burn in the fires of hell from everlasting unto everlasting. Repent!"

The bereaved fell upon their knees before him and clasped their hands and bowed their gray heads, adoring. But their tongues clung to the roof of their mouths, and they were dumb.

"Speak! that I may bear the message to the chancery of heaven and bring again the decree from which there is no appeal."

Then they bowed their heads yet lower, and one said:

"Our sin is great, and we suffer shame; but only perfect and final repentance can make us whole; and we are poor creatures who have learned our human weakness, and we know that if we were in those hard straits again our hearts would fail again, and we should sin as before. The strong could prevail, and so be saved, but we are lost."

They lifted their heads in supplication. The angel was gone. While they marvelled and wept he came again; and bending low, he whispered the decree.

X

Was it Heaven? Or Hell?

The Mysterious Stranger

CHAPTER I

IT was in 1590—winter. Austria was far away from the world, and asleep; it was still the Middle Ages in Austria, and promised to remain so forever. Some even set it away back centuries upon centuries and said that by the mental and spiritual clock it was still the Age of Belief in Austria. But they meant it as a compliment, not a slur, and it was so taken, and we were all proud of it. I remember it well, although I was only a boy; and I remember, too, the pleasure it gave me.

Yes, Austria was far from the world, and asleep, and our village was in the middle of that sleep, being in the middle of Austria. It drowsed in peace in the deep privacy of a hilly and woodsy solitude where news from the world hardly ever came to disturb its dreams, and was infinitely content. At its front flowed the tranquil river, its surface painted with cloud forms and the reflections of drifting arks and stoneboats; behind it rose the woody steeps to the base of the lofty precipice; from the top of the precipice frowned a vast castle, its long stretch of towers and bastions mailed in vines; beyond the river, a league to the left, was a tumbled expanse of forest-clothed hills cloven by winding gorges where the sun never penetrated; and to the right a precipice overlooking the river, and between it and the hills just spoken of lay a far-reaching plain dotted with little homesteads nested among orchards and shade trees.

The whole region for leagues around was the hereditary property of a prince, whose servants kept the castle always in perfect condition for occupancy, but neither he nor his family came there oftener than once in five years. When they came it was as if the lord of the world had arrived, and had brought all the glories of its kingdoms along; and when they went they left a calm behind which was like the deep sleep which follows an orgy.

Eseldorf was a paradise for us boys. We were not over-much pestered with schooling. Mainly we were trained to be good Christians; to revere the Virgin, the Church, and the saints above everything. Beyond these matters we were not required to know much; and, in fact, not allowed to. Knowledge was not good for the common people, and could make them discontented with the lot which God had appointed for them, and God would not endure discontentment with His plans. We had two priests. One of them, Father Adolf, was a very zealous and strenuous priest, much considered.

There may have been better priests, in some ways, than Father Adolf, but there was never one in our commune who was held in more solemn and awful respect. This was because he had absolutely no fear of the Devil. He was the only Christian I have ever known of whom that could be truly said. People stood in deep dread of him on that account; for they thought that there must be something supernatural about him, else he could not be so bold and so confident. All men speak in bitter disapproval of the Devil, but they do it reverently, not flippantly; but Father Adolf's way was very different; he called him by every name he could lay his tongue to, and it made everyone shudder that heard him; and often he would even speak of him scornfully and scoffingly; then the people crossed themselves and went quickly out of his presence, fearing that something fearful might happen.

Father Adolf had actually met Satan face to face more than once, and defied him. This was known to be so. Father Adolf said it himself. He never made any secret of it, but spoke it right out. And that he was speaking true there was proof in at least one instance, for on that occasion he quarreled with the enemy, and intrepidly threw his bottle at him; and there, upon the wall of his study, was the ruddy splotch where it struck and broke.

But it was Father Peter, the other priest, that we all loved best and were sorriest for. Some people charged him with talking around in conversation that God was all goodness and would find a way to save all his poor human children. It was a horrible thing to say, but there was never any absolute proof that Father Peter said it; and it was out of character for him to say it, too, for he was always good and gentle and truthful. He wasn't charged with saying it in the pulpit, where all the congregation could hear and testify, but only outside, in talk; and it is easy for enemies to manufacture *that*. Father Peter had an enemy and a very powerful one, the astrologer who lived in a tumbled old tower up the valley, and put in his nights studying the stars. Everyone knew he could foretell wars and famines, though that was not so hard, for there was always a war and generally a famine somewhere. But he could also read any man's life through the stars in a big book he had, and find lost property, and everyone in the village except Father Peter stood in awe of him. Even Father Adolf, who had defied the Devil, had a wholesome respect for the astrologer when he came through our village wearing his tall, pointed hat and his long, flowing robe with stars on it, carrying his big book, and a staff which was known to have magic power. The bishop himself sometimes listened to the astrologer, it was said, for, besides studying the stars and prophesying, the astrologer made a great show of piety, which would impress the bishop, of course.

But Father Peter took no stock in the astrologer. He denounced him openly as a charlatan—a fraud with no valuable knowledge of any kind, or powers beyond those of an ordinary and rather inferior human being, which naturally made the astrologer hate Father Peter and wish to ruin him. It was the astrologer, as we all believed, who originated the story about Father Peter's shocking remark and carried it to the bishop. It was said that Father Peter had made the remark to his niece, Marget, though Marget denied it and implored the bishop to believe her and spare her old uncle from poverty and disgrace. But the bishop wouldn't listen. He suspended Father Peter indefinitely, though he wouldn't go so far as to excommunicate him on the evidence of only one witness; and now Father Peter had been out a couple of years, and our other priest, Father Adolf, had his flock.

Those had been hard years for the old priest and Marget. They had been favorites, but of course that changed when they came under the shadow of the bishop's frown. Many of their friends fell away entirely, and the rest became cool and distant. Marget was a lovely girl of eighteen when the trouble came, and she had the best head in the village, and the most in it. She taught the harp, and earned all her clothes and pocket money by her own industry. But her scholars fell off one by one now; she was forgotten when there were dances and parties among the youth of the village; the young fellows stopped coming to the house, all except Wilhelm Meidling —and he could have been spared; she and her uncle were sad and forlorn in their neglect and disgrace, and the sunshine was gone out of their lives. Matters went worse and worse, all through the two years. Clothes were wearing out, bread was harder and harder to get. And now, at last, the very end was come. Solomon Isaacs had lent all the money he was willing to put on the house, and gave notice that tomorrow he would foreclose.

CHAPTER II

THREE of us boys were always together, and had been so from the cradle, being fond of one another from the beginning, and this affection deepened as the years went on—Nikolaus Bauman, son of the principal judge of the local court; Seppi Wohlmeyer, son of the keeper of the principal inn, the "Golden Stag," which had a nice garden, with shade trees reaching down to the riverside, and pleasure boats for hire; and I was the third—Theodor Fischer, son of the church organist, who was also leader of the village musicians, teacher of the violin, composer, tax-collector of the commune, sexton, and in other ways a useful citizen, and respected by all. We knew the hills and the woods as well as the birds knew them; for we were always roaming them when we had leisure—at least, when we were not swimming or boating or fishing, or playing on the ice or sliding downhill.

And we had the run of the castle park, and very few had that. It was because we were pets of the oldest serving-man in the castle—Felix Brandt; and often we went there, nights, to hear him talk about old times and strange things, and to smoke with him (he taught us that) and to drink coffee; for he had served in the wars, and was at the siege of Vienna; and there, when the Turks were defeated and driven away, among the captured things were bags of coffee, and the Turkish prisoners explained the character of it and how to make a pleasant drink out of it, and now he always kept coffee by him, to drink himself and also to astonish the ignorant with. When it stormed he kept us all night; and while it thundered and lightened outside he told us about ghosts and horrors of every kind, and of battles and murders and mutilations, and such things, and made it pleasant and cozy inside; and he told these things from his own experience largely. He had seen many ghosts in his time, and witches and enchanters, and once he was lost in a fierce storm at midnight in the mountains, and by the glare of the lightning had seen the Wild Huntsman rage on the blast with his specter dogs chasing after him through the driving cloud rack. Also he had seen an incubus once, and several times he had seen the great bat that sucks the blood from the necks of people while they are asleep, fanning them softly with its wings and so keeping them drowsy till they die.

He encouraged us not to fear supernatural things, such as ghosts, and said they did no harm, but only wandered about because they were lonely and distressed and wanted kindly notice and compassion; and in time we learned not to be afraid, and even went down with him in the night to the haunted chamber in the dungeons of the castle. The ghost appeared only once, and it went by very dim to the sight and floated noiseless through the air, and then disappeared; and we scarcely trembled, he had taught us so well. He said it came up sometimes in the night and woke him by passing its clammy hand over his face, but it did him no hurt; it only wanted sympathy and notice. But the strangest thing was that he had seen angels—actual angels out of heaven—and had talked with them. They had no wings, and wore clothes, and talked and looked and acted just like any natural person, and you would never know them for angels except for the wonderful things they did which a mortal could not do, and the way they suddenly disappeared while you were talking with them, which was also a thing which no mortal could do. And he said they were pleasant and cheerful, not gloomy and melancholy, like ghosts.

It was after that kind of a talk one May night that we got up next morning and had a good breakfast with him and then went down and crossed the bridge and went away up into the hills on the left to a woody hilltop which was a favorite place of ours, and there we stretched out on the grass in the shade to rest and smoke and talk over these strange things, for they were in our minds yet, and impressing us. But we couldn't smoke, because we had been heedless and left our flint and steel behind.

Soon there came a youth strolling toward us through the trees, and he sat down and began to talk in a friendly way, just as if he knew us. But we did not answer him, for he was a stranger and we were not used to strangers and were shy of them. He had new and good clothes on, and was handsome and had a winning face and a pleasant voice, and was easy and graceful and unembarrassed, not slouchy and awkward and diffident, like other boys. We wanted to be friendly with him, but didn't know how to begin. Then I thought of the pipe, and wondered if it would be taken as kindly meant if I offered it to him. But I remembered that we had no fire, so I was sorry and disappointed. But he looked up bright and pleased, and said:

"Fire? Oh, that is easy; I will furnish it."

I was so astonished I couldn't speak; for I had not said anything. He took the pipe and blew his breath on it, and the tobacco glowed red, and spirals of blue smoke rose up. We jumped up and were going to run, for that was natural; and we did run a few steps, although he was yearningly pleading for us to stay, and giving us his word that he would not do us any harm, but only wanted to be friends with us and have company. So we stopped and stood, and wanted to go back, being full of curiosity and wonder, but afraid to venture. He went on coaxing, in his soft, persuasive way; and when we saw that the pipe did not blow up and nothing happened, our confidence returned by little and little, and presently our curiosity got to be stronger than our fear, and we ventured back—but slowly, and ready to fly at any alarm.

He was bent on putting us at ease, and he had the right art; one could not remain doubtful and timorous where a person was so earnest and simple and gentle, and talked so alluringly as he did; no, he won us over, and it was not long before we were content and comfortable and chatty, and glad we had found this new friend. When the feeling of constraint was all gone we asked him how he had learned to do that strange thing, and he said he hadn't learned it at all; it came natural to him—like other things—other curious things.

"What ones?"

"Oh, a number; I don't know how many."

"Will you let us see you do them?"

"Do—please!" the others said.

"You won't run away again?"

"No—indeed we won't. Please do. Won't you?"

"Yes, with pleasure; but you mustn't forget your promise, you know."

We said we wouldn't, and he went to a puddle and came back with water in a cup which he had made out of a leaf, and blew upon it and threw it out, and it was a lump of ice the shape of the cup. We were astonished and charmed, but not afraid any more; we were very glad to be there, and asked him to go on and do some more things. And he did. He said he would give us any kind of fruit we liked, whether it was in season or not. We all spoke at once:

"Orange!"

"Apple!"

"Grapes!"

"They are in your pockets," he said, and it was true. And they were of the best, too, and we ate them and wished we had more, though none of us said so.

"You will find them where those came from," he said, "and everything else your appetites call for; and you need not name the thing you wish; as long as I am with you, you have only to wish and find."

And he said true. There was never anything so wonderful and so interesting. Bread, cakes, sweets, nuts—whatever one wanted, it was there. He ate nothing himself, but sat and chatted, and did one curious thing after another to amuse us. He made a tiny toy squirrel out of clay, and it ran up a tree and sat on a limb overhead and barked down at us. Then he made a dog that was not much larger than a mouse, and it treed the squirrel and danced about the tree, excited and barking, and was as alive as any dog could be. It frightened the squirrel from tree to tree and followed it up until both were out of sight in the forest. He made birds out of clay and set them free, and they flew away, singing.

At last I made bold to ask him to tell us who he was. "An angel," he said, quite simply, and set another bird free and clapped his hands and made it fly away.

A kind of awe fell upon us when we heard him say that, and we were afraid again; but he said we need not be troubled, there was no occasion for us to be afraid of an angel, and he liked us, anyway. He went on chatting as simply and unaffectedly as ever; and while he talked he made a crowd of little men and women the size of your finger, and they went diligently to work and cleared and leveled off a space a couple of yards square in the grass and began to build a cunning little castle in it, the women mixing the mortar and carrying it up the scaffoldings in pails on their heads, just as our workwomen have always done, and the men laying the courses of masonry—five hundred of these toy people swarming briskly about and working diligently and wiping the sweat off their faces as natural as life. In the absorbing interest of watching those five hundred little people make the castle grow step by step and course by course, and take shape and symmetry, that feeling and awe soon passed away and we were quite comfortable and at home again. We asked if we might make some people, and he said yes, and told Seppi to make some cannon for the walls, and told Nikolaus to make some halberdiers, with breastplates and greaves and helmets, and I was to make some cavalry, with horses, and in allotting these tasks he called us by our names, but did not say how he knew them. Then Seppi asked him what his own name was, and he said, tranquilly, "Satan," and held out a chip and caught a little woman on it who was falling from the scaffolding and put her back where she belonged, and said, "She is an idiot to step backward like that and not notice what she is about."

It caught us suddenly, that name did, and our work dropped out of our hands and broke to pieces—a cannon, a halberdier, and a horse. Satan laughed, and asked what was the matter. I said, "Nothing, only it seemed a strange name for an angel." He asked why.

"Because it's—it's well, it's his name, you know."

"Yes—he is my uncle."

He said it placidly, but it took our breath for a moment and made our hearts beat. He did not seem to notice that, but mended our halberdiers and things with a touch, handing them to us finished, and said, "Don't you remember?—he was an angel himself, once."

"Yes—it's true," said Seppi; "I didn't think of that."

"Before the Fall he was blameless."

"Yes," said Nikolaus, "he was without sin."

"It is a good family—ours," said Satan; "there is not a better. He is the only member of it that has ever sinned."

I should not be able to make anyone understand how exciting it all was. You know that kind of quiver that trembles around through you when you are seeing something so strange and enchanting and wonderful that it is just a fearful joy to be alive and look at it; and you know how you gaze, and your lips turn dry and your breath comes short, but you wouldn't be anywhere but there, not for the world. I was bursting to ask one question—I had it on my tongue's end and could hardly hold it back—but I was ashamed to ask it; it might be a rudeness. Satan set an ox down that he had been making, and smiled up at me and said:

"It wouldn't be a rudeness, and I should forgive it if it was. Have I seen him? Millions of times. From the time that I was a little child a thousand years old I was his second favorite among the nursery angels of our blood and lineage—to use a human phrase—yes, from that time until the Fall, eight thousand years, measured as you count time."

"Eight—thousand!"

"Yes." He turned to Seppi, and went on as if answering something that was in Seppi's mind: "Why, naturally I look like a boy, for that is what I am. With us what you call time is a spacious thing; it takes a long stretch of it to grow an angel to full age." There was a question in my mind, and he turned to me and answered it, "I am sixteen thousand years old—counting as you count." Then he turned to Nikolaus and said: "No, the Fall did not affect me nor the rest of the relationship. It was only he that I was named for who ate of the fruit of the tree and then beguiled the man and the woman with it. We others are still ignorant of sin; we are not able to commit it; we are without blemish, and shall abide in that estate always. We—" Two of the little workmen were quarreling, and in buzzing little bumblebee voices they were cursing and swearing at each other; now came blows and blood; then they locked themsleves together in a life-and-death struggle. Satan reached out his hand and crushed the life out of them with his fingers, threw them away, wiped the red from his fingers on his handkerchief, and went on talking where he had left off: "We cannot do wrong; neither have we any disposition to do it, for we do not know what it is."

It seemed a strange speech, in the circumstances, but we barely noticed that, we were so shocked and grieved at the wanton murder he had committed—for murder it was, that was its true name, and it was without palliation or excuse, for the men had not wronged him in any way. It made us miserable, for we loved him, and had thought him so noble and so beautiful and gracious, and had honestly believed he was an angel; and to have him do this cruel thing—ah, it lowered him so, and we had had such pride in him. He went right on talking, just as if nothing had happened, telling about his travels, and the interesting things he had seen in the big worlds of our solar system and of other solar systems far away in the remotenesses of space, and about the customs of the immortals that inhabit them, somehow fascinating us, enchanting us, charming us in spite of the pitiful scene that

was now under our eyes, for the wives of the little dead
men had found the crushed and shapeless bodies and
were crying over them, and sobbing and lamenting, and
a priest was kneeling there with his hands crossed upon
his breast, praying; and crowds and crowds of pitying
friends were massed about them, reverently uncovered,
with their bare heads bowed, and many with the tears
running down—a scene which Satan paid no attention to
until the small noise of the weeping and praying began to
annoy him, then he reached out and took the heavy board
seat out of our swing and brought it down and mashed
all those people into the earth just as if they had been
flies, and went on talking just the same.

An angel, and kill a priest! An angel who did not
know how to do wrong, and yet destroys in cold blood
hundreds of helpless poor men and women who had
never done him any harm! It made us sick to see that
awful deed, and to think that none of those poor creatures was prepared except the priest, for none of them had
ever heard a mass or seen a church. And we were witnesses; we had seen these murders done and it was our duty
to tell, and let the law take its course.

But he went on talking right along, and worked his
enchantments upon us again with that fatal music of his
voice. He made us forget everything; we could only listen
to him, and love him, and be his slaves, to do with us as
he would. He made us drunk with the joy of being with
him, and of looking into the heaven of his eyes, and of
feeling the ecstasy that thrilled our veins from the touch
of his hand.

CHAPTER III

THE Stranger had seen everything, he had been everywhere, he knew everything, and he forgot nothing.
What another must study, he learned at a glance; there
were no difficulties for him. And he made things live before you when he told about them. He saw the world
made; he saw Adam created; he saw Samson surge
against the pillars and bring the temple down in ruins
about him; he saw Caesar's death; he told of the daily life
in heaven; he had seen the damned writhing in the red

waves of hell; and he made us see all these things, and it was as if we were on the spot and looking at them with our own eyes. And we felt them, too, but there was no sign that they were anything to him beyond mere entertainments. Those visions of hell, those poor babes and women and girls and lads and men shrieking and supplicating in anguish—why, we could hardly bear it, but he was as bland about it as if it had been so many imitation rats in an artificial fire.

And always when he was talking about men and women here on the earth and their doings—even their grandest and sublimest—we were secretly ashamed, for his manner showed that to him they and their doings were of paltry poor consequence; often you would think he was talking about flies, if you didn't know. Once he even said, in so many words, that our people down here were quite interesting to him, notwithstanding they were so dull and ignorant and trivial and conceited, and so diseased and rickety, and such a shabby, poor, worthless lot all around. He said it in a quite matter-of-course way and without bitterness, just as a person might talk about bricks or manure or any other thing that was of no consequence and hadn't feelings. I could see he meant no offense, but in my thoughts I set it down as not very good manners.

"Manners!" he said. "Why, it is merely the truth, and truth is good manners; manners are a fiction. The castle is done. Do you like it?"

Anyone would have been obliged to like it. It was lovely to look at, it was so shapely and fine, and so cunningly perfect in all its particulars, even to the little flags waving from the turrets. Satan said we must put the artillery in place now, and station the halberdiers and display the cavalry. Our men and horses were a spectacle to see, they were so little like what they were intended for; for, of course, we had no art in making such things. Satan said they were the worst he had seen; and when he touched them and made them alive, it was just ridiculous the way they acted, on account of their legs not being of uniform lengths. They reeled and sprawled around as if they were drunk, and endangered everybody's lives around them, and finally fell over and lay helpless and kicking. It made us all laugh, though it was a shameful thing to see. The guns were charged with dirt, to fire a salute, but they were so crooked and so badly made that they all burst when they went off, and killed some of the gunners and crippled the others. Satan said we would have a storm now, and an earthquake, if we liked, but we must stand off a piece, out of danger. We wanted to call the people away, too, but he said never mind them; they were of no consequence, and we could make more, some time or other, if we needed them.

A small storm cloud began to settle down black over the castle, and the miniature lightning and thunder began to play, and the ground to quiver, and the wind to pipe and wheeze, and the rain to fall, and all the people flocked into the castle for shelter. The cloud settled down blacker and blacker, and one could see the castle only dimly through it; the lightning blazed out flash upon flash and pierced the castle and set it on fire, and the flames shone out red and fierce through the cloud, and the people came flying out, shrieking, but Satan brushed them back, paying no attention to our begging and crying and imploring; and in the midst of the howling of the wind and volleying of the thunder the magazine blew up, the earthquake rent the ground wide, and the castle's wreck and ruin tumbled into the chasm, which swallowed it from sight and closed upon it, with all that innocent life, not one of the five hundred poor creatures escaping. Our hearts were broken; we could not keep from crying.

"Don't cry," Satan said; "they were of no value."

"But they are gone to hell!"

"Oh, it is no matter; we can make plenty more."

It was of no use to try to move him; evidently he was wholly without feelings, and could not understand. He was full of bubbling spirits, and as gay as if this were a wedding instead of a fiendish massacre. And he was bent on making us feel as he did, and of course his magic accomplished his desire. It was no trouble to him; he did whatever he pleased with us. In a little while we were dancing on that grave, and he was playing to us on a strange, sweet instrument which he took out of his pocket; and the music—but there is no music like that, unless perhaps in heaven, and that was where he brought

it from, he said. It made one mad, for pleasure; and
we could not take our eyes from him, and the looks that
went out of our eyes came from our hearts, and their
dumb speech was worship. He brought the dance from
heaven, too, and the bliss of paradise was in it.

Presently he said he must go away on an errand. But
we could not bear the thought of it, and clung to him,
and pleaded with him to stay; and that pleased him, and
he said so, and said he would not go yet, but would wait
a little while and we would sit down and talk a few minutes longer; and he told us Satan was only his real name,
and he was to be known by it to us alone, but he had
chosen another one to be called by in the presence of
others; just a common one, such as people have—Philip
Traum.

It sounded so odd and mean for such a being! But it
was his decision, and we said nothing; his decision was
sufficient.

We had seen wonders this day; and my thoughts began
to run on the pleasure it would be to tell them when I
got home, but he noticed those thoughts, and said:

"No, all these matters are a secret among us four. I
do not mind your trying to tell them, if you like, but I
will protect your tongues, and nothing of the secret will
escape from them."

It was a disappointment, but it couldn't be helped, and
it cost us a sigh or two. We talked pleasantly along, and
he was always reading our thoughts and responding to
them, and it seemed to me that this was the most wonderful of all the things he did, but he interrupted my
musings and said:

"No, it would be wonderful for you, but it is not
wonderful for me. I am not limited like you. I am not
subject to human conditions. I can measure and understand your human weaknesses, for I have studied them;
but I have none of them. My flesh is not real, although
it would seem firm to your touch; my clothes are not real;
I am a spirit. Father Peter is coming." We looked
around, but did not see anyone. "He is not in sight yet,
but you will see him presently."

"Do you know him, Satan?"

"No."

"Won't you talk with him when he comes? He is not ignorant and dull, like us, and he would so like to talk with you. Will you?"

"Another time, yes, but not now. I must go on my errand after a little. There he is now; you can see him. Sit still, and don't say anything."

We looked up and saw Father Peter approaching through the chestnuts. We three were sitting together in the grass, and Satan sat in front of us in the path. Father Peter came slowly along with his head down, thinking, and stopped within a couple of yards of us and took off his hat and got out his silk handkerchief, and stood there mopping his face and looking as if he were going to speak to us, but he didn't. Presently he muttered, "I can't think what brought me here; it seems as if I were in my study a minute ago—but I suppose I have been dreaming along for an hour and have come all this stretch without noticing; for I am not myself in these troubled days." Then he went mumbling along to himself and walked straight through Satan, just as if nothing were there. It made us catch our breath to see it. We had the impulse to cry out, the way you nearly always do when a startling thing happens, but something mysteriously restrained us and we remained quiet, only breathing fast. Then the trees hid Father Peter after a little, and Satan said:

"It is as I told you—I am only a spirit."

"Yes, one perceives it now," said Nikolaus, "but we are not spirits. It is plain he did not see you, but were we invisible, too? He looked at us, but he didn't seem to see us."

"No, none of us was visible to him, for I wished it so."

It seemed almost too good to be true, that we were actually seeing these romantic and wonderful things, and that it was not a dream. And there he sat, looking just like anybody—so natural and simple and charming, and chatting along again the same as ever, and—well, words cannot make you understand what we felt. It was an ecstasy; and an ecstasy is a thing that will not go into words; it feels like music, and one cannot tell about music so that another person can get the feeling of it. He was back in the old ages once more now, and making them

live before us. He had seen so much, so much! It was just
a wonder to look at him and try to think how it must
seem to have such experience behind one.

But it made you seem sorrowfully trivial, and the
creature of a day, and such a short and paltry day, too.
And he didn't say anything to raise up your drooping
pride—no, not a word. He always spoke of men in the
same old indifferent way—just as one speaks of bricks
and manure piles and such things; you could see that
they were of no consequence to him, one way or the
other. He didn't mean to hurt us, you could see that; just
as we don't mean to insult a brick when we disparage it;
a brick's emotions are nothing to us; it never occurs to
us to think whether it has any or not.

Once when he was bunching the most illustrious kings
and conquerors and poets and prophets and pirates and
beggars together—just a brick pile—I was shamed into
putting in a word for man, and asked him why he made
so much difference between men and himself. He had to
struggle with that a moment; he didn't seem to understand how I could ask such a strange question. Then he
said:

"The difference between man and me? The difference
between a mortal and an immortal? Between a cloud and
a spirit?" He picked up a wood louse that was creeping
along a piece of bark: "What is the difference between
Caesar and this?"

I said, "One cannot compare things which by their
nature and by the interval between them are not comparable."

"You have answered your own question," he said. "I
will expand it. Man is made of dirt—I saw him made. I
am not made of dirt. Man is a museum of diseases, a
home of impurities; he comes today and is gone tomorrow; he begins as dirt and departs as stench; I am of the
aristocracy of the Imperishables. And man has the
Moral Sense. You understand? He has the *Moral Sense.*
That would seem to be difference enough between us,
all by itself."

He stopped there, as if that settled the matter. I was
sorry, for at that time I had but a dim idea of what the
Moral Sense was. I merely knew that we were proud of

having it, and when he talked like that about it, it
wounded me, and I felt as a girl feels who thinks her dearest finery is being admired and then overhears strangers
making fun of it. For a while we were all silent, and I,
for one, was depressed. Then Satan began to chat again,
and soon he was sparkling along in such a cheerful and
vivacious vein that my spirits rose once more. He told
some very cunning things that put us in a gale of laughter; and when he was telling about the time that Samson
tied the torches to the foxes' tails and set them loose in
the Philistines' corn, and Samson sitting on the fence
slapping his thighs and laughing, with the tears running
down his cheeks, and lost his balance and fell off the
fence, the memory of that picture got him to laughing,
too, and we did have a most lovely and jolly time. By
and by he said:

"I am going on my errand now."

"Don't!" we all said. "Don't go; stay with us. You won't
come back."

"Yes, I will; I give you my word."

"When? Tonight? Say when."

"It won't be long. You will see."

"We like you."

"And I you. And as a proof of it I will show you something fine to see. Usually when I go I merely vanish;
but now I will dissolve myself and let you see me do
it."

He stood up, and it was quickly finished. He thinned
away and thinned away until he was a soap bubble, except that he kept his shape. You could see the bushes
through him as clearly as you see things through a soap
bubble, and all over him played and flashed the delicate
iridescent colors of the bubble, and along with them
was that thing shaped like a window sash which you always see on the globe of the bubble. You have seen a
bubble strike the carpet and lightly bound along two or
three times before it bursts. He did that. He sprang—
touched the grass—bounded—floated along—touched
again—and so on, and presently exploded—puff! and in
his place was vacancy.

It was a strange and beautiful thing to see. We did not
say anything, but sat wondering and dreaming and blink-

ing; and finally Seppi roused up and said, mournfully sighing:

"I suppose none of it has happened."

Nikolaus sighed and said about the same.

I was miserable to hear them say it, for it was the same cold fear that was in my own mind. Then we saw poor old Father Peter wandering along back, with his head bent down, searching the ground. When he was pretty close to us he looked up and saw us, and said, "How long have you been here, boys?"

"A little while, Father."

"Then it is since I came by, and maybe you can help me. Did you come up by the path?"

"Yes, Father."

"That is good. I came the same way. I have lost my wallet. There wasn't much in it, but a very little is much to me, for it was all I had. I suppose you haven't seen anything of it?"

"No, Father, but we will help you hunt."

"It is what I was going to ask you. Why, here it is!"

We hadn't noticed it; yet there it lay, right where Satan stood when he began to melt—if he did melt and it wasn't a delusion. Father Peter picked it up and looked very much surprised.

"It is mine," he said, "but not the contents. This is fat; mine was flat; mine was light; this is heavy." He opened it; it was stuffed as full as it could hold with gold coins. He let us gaze our fill; and of course we did gaze, for we had never seen so much money at one time before. All our mouths came open to say "Satan did it!" but nothing came out. There it was, you see—we couldn't tell what Satan didn't want told; he had said so himself.

"Boys, did you do this?"

It made us laugh. And it made him laugh, too, as soon as he thought what a foolish question it was.

"Who has been here?"

Our mouths came open to answer, but stood so for a moment, because we couldn't say "Nobody," for it wouldn't be true, and the right word didn't seem to come; then I thought of the right one, and said it:

"Not a human being."

"That is so," said the others, and let their mouths go shut.

"It is not so," said Father Peter, and looked at us very severely. "I came by here a while ago, and there was no one here, but that is nothing; someone has been here since. I don't mean to say that the person didn't pass here before you came, and I don't mean to say you saw him, but someone did pass, that I know. On your honor—you saw no one?"

"Not a human being."

"That is sufficient; I know you are telling me the truth."

He began to count the money on the path, we on our knees eagerly helping to stack it in little piles.

"It's eleven hundred ducats odd!" he said. "Oh dear! if it were only mine—and I need it so!" And his voice broke and his lips quivered.

"It is yours, sir!" we all cried out at once, "every heller!"

"No—it isn't mine. Only four ducats are mine; the rest . . . !" He fell to dreaming, poor old soul, and caressing some of the coins in his hands, and forgot where he was, sitting there on his heels with his old gray head bare; it was pitiful to see. "No," he said, waking up, "it isn't mine. I can't account for it. I think some enemy . . . it must be a trap."

Nikolaus said: "Father Peter, with the exception of the astrologer you haven't a real enemy in the village—nor Marget, either. And not even a half-enemy that's rich enough to chance eleven hundred ducats to do you a mean turn. I'll ask you if that's so or not?"

He couldn't get around that argument, and it cheered him up. "But it isn't mine, you see—it isn't mine, in any case."

He said it in a wistful way, like a person that wouldn't be sorry, but glad, if anybody would contradict him.

"It is yours, Father Peter, and we are witness to it. Aren't we, boys?"

"Yes, we are—and we'll stand by it, too."

"Bless your hearts, you do almost persuade me; you do, indeed. If I had only a hundred-odd ducats of it! The house is mortgaged for it, and we've no home for our heads if we don't pay tomorrow. And that four ducats is all we've got in the—"

"It's yours, every bit of it, and you've got to take it—we are bail that it's all right. Aren't we, Theodor? Aren't we, Seppi?"

We two said yes, and Nikolaus stuffed the money back into the shabby old wallet and made the owner take it. So he said he would use two hundred of it, for his house was good enough security for that, and would put the rest at interest till the rightful owner came for it; and on our side we must sign a paper showing how he got the money—a paper to show to the villagers as proof that he had not got out of his troubles dishonestly.

CHAPTER IV

IT made immense talk next day, when Father Peter paid Solomon Isaacs in gold and left the rest of the money with him at interest. Also, there was a pleasant change; many people called at the house to congratulate him, and a number of cool old friends became kind and friendly again; and, to top all, Marget was invited to a party.

And there was no mystery; Father Peter told the whole circumstance just as it happened, and said he could not account for it, only it was the plain hand of Providence, so far as he could see.

One or two shook their heads and said privately it looked more like the hand of Satan; and really that seemed a surprisingly good guess for ignorant people like that. Some came slyly buzzing around and tried to coax us boys to come out and "tell the truth"; and promised they wouldn't ever tell, but only wanted to know for their own satisfaction, because the whole thing was so curious. They even wanted to buy the secret, and pay money for it; and if we could have invented something that would answer—but we couldn't; we hadn't the ingenuity, so we had to let the chance go by, and it was a pity.

We carried that secret around without any trouble, but the other one, the big one, the splendid one, burned the very vitals of us, it was so hot to get out and we so hot to let it out and astonish people with it. But we had to keep it in; in fact, it kept itself in. Satan said it would, and it did. We went off every day and got to ourselves in the woods so that we could talk about Satan, and really that was the only subject we thought of or cared anything about; and day and night we watched for him and hoped he would come, and we got more and more impatient all the time. We hadn't any interest in the other boys any more, and wouldn't take part in their games and enterprises. They seemed so tame, after Satan; and their doings so trifling and commonplace after his adventures in antiquity and the constellations, and his miracles and meltings and explosions, and all that.

During the first day we were in a state of anxiety on account of one thing, and we kept going to Father Peter's house on one pretext or another to keep track of it. That was the gold coin; we were afraid it would crumble and turn to dust, like fairy money. If it did— But it didn't. At the end of the day no complaint had been made about it, so after that we were satisfied that it was real gold, and dropped the anxiety out of our minds.

There was a question which we wanted to ask Father Peter, and finally we went there the second evening, a little diffidently, after drawing straws, and I asked it as casually as I could, though it did not sound as casual as I wanted, because I didn't know how:

"What is the Moral Sense, sir?"

He looked down, surprised, over his great spectacles, and said, "Why, it is the faculty which enables us to distinguish good from evil."

It threw some light, but not a glare, and I was a little disappointed, also to some degree embarrassed. He was waiting for me to go on, so, in default of anything else to say, I asked, "Is it valuable?"

"Valuable? Heavens, lad, it is the one thing that lifts man above the beasts that perish and makes him heir to immortality!"

This did not remind me of anything further to say, so I got out, with the other boys, and we went away with that indefinite sense you have often had of being filled but not fatted. They wanted me to explain, but I was tired.

We passed out through the parlor, and there was Marget at the spinet teaching Marie Lueger. So one of the de-

serting pupils was back; and an influential one, too; the
others would follow. Marget jumped up and ran and
thanked us again, with tears in her eyes—this was the
third time—for saving her and her uncle from being
turned into the street, and we told her again we hadn't
done it; but that was her way, she never could be grateful
enough for anything a person did for her; so we let her
have her say. And as we passed through the garden,
there was Wilhelm Meidling sitting there waiting, for it
was getting toward the edge of the evening, and he would
be asking Marget to take a walk along the river with him
when she was done with the lesson. He was a young
lawyer, and succeeding fairly well and working his way
along, little by little. He was very fond of Marget, and she
of him. He had not deserted along with the others, but
had stood his ground all through. His faithfulness
was not lost on Marget and her uncle. He hadn't so very
much talent, but he was handsome and good, and these
are a kind of talents themselves and help along. He asked
us how the lesson was getting along, and we told him it
was about done. And maybe it was so; we didn't know
anything about it, but we judged it would please him,
and it did, and didn't cost us anything.

CHAPTER V

On the fourth day comes the astrologer from his crumbling old tower up the valley, where he had heard the
news, I reckon. He had a private talk with us, and we told
him what we could, for we were mightily in dread of
him. He sat there studying and studying awhile to himself; then he asked:

"How many ducats did you say?"

"Eleven hundred and seven, sir."

Then he said, as if he were talking to himself: "It is
ver-y singular. Yes . . . very strange. A curious coinci-
dence." Then he began to ask questions, and went over the
whole ground from the beginning, we answering. By
and by he said: "Eleven hundred and six ducats. It is a
large sum."

"Seven," said Seppi, correcting him.

"Oh, seven, was it? Of course a ducat more or less

isn't of consequence, but you said eleven hundred and six before."

It would not have been safe for us to say he was mistaken, but we knew he was. Nikolaus said, "We ask pardon for the mistake, but we meant to say seven."

"Oh, it is no matter, lad; it was merely that I noticed the discrepancy. It is several days, and you cannot be expected to remember precisely. One is apt to be inexact when there is no particular circumstances to impress the count upon the memory."

"But there was one, sir," said Seppi, eagerly.

"What was it, my son?" asked the astrologer, indifferently.

"First, we all counted the piles of coin, each in turn, and all made it the same—eleven hundred and six. But I had slipped one out, for fun, when the count began, and now I slipped it back and said, 'I think there is a mistake —there are eleven hundred and seven; let us count again.' We did, and of course I was right. They were astonished; then I told how it came about."

The astrologer asked us if this was so, and we said it was.

"That settles it," he said. "I know the thief now. Lads, the money was stolen."

Then he went away, leaving us very much troubled, and wondering what he could mean. In about an hour we found out; for by that time it was all over the village that Father Peter had been arrested for stealing a great sum of money from the astrologer. Everybody's tongue was loose and going. Many said it was not in Father Peter's character and must be a mistake; but the others shook their heads and said misery and want could drive a suffering man to almost anything. About one detail there were no differences; all agreed that Father Peter's account of how the money came into his hands was just about unbelievable—it had such an impossible look. They said it might have come into the astrologer's hands in some such way, but into Father Peter's, never! Our characters began to suffer now. We were Father Peter's only witnesses; how much did he probably pay us to back up his fantastic tale? People talked that kind of talk to us pretty freely and frankly, and were full of scoffings when we begged them to believe really we had told only

the truth. Our parents were harder on us than anyone
else. Our fathers said we were disgracing our families, and
they commanded us to purge ourselves of our lie, and
there was no limit to their anger when we continued to
say we had spoken true. Our mothers cried over us
and begged us to give back our bribe and get back our
honest names and save our families from shame, and
come out and honorably confess. And at last we were
so worried and harassed that we tried to tell the whole
thing, Satan and all—but no, it wouldn't come out. We
were hoping and longing all the time that Satan would
come and help us out of our trouble, but there was no
sign of him.

Within an hour after the astrologer's talk with us,
Father Peter was in prison and the money sealed up and
in the hands of the officers of the law. The money was
in a bag, and Solomon Isaacs said he had not touched
it since he had counted it; his oath was taken that it was
the same money, and that the amount was eleven hundred and seven ducats. Father Peter claimed trial by the
ecclesiastical court, but our other priest, Father Adolf,
said an ecclesiastical court hadn't jurisdiction over a suspended priest. The bishop upheld him. That settled it; the
case would go to trial in the civil court. The court
would not sit for some time to come. Wilhelm Meidling
would be Father Peter's lawyer and do the best he could,
of course, but he told us privately that a weak case on
his side and all the power and prejudice on the other
made the outlook bad.

So Marget's new happiness died a quick death. No
friends came to condole with her, and none were expected; an unsigned note withdrew her invitation to the party.
There would be no scholars to take lessons. How could she
support herself? She could remain in the house, for the
mortgage was paid off, though the government and not
poor Solomon Isaacs had the mortgage money in its grip
for the present. Old Ursula, who was cook, chamber-
maid, housekeeper, laundress, and everything else for
Father Peter, and had been Marget's nurse in earlier years,
said God would provide. But she said that from habit,
for she was a good Christian. She meant to help in the
providing, to make sure, if she could find a way.

We boys wanted to go and see Marget and show friendliness for her, but our parents were afraid of offending the community and wouldn't let us. The astrologer was going around inflaming everybody against Father Peter, and saying he was an abandoned thief and had stolen eleven hundred and seven gold ducats from him. He said he knew he was a thief from that fact, for it was exactly the sum he had lost and which Father Peter pretended he had "found."

In the afternoon of the fourth day after the catastrophe old Ursula appeared at our house and asked for some washing to do, and begged my mother to keep this secret, to save Marget's pride, who would stop this project if she found it out, yet Marget had not enough to eat and was growing weak. Ursula was growing weak herself, and showed it; and she ate of the food that was offered her like a starving person, but could not be persuaded to carry any home, for Marget would not eat charity food. She took some clothes down to the stream to wash them, but we saw from the window that handling the bat was too much for her strength; so she was called back and a trifle of money offered her, which she was afraid to take lest Marget should suspect; then she took it, saying she would explain that she found it in the road. To keep it from being a lie and damning her soul, she got me to drop it while she watched; then she went along by there and found it, and exclaimed with surprise and joy, and picked it up and went her way. Like the rest of the village, she could tell everyday lies fast enough and without taking any precautions against fire and brimstone on their account; but this was a new kind of lie, and it had a dangerous look because she hadn't had any practice in it. After a week's practice it wouldn't have given her any trouble. It is the way we are made.

I was in trouble, for how would Marget live? Ursula could not find a coin in the road every day—perhaps not even a second one. And I was ashamed, too, for not having been near Marget, and she so in need of friends; but that was my parents' fault, not mine, and I couldn't help it.

I was walking along the path, feeling very downhearted, when a most cheery and tingling freshening-up sensa-

tion went rippling through me, and I was too glad for any
words, for I knew by that sign that Satan was by. I had
noticed it before. Next moment he was alongside of me
and I was telling him all my trouble and what had been
happening to Marget and her uncle. While we were talking we turned a curve and saw old Ursula resting in the
shade of a tree, and she had a lean stray kitten in her
lap and was petting it. I asked her where she got it, and
she said it came out of the woods and followed her; and
she said it probably hadn't any mother or any friends
and she was going to take it home and take care of it.
Satan said:

"I understand you are very poor. Why do you want
to add another mouth to feed? Why don't you give it to
some rich person?"

Ursula bridled at this and said: "Perhaps you would
like to have it. You must be rich, with your fine clothes
and quality airs." Then she sniffed and said: "Give it to
the rich—the idea! The rich don't care for anybody but
themselves; it's only the poor that have feeling for the
poor, and help them. The poor and God. God will provide
for this kitten."

"What makes you think so?"

Ursula's eyes snapped with anger. "Because I know it!"
she said. "Not a sparrow falls to the ground without His
seeing it."

"But it falls, just the same. What good is seeing it
fall?"

Old Ursula's jaws worked, but she could not get
any word out for the moment, she was so horrified. When
she got her tongue she stormed out, "Go about your
business, you puppy, or I will take a stick to you!"

I could not speak, I was so scared. I knew that with
his notions about the human race Satan would consider it a matter of no consequence to strike her dead,
there being "plenty more"; but my tongue stood still, I
could give her no warning. But nothing happened;
Satan remained tranquil—tranquil and indifferent. I suppose he could not be insulted by Ursula any more than
the king could be insulted by a tumblebug. The old
woman jumped to her feet when she made her remark,
and did it as briskly as a young girl. It had been many

years since she had done the like of that. That was Satan's influence; he was a fresh breeze to the weak and the sick, wherever he came. His presence affected even the lean kitten, and it skipped to the ground and began to chase a leaf. This surprised Ursula, and she stood looking at the creature and nodding her head wonderingly, her anger quite forgotten.

"What's come over it?" she said. "A while ago it could hardly walk."

"You have not seen a kitten of that breed before," said Satan.

Ursula was not proposing to be friendly with the mocking stranger, and she gave him an ungentle look and retorted: "Who asked you to come here and pester me, I'd like to know? And what do you know about what I've seen and what I haven't seen?"

"You haven't seen a kitten with the hair-spines on its tongue pointing to the front, have you?"

"No—nor you, either."

"Well, examine this one and see."

Ursula was become pretty spry, but the kitten was spryer, and she could not catch it, and had to give it up. Then Satan said:

"Give it a name, and maybe it will come."

Ursula tried several names, but the kitten was not interested.

"Call it Agnes. Try that."

The creature answered to the name and came. Ursula examined its tongue. "Upon my word, it's true!" she said. "I have not seen this kind of a cat before. Is it yours?"

"No."

"Then how did you know its name so pat?"

"Because all cats of that breed are named Agnes; they will not answer to any other."

Ursula was impressed. "It is the most wonderful thing!" Then a shadow of trouble came into her face, for her superstitions were aroused, and she reluctantly put the creature down, saying: "I suppose I must let it go; I am not afraid—no, not exactly that, though the priest— well, I've heard people—indeed, many people . . . And, besides, it is quite well now and can take care of itself." She sighed, and turned to go, murmuring: "It is such a pretty one, too, and would be such company—and the house is so sad and lonesome these troubled days. . . . Miss Marget so mournful and just a shadow, and the old master shut up in jail."

"It seems a pity not to keep it," said Satan.

Ursula turned quickly—just as if she were hoping someone would encourage her.

"Why?" she asked, wistfully.

"Because this breed brings luck."

"Does it? Is it true? Young man, do you know it to be true? How does it bring luck?"

"Well, it brings money, anyway."

Ursula looked disappointed. "Money? A cat bring money? The idea! You could never sell it here; people do not buy cats here; one can't even give them away." She turned to go.

"I don't mean sell it. I mean have an income from it. This kind is called the Lucky Cat. Its owner finds four silver groschen in his pocket every morning."

I saw the indignation rising in the old woman's face. She was insulted. This boy was making fun of her. That was her thought. She thrust her hands into her pockets and straightened up to give him a piece of her mind. Her temper was all up, and hot. Her mouth came open and let out three words of a bitter sentence . . . then it fell silent, and the anger in her face turned to surprise or wonder or fear, or something, and she slowly brought out her hands from her pocket and opened them and held them so. In one was my piece of money, in the other lay four silver groschen. She gazed a little while, perhaps to see if the groschen would vanish away; then she said, fervently:

"It's true—it's true—and I'm ashamed and beg forgiveness, O dear master and benefactor!" And she ran to Satan and kissed his hand, over and over again, according to the Austrian custom.

In her heart she probably believed it was a witch-cat and an agent of the Devil; but no matter, it was all the more certain to be able to keep its contract and furnish a daily good living for the family, for in matters of finance even the piousest of our peasants would have more confidence in an arrangement with the Devil than with an archangel. Ursula started homeward, with Agnes in her arms, and I said I wished I had her privilege of seeing Marget.

Then I caught my breath, for we were there. There in the parlor, and Marget standing looking at us, astonished. She was feeble and pale, but I knew that those conditions would not last in Satan's atmosphere, and it turned out so. I introduced Satan—that is, Philip Traum—and we sat down and talked. There was no constraint. We were simple folk, in our village, and when a stranger was a pleasant person we were soon friends. Marget wondered how we got in without her hearing us. Traum said the door was open, and we walked in and waited until she should turn around and greet us. This was not true; no door was open; we entered through the walls or the roof or down the chimney, or somehow; but no matter, what Satan wished a person to believe, the person was sure to believe, and so Marget was quite satisfied with that explanation. And then the main part of her mind was on Traum, anyway; she couldn't keep her eyes off him, he was so beautiful. That gratified me, and made me proud. I hoped he would show off some, but he didn't. He seemed only interested in being friendly and telling lies. He said he was an orphan. That made Marget pity him. The water came into her eyes. He said he had never known his mamma; she passed away while he was a young thing; and said his papa was in shattered health, and had no property to speak of—in fact, none of any earthly value—but he had an uncle in business down in the tropics, and he was very well off and had a monopoly, and it was from this uncle that he drew his support. The very mention of a kind uncle was enough to remind Marget of her own, and her eyes filled again. She said she hoped their two uncles would meet, some day. It made me shudder. Philip said he hoped so, too; and that made me shudder again.

"Maybe they will," said Marget. "Does your uncle travel much?"

"Oh yes, he goes all about; he has business everywhere."

And so they went on chatting, and poor Marget forgot her sorrows for one little while, anyway. It was probably

the only really bright and cheery hour she had known
lately. I saw she liked Philip, and I knew she would. And
when he told her he was studying for the ministry I could
see that she liked him better than ever. And then, when
he promised to get her admitted to the jail so that she
could see her uncle, that was the capstone. He said he
would give the guards a little present, and she must always go in the evening after dark, and say nothing,
"but just show this paper and pass in, and show it again
when you come out"—and he scribbled some queer marks
on the paper and gave it to her, and she was ever so
thankful, and right away was in a fever for the sun to go
down; for in that old, cruel time prisoners were not allowed to see their friends, and sometimes they spent
years in the jails without ever seeing a friendly face.
I judged that the marks on the paper were an enchant-
ment, and that the guards would not know what they
were doing, nor have any memory of it afterward; and
that was indeed the way of it. Ursula put her head in at
the door now and said:

"Supper's ready, miss." Then she saw us and looked
frightened, and motioned me to come to her, which I
did, and she asked if we had told about the cat. I said
no, and she was relieved, and said please don't; for if
Miss Marget knew, she would think it was an unholy
cat and would send for a priest and have its gifts all
purified out of it, and then there wouldn't be any more
dividends. So I said we wouldn't tell, and she was satisfied. Then I was beginning to say goodbye to Marget, but
Satan interrupted and said, ever so politely—well, I
don't remember just the words, but anyway he as good
as invited himself to supper, and me, too. Of course
Marget was miserably embarrassed, for she had no reason
to suppose there would be half enough for a sick bird.
Ursula heard him, and she came straight into the room,
not a bit pleased. At first she was astonished to see
Marget looking so fresh and rosy, and said so; then she
spoke up in her native tongue, which was Bohemian, and
said—as I learned afterward—"Send him away, Miss Marget; there's not victuals enough."

Before Marget could speak, Satan had the word, and
was talking back at Ursula in her own language—which

was a surprise to her, and for her mistress, too. He said, "Didn't I see you down the road a while ago?"

"Yes, sir."

"Ah, that pleases me; I see you remember me." He stepped to her and whispered: "I told you it is a Lucky Cat. Don't be troubled; it will provide."

That sponged the slate of Ursula's feelings clean of its anxieties, and a deep, financial joy shone in her eyes. The cat's value was augmenting. It was getting full time for Marget to take some sort of notice of Satan's invitation, and she did it in the best way, the honest way that was natural to her. She said she had little to offer, but that we were welcome if we would share it with her.

We had supper in the kitchen, and Ursula waited at table. A small fish was in the frying pan, crisp and brown and tempting, and one could see that Marget was not expecting such respectable food as this. Ursula brought it, and Marget divided it between Satan and me, declining to take any of it herself; and was beginning to say she did not care for fish today, but she did not finish the remark. It was because she noticed that another fish had appeared in the pan. She looked surprised, but did not say anything. She probably meant to inquire of Ursula about this later. There were other surprises: flesh and game and wines and fruits—things which had been strangers in that house lately; but Marget made no exclamations, and now even looked unsurprised, which was Satan's influence, of course. Satan talked right along, and was entertaining, and made the time pass pleasantly and cheerfully; and although he told a good many lies, it was no harm in him, for he was only an angel and did not know any better. They do not know right from wrong; I knew this, because I remembered what he had said about it. He got on the good side of Ursula. He praised her to Marget, confidentially, but speaking just loud enough for Ursula to hear. He said she was a fine woman, and he hoped some day to bring her and his uncle together. Very soon Ursula was mincing and simpering around in a ridiculous, girly way, and smoothing out her gown and prinking at herself like a foolish old hen, and all the time pretending she was not hearing what Satan was saying. I was ashamed, for it showed us to be what Satan considered us, a silly race and trivial. Satan said his uncle entertained a great deal, and to have a clever woman presiding over the festivities would double the attractions of the place.

"But your uncle is a gentleman, isn't he?" asked Marget.

"Yes," said Satan, indifferently; "some even call him a Prince, out of compliment, but he is not bigoted; to him personal merit is everything, rank nothing."

My hand was hanging down by my chair; Agnes came along and licked it; by this act a secret was revealed. I started to say, "It is all a mistake; this is just a common, ordinary cat; the hair-needles on her tongue point inward, not outward." But the words did not come, because they couldn't. Satan smiled upon me, and I understood.

When it was dark Marget took food and wine and fruit, in a basket, and hurried away to the jail, and Satan and I walked toward my home. I was thinking to myself that I should like to see what the inside of the jail was like; Satan overheard the thought, and the next moment we were in the jail. We were in the torture chamber, Satan said. The rack was there, and the other instruments, and there was a smoky lantern or two hanging on the walls and helping to make the place look dim and dreadful. There were people there—and executioners—but as they took no notice of us, it meant that we were invisible. A young man lay bound, and Satan said he was suspected of being a heretic, and the executioners were about to inquire into it. They asked the man to confess to the charge, and he said he could not, for it was not true. Then they drove splinter after splinter under his nails, and he shrieked with the pain. Satan was not disturbed, but I could not endure it, and had to be whisked out of there. I was faint and sick, but the fresh air revived me, and we walked toward my home. I said it was a brutal thing.

"No, it was a human thing. You should not insult the brutes by such a misuse of that word; they have not deserved it," and he went on talking like that. "It is like your paltry race—always lying, always claiming virtues which it hasn't got, always denying them to the higher animals, which alone possess them. No brute ever does a cruel thing—that is the monopoly of those with the Moral Sense. When a brute inflicts pain he does it innocently; it is not wrong; for him there is no such thing as wrong. And he does not inflict pain for the pleasure of inflicting it—only man does that. Inspired by that mongrel Moral Sense of his! A sense whose function is to distinguish between right and wrong, with liberty to choose which of them he will do. Now what advantage can he get out of that? He is always choosing, and in nine cases out of ten he prefers the wrong. There shouldn't be any wrong; and without the Moral Sense there couldn't be any. And yet he is such an unreasoning creature that he is not able to perceive that the Moral Sense degrades him to the bottom layer of animated beings and is a shameful possession. Are you feeling better? Let me show you something."

CHAPTER VI

IN a moment we were in a French Village. We walked through a great factory of some sort, where men and women and little children were toiling in heat and dirt and a fog of dust; and they were clothed in rags, and drooped at their work, for they were worn and half starved, and weak and drowsy. Satan said:

"It is some more Moral Sense. The proprietors are rich, and very holy; but the wage they pay to these poor brothers and sisters of theirs is only enough to keep them from dropping dead with hunger. The work hours are fourteen per day, winter and summer—from six in the morning till eight at night—little children and all. And they walk to and from the pigsties which they inhabit—four miles each way, through mud and slush, rain, snow, sleet, and storm, daily, year in and year out. They get four hours of sleep. They kennel together, three families in a room, in unimaginable filth and stench; and disease comes, and they die off like flies. Have they committed a crime, these mangy things? No. What have they done, that they are punished so? Nothing at all, except getting themselves born into your foolish race. You have seen how they treat a misdoer there in the jail; now you see how they treat the innocent and the worthy. Is your race logical? Are these ill-smelling innocents better off than that heretic? Indeed, no; his punishment is trivial compared with theirs. They broke him on the wheel and smashed him to rags and pulp after we left, and he is dead now, and free of your precious race; but these poor slaves here—why, they have been dying for years, and some of them will not escape from life for years to come. It is the Moral Sense which teaches the factory proprietors the difference between right and wrong—you perceive the result. They think themselves better than dogs. Ah, you are such an illogical, unreasoning race! And paltry—oh, unspeakably!"

Then he dropped all seriousness and just overstrained himself making fun of us, and deriding our pride in our warlike deeds, our great heroes, our imperishable fames, our mighty kings, our ancient aristocracies, our venerable history—and laughed and laughed till it was enough to make a person sick to hear him; and finally he sobered a little and said, "But, after all, it is not all ridiculous; there is a sort of pathos about it when one remembers how few are your days, how childish your pomps, and what shadows you are!"

Presently all things vanished suddenly from my sight, and I knew what it meant. The next moment we were walking along in our village; and down toward the river I saw the twinkling lights of the Golden Stag. Then in the dark I heard a joyful cry:

"He's come again!"

It was Seppi Wohlmeyer. He had felt his blood leap and his spirits rise in a way that could mean only one thing, and he knew Satan was near, although it was too dark to see him. He came to us, and we walked along together, and Seppi poured out his gladness like water. It was as if he were a lover and had found his sweetheart who had been lost. Seppi was a smart and animated boy, and had enthusiasm and expression, and was a contrast to Nikolaus and me. He was full of the last new mystery, now—the disappearance of Hans Oppert, the village loafer. People were beginning to be curious about it, he said. He did not say anxious—curious was the right word, and strong enough. No one had seen Hans for a couple of days.

"Not since he did that brutal thing, you know," he said.

"What brutal thing?" It was Satan that asked.

"Well, he is always clubbing his dog, which is a good dog, and his only friend, and is faithful, and loves him, and does no one any harm; and two days ago he was at it again, just for nothing—just for pleasure—and the dog was howling and begging, and Theodor and I begged, too, but he threatened us, and struck the dog again with all his might and knocked one of his eyes out, and he said to us, 'There, I hope you are satisfied now; that's what you have got for him by your damned meddling'—and he laughed, the heartless brute." Seppi's voice trembled with pity and anger. I guessed what Satan would say, and he said it.

"There is that misused word again—that shabby slander. Brutes do not act like that, but only men."

"Well, it was inhuman, anyway."

"No, it wasn't, Seppi; it was human—quite distinctly human. It is not pleasant to hear you libel the higher animals by attributing to them dispositions which they are free from, and which are found nowhere but in the human heart. None of the higher animals is tainted with the disease called the Moral Sense. Purify your language, Seppi; drop those lying phrases out of it."

He spoke pretty sternly—for him—and I was sorry I hadn't warned Seppi to be more particular about the word he used. I knew how he was feeling. He would not want to offend Satan; he would rather offend all his kin. There was an uncomfortable silence, but relief soon came for that poor dog came along now, with his eye hanging down, and went straight to Satan, and began to moan and mutter brokenly, and Satan began to answer in the same way, and it was plain that they were talking together in the dog language. We all sat down in the grass, in the moonlight, for the clouds were breaking away now, and Satan took the dog's head in his lap and put the eye back in its place, and the dog was comfortable, and he wagged his tail and licked Satan's hand, and looked thankful and said the same; I knew he was saying it, though I did not understand the words. Then the two talked together a bit, and Satan said:

"He says his master was drunk."

"Yes, he was," said we.

"And an hour later he fell over the precipice there beyond the Cliff Pasture."

"We know the place; it is three miles from here."

"And the dog has been often to the village, begging people to go there, but he was only driven away and not listened to."

We remembered it, but hadn't understood what he wanted.

"He only wanted help for the man who had misused him, and he thought only of that, and has had no food nor sought any. He has watched by his master two nights. What do you think of your race? Is heaven reserved for it, and this dog ruled out, as your teachers tell you? Can your race add anything to this dog's stock of morals and magnanimities?" He spoke to the creature, who jumped up, eager and happy, and apparently ready for orders and impatient to execute them. "Get some men; go with the dog—he will show you that carrion; and take a priest along to arrange about insurance, for death is near."

With the last word he vanished, to our sorrow and disappointment. We got the men and Father Adolf, and we saw the man die. Nobody cared but the dog; he mourned and grieved, and licked the dead face, and could not be comforted. We buried him where he was, and without a coffin, for he had no money, and no friend but the dog. If we had been an hour earlier the priest would have been in time to send that poor creature to heaven, but now he was gone down into the awful fires, to burn forever. It seemed such a pity that in a world where so many people have difficulty to put in their time, one little hour could not have been spared for this poor creature who needed it so much, and to whom it would have made the difference between eternal joy and eternal pain. It gave an appalling idea of the value of an hour, and I thought I could never waste one again without remorse and terror. Seppi was depressed and grieved, and said it must be so much better to be a dog and not run such awful risks. We took this one home with us and kept him for our own. Seppi had a very good thought as we were walking along, and it cheered us up and made us feel much better. He said the dog had for-

given the man that had wronged him so, and maybe God
would accept that absolution.

There was a very dull week, now, for Satan did not
come, nothing much was going on, and we boys could
not venture to go and see Marget, because the nights were
moonlit and our parents might find us out if we tried.
But we came across Ursula a couple of times taking a
walk in the meadows beyond the river to air the cat, and
we learned from her that things were going well. She
had natty new clothes on and bore a prosperous look.
The four groschen a day were arriving without a break,
but were not being spent for food and wine and such
things—the cat attended to all that.

Marget was enduring her forsakenness and isolation
fairly well, all things considered, and was cheerful, by
help of Wilhelm Meidling. She spent an hour or two
every night in the jail with her uncle, and had fattened
him up with the cat's contributions. But she was curious
to know more about Philip Traum, and hoped I would
bring him again. Ursula was curious about him herself,
and asked a good many questions about his uncle. It
made the boys laugh, for I had told them the nonsense
Satan had been stuffing her with. She got no satisfaction
out of us, our tongues being tied.

Ursula gave us a small item of information: money
being plenty now, she had taken on a servant to help
about the house and run errands. She tried to tell it in a
commonplace, matter-of-course way, but she was so set
up by it and so vain of it that her pride in it leaked
out pretty plainly. It was beautiful to see her veiled delight in this grandeur, poor old thing, but when we heard
the name of the servant we wondered if she had been
altogether wise; for although we were young, and often
thoughtless, we had fairly good perception on some matters. This boy was Gottfried Narr, a dull, good creature,
with no harm in him and nothing against him personally;
still, he was under a cloud, and properly so, for it had
not been six months since a social blight had mildewed
the family—his grandmother had been burned as a
witch. When that kind of a malady is in the blood it
does not always come out with just one burning. Just now
was not a good time for Ursula and Marget to be having

dealings with a member of such a family, for the witch-terror had risen higher during the past year than it had ever reached in the memory of the oldest villagers. The mere mention of a witch was almost enough to frighten us out of our wits. This was natural enough, because of late years there were more kinds of witches than there used to be; in old times it had been only old women, but of late years they were of all ages—even children of eight and nine; it was getting so that anybody might turn out to be a familiar of the Devil—age and sex hadn't anything to do with it. In our little region we had tried to extirpate the witches, but the more of them we burned the more of the breed rose up in their places.

Once, in a school for girls only ten miles away, the teachers found that the back of one of the girls was all red and inflamed, and they were greatly frightened, believing it to be the Devil's marks. The girl was scared, and begged them not to denounce her, and said it was only fleas; but of course it would not do to let the matter rest there. All the girls were examined, and eleven out of the fifty were badly marked, the rest less so. A commission was appointed, but the eleven only cried for their mothers and would not confess. Then they were shut up, each by herself, in the dark, and put on black bread and water for ten days and nights; and by that time they were haggard and wild, and their eyes were dry and they did not cry any more, but only sat and mumbled, and would not take the food. Then one of them confessed, and said they had often ridden through the air on broomsticks to the witches' Sabbath, and in a bleak place high up in the mountains had danced and drunk and caroused with several hundred other witches and the Evil One, and all had conducted themselves in a scandalous way and had reviled the priests and blasphemed God. That is what she said—not in narrative form, for she was not able to remember any of the details without having them called to her mind one after the other; but the commission did that, for they knew just what questions to ask, they being all written down for the use of witch-commissioners two centuries before. They asked, "Did you do so and so?" and she always said yes, and looked weary and tired, and took no interest in it. And so when the other ten heard that this one confessed, they confessed, too, and answered yes to the questions. Then they were burned at the stake all together, which was just and right; and everybody went from all the countryside to see it. I went, too; but when I saw that one of them was a bonny, sweet girl I used to play with, and looked so pitiful there chained to the stake, and her mother crying over her and devouring her with kisses and clinging around her neck, and saying, "Oh, my God! oh, my God!" it was too dreadful, and I went away.

It was bitter cold weather when Gottfried's grandmother was burned. It was charged that she had cured bad headaches by kneading the person's head and neck with her fingers—as she said—but really by the Devil's help, as everybody knew. They were going to examine her but she stopped them, and confessed straight off that her power was from the Devil. So they appointed to burn her next morning, early, in our market square. The officer who was to prepare the fire was there first, and prepared it. She was there next—brought by the constables, who left her and went to fetch another witch. Her family did not come with her. They might be reviled, maybe stoned, if the people were excited. I came, and gave her an apple. She was squatting at the fire, warming herself and waiting; and her old lips and hands were blue with the cold. A stranger came next. He was a traveler, passing through; and he spoke to her gently, and, seeing nobody but me there to hear, said he was sorry for her. And he asked if what she confessed was true, and she said no. He looked surprised and still more sorry then, and asked her:

"Then why did you confess?"

"I am old and very poor," she said, "and I work for my living. There was no way but to confess. If I hadn't they might have set me free. That would ruin me, for no one would forget that I had been suspected of being a witch, and so I would get no more work, and wherever I went they would set the dogs on me. In a little while I would starve. The fire is best; it is soon over. You have been good to me, you two, and I thank you."

She snuggled closer to the fire, and put out her hands

to warm them, the snowflakes descending soft and still on her old gray head and making it white and whiter. The crowd was gathering now, and an egg came flying and struck her in the eye, and broke and ran down her face. There was a laugh at that.

I told Satan all about the eleven girls and the old woman, once, but it did not affect him. He only said it was the human race, and what the human race did was of no consequence. And he said he had seen it made; and it was not made of clay; it was made of mud—part of it was, anyway. I knew what he meant by that—the Moral Sense. He saw the thought in my head, and it tickled him and made him laugh. Then he called a bullock out of a pasture and petted it and talked with it, and said:

"There—he wouldn't drive children mad with hunger and fright and loneliness, and then burn them for confessing to things invented for them which had never happened. And neither would he break the hearts of innocent, poor old women and make them afraid to trust themselves among their own race; and he would not insult them in their death agony. For he is not besmirched with the Moral Sense, but is as the angels are, and knows no wrong, and never does it."

Lovely as he was, Satan could be cruelly offensive when he chose; and he always chose when the human race was brought to his attention. He always turned up his nose at it, and never had a kind word for it.

Well, as I was saying, we boys doubted if it was a good time for Ursula to be hiring a member of the Narr family. We were right. When the people found it out they were naturally indignant. And, moreover, since Marget and Ursula hadn't enough to eat themselves, where was the money coming from to feed another mouth? That is what they wanted to know; and in order to find out they stopped avoiding Gottfried and began to seek his society and have sociable conversations with him. He was pleased—not thinking any harm and not seeing the trap—and so he talked innocently along, and was no discreeter than a cow.

"Money!" he said; "they've got plenty of it. They pay me two groschen a week, besides my keep. And they

live on the fat of the land, I can tell you; t̶...
himself can't beat their table."

This astonishing statement was conveyed by the
oger to Father Adolf on a Sunday morning when he was
returning from mass. He was deeply moved, and said:

"This must be looked into."

He said there must be witchcraft at the bottom of it,
and told the villagers to resume relations with Marget
and Ursula in a private and unostentatious way, and keep
both eyes open. They were told to keep their own coun-
sel, and not rouse the suspicions of the household. The
villagers were at first a bit reluctant to enter such a
dreadful place, but the priest said they would be under
his protection while there, and no harm could come to
them, particularly if they carried a trifle of holy water
along and kept their beads and crosses handy. This satisfied them and made them willing to go; envy and malice
made the baser sort even eager to go.

And so poor Marget began to have company again,
and was as pleased as a cat. She was like most anybody
else—just human, and happy in her prosperities and not
averse from showing them off a little; and she was hu-
manly grateful to have the warm shoulder turned to her
and be smiled upon by her friends and the village again;
for of all the hard things to bear, to be cut by your neighbors and left in contemptuous solitude is maybe the hard-
est.

The bars were down, and we could all go there now,
and we did—our parents and all—day after day. The cat
began to strain herself. She provided the top of everything for those companies, and in abundance—among
them many a dish and many a wine which they had not
tasted before and which they had not even heard of except at secondhand from the prince's servants. And the
tableware was much above ordinary, too.

Marget was troubled at times, and pursued Ursula with
questions to an uncomfortable degree; but Ursula stood
her ground and stuck to it that it was Providence, and
said no word about the cat. Marget knew that nothing
was impossible to Providence, but she could not help
having doubts that this effort was from there, though she
was afraid to say so, lest disaster come of it. Witchcraft

occurred to her, but she put the thought aside, for this was before Gottfried joined the household, and she knew Ursula was pious and a bitter hater of witches. By the time Gottfried arrived Providence was established, unshakably intrenched, and getting all the gratitude. The cat made no murmur, but went on composedly improving in style and prodigality by experience.

In any community, big or little, there is always a fair proportion of people who are not malicious or unkind by nature, and who never do unkind things except when they are overmastered by fear, or when their self-interest is greatly in danger, or some such matter as that. Eseldorf had its proportion of such people, and ordinarily their good and gentle influence was felt, but these were not ordinary times—on account of the witch-dread—and so we did not seem to have any gentle and compassionate hearts left, to speak of. Every person was frightened at the unaccountable state of things at Marget's house, not doubting that witchcraft was at the bottom of it, and fright frenzied their reason. Naturally there were some who pitied Marget and Ursula for the danger that was gathering about them, but naturally they did not say so; it would not have been safe. So the others had it all their own way, and there was none to advise the ignorant girl and the foolish woman and warn them to modify their doings. We boys wanted to warn them, but we backed down when it came to the pinch, being afraid. We found that we were not manly enough nor brave enough to do a generous action when there was a chance that it could get us into trouble. Neither of us confessed this poor spirit to the others, but did as other people would have done—dropped the subject and talked about something else. And I knew we all felt mean, eating and drinking Marget's fine things along with those companies of spies, and petting her and complimenting her with the rest, and seeing with self-reproach how foolishly happy she was, and never saying a word to put her on her guard. And, indeed, she was happy, and as proud as a princess, and so grateful to have friends again. And all the time these people were watching with all their eyes and reporting all they saw to Father Adolf.

But he couldn't make head or tail of the situation.

There must be an enchanter somewhere on the premises, but who was it? Marget was not seen to do any jugglery, nor was Ursula, nor yet Gottfried; and still the wines and dainties never ran short, and a guest could not call for a thing and not get it. To produce these effects was usual enough with witches and enchanters—that part of it was not new; but to do it without any incantations, or even any rumblings or earthquakes or lightnings or apparitions —that was new, novel, wholly irregular. There was nothing in the books like this. Enchanted things were always unreal. Gold turned to dirt in an unenchanted atmosphere, food withered away and vanished. But this test failed in the present case. The spies brought samples: Father Adolf prayed over them, exorcised them, but it did no good; they remained sound and real, they yielded to natural decay only, and took the usual time to do it.

Father Adolf was not merely puzzled, he was also exasperated; for these evidences very nearly convinced him —privately—that there was no witchcraft in the matter. It did not wholly convince him, for this could be a new kind of witchcraft. There was a way to find out as to this: if this prodigal abundance of provender was not brought in from the outside, but produced on the premises, there was witchcraft, sure.

CHAPTER VII

MARGET announced a party, and invited forty people; the date for it was seven days away. This was a fine opportunity. Marget's house stood by itself, and it could be easily watched. All the week it was watched night and day. Marget's household went out and in as usual, but they carried nothing in their hands, and neither they nor others brought anything to the house. This was ascertained. Evidently rations for forty people were not being fetched. If they were furnished any sustenance it would have to be made on the premises. It was true that Marget went out with a basket every evening, but the spies ascertained that she always brought it back empty.

The guests arrived at noon and filled the place. Father Adolf followed; also, after a little, the astrologer, without invitation. The spies had informed him that neither at the back nor the front had any parcels been brought in. He entered, and found the eating and drinking going on finely, and everything progressing in a lively and festive way. He glanced around and perceived that many of the cooked delicacies and all of the native and foreign fruits were of a perishable character, and he also recognized that these were fresh and perfect. No apparitions, no incantations, no thunder. That settled it. This was witchcraft. And not only that, but of a new kind—a kind never dreamed of before. It was a prodigious power, an illustrious power; he resolved to discover its secret. The announcement of it would resound throughout the world, penetrate to the remotest lands, paralyze all the nations with amazement—and carry his name with it, and make him renowned forever. It was a wonderful piece of luck, a splendid piece of luck; the glory of it made him dizzy.

All the house made room for him; Marget politely seated him; Ursula ordered Gottfried to bring a special table for him. Then she decked it and furnished it, and asked for his orders.

"Bring me what you will," he said.

The two servants brought supplies from the pantry, together with white wine and red—a bottle of each. The astrologer, who very likely had never seen such delicacies before, poured out a beaker of red wine, drank it off, poured another, then began to eat with a grand appetite.

I was not expecting Satan, for it was more than a week since I had seen or heard of him, but now he came in—I knew it by the feel, though people were in the way and I could not see him. I heard him apologizing for intruding; and he was going away, but Marget urged him to stay, and he thanked her and stayed. She brought him along, introducing him to the girls, and to Meidling, and to some of the elders; and there was quite a rustle of whispers: "It's the young stranger we hear so much about and can't get sight of, he is away so much." "Dear, dear, but he is beautiful—what is his name?" "Philip Traum." "Ah, it fits him!" (You see, "Traum" is German for "Dream.") "What does he do?" "Studying for the ministry, they say." "His face is his fortune—he'll be a cardinal some day." "Where is his home?" "Away down somewhere in the tropics, they say—has a rich uncle down there." And so on. He made his way at once; everybody was anxious to know him and talk with him. Everybody noticed how cool and fresh it was, all of a sudden, and wondered at it, for they could see that the sun was beating down the same as before, outside, and the sky was clear of clouds, but no one guessed the reason, of course.

The astrologer had drunk his second beaker; he poured out a third. He set the bottle down, and by accident overturned it. He seized it before much was spilled, and held it up to the light, saying, "What a pity—it is royal wine." Then his face lighted with joy or triumph, or something, and he said, "Quick! Bring a bowl."

It was brought—a four-quart one. He took up that two-pint bottle and began to pour; went on pouring, the red liquor gurgling and gushing into the white bowl and rising higher and higher up its sides, everybody staring and holding their breath—and presently the bowl was full to the brim.

"Look at the bottle," he said, holding it up; "it is full yet!" I glanced at Satan, and in that moment he vanished. Then Father Adolf rose up, flushed and excited, crossed himself, and began to thunder in his great voice, "This house is bewitched and accursed!" People began to cry and shriek and crowd toward the door. "I summon this detected household to—"

His words were cut off short. His face became red, then purple, but he could not utter another sound. Then I saw Satan, a transparent film, melt into the astrologer's body; then the astrologer put up his hand, and apparently in his own voice said, "Wait—remain where you are." All stopped where they stood. "Bring a funnel!" Ursula brought it, trembling and scared, and he stuck it in the bottle and took up the great bowl and began to pour the wine back, the people gazing and dazed with astonishment, for they knew the bottle was already full before he began. He emptied the whole of the bowl into the bottle, then smiled out over the room, chuckled, and said, indifferently: "It is nothing—anybody can do it! With my powers I can even do much more."

A frightened cry burst out everywhere, "Oh, my God, he is possessed!" and there was a tumultuous rush for the door which swiftly emptied the house of all who did not belong in it except us boys and Meidling. We boys knew the secret, and would have told it if we could, but we couldn't. We were very thankful to Satan for furnishing that good help at the needful time.

Marget was pale, and crying; Meidling looked kind of petrified; Ursula the same; but Gottfried was the worst— he couldn't stand, he was so weak and scared. For he was of a witch family, you know, and it would be bad for him to be suspected. Agnes came loafing in, looking pious and unaware, and wanted to rub up against Ursula and be petted, but Ursula was afraid of her and shrank away from her, but pretending she was not meaning any incivility, for she knew very well it wouldn't answer to have strained relations with that kind of a cat. But we boys took Agnes and petted her, for Satan would not have befriended her if he had not had a good opinion of her, and that was indorsement enough for us. He seemed to trust anything that hadn't the Moral Sense.

Outside, the guests, panic-stricken, scattered in every direction and fled in a pitiable state of terror; and such a tumult as they made with their running and sobbing and shrieking and shouting that soon all the village came flocking from their houses to see what had happened, and they thronged the street and shouldered and jostled one another in excitement and fright; and then Father Adolf appeared, and they fell apart in two walls like the cloven Red Sea, and presently down this lane the astrologer came striding and mumbling, and where he passed the lanes surged back in packed masses, and fell silent with awe, and their eyes stared and their breasts heaved, and several women fainted; and when he was gone by the crowd swarmed together and followed him at a distance, talking excitedly and asking questions and finding out the facts. Finding out the facts and passing them on to others, with improvements—improvements which soon enlarged the bowl of wine to a barrel, and made the one bottle hold it all and yet remain empty to the last.

When the astrologer reached the market square he went straight to a juggler, fantastically dressed, who was keeping three brass balls in the air, and took them from him and faced around upon the approaching crowd and said: "This poor clown is ignorant of his art. Come forward and see an expert perform."

So saying, he tossed the balls up one after another and set them whirling in a slender bright oval in the air, and added another, then another and another, and soon —no one seeing whence he got them—adding, adding, adding, the oval lengthening all the time, his hands moving so swiftly that they were just a web or a blur and not distinguishable as hands; and such as counted said there were now a hundred balls in the air. The spinning great oval reached up twenty feet in the air and was a shining and glinting and wonderful sight. Then he folded his arms and told the balls to go on spinning without his help—and they did it. After a couple of minutes he said, "There, that will do," and the oval broke and came crashing down, and the balls scattered abroad and rolled every whither. And wherever one of them came the people fell back in dread, and no one would touch it. It made him laugh, and he scoffed at the people and called them cowards and old women. Then he turned and saw the tightrope, and said foolish people were daily wasting their money to see a clumsy and ignorant varlet degrade that beautiful art; now they should see the work of a master. With that he made a spring into the air and lit firm on his feet on the rope. Then he hopped the whole length of it back and forth on one foot, with his hands clasped over his eyes; and next he began to throw somersaults, both backward and forward, and threw twenty-seven.

The people murmured, for the astrologer was old, and always before had been halting of movement and at times even lame, but he was nimble enough now and went on with his antics in the liveliest manner. Finally he sprang lightly down and walked away, and passed up the road and around the corner and disappeared. Then that great, pale, silent, solid crowd drew a deep breath and looked into one another's faces as if they said: "Was it real? Did you see it, or was it only I—and I was dreaming?" Then they broke into a low murmur of talking, and fell apart in couples, and moved toward their homes, still talking in that awed way, with faces close together and laying a hand on an arm and making other such gestures as people make when they have been deeply impressed by something.

We boys followed behind our fathers, and listened, catching all we could of what they said; and when they sat down in our house and continued their talk they still had us for company. They were in a sad mood, for it was certain, they said, that disaster for the village must follow this awful visitation of witches and devils. Then my father remembered that Father Adolf had been struck dumb at the moment of his denunciation.

"They have not ventured to lay their hands upon an anointed servant of God before," he said; "and how they could have dared it this time I cannot make out, for he wore his crucifix. Isn't it so?"

"Yes," said the others, "we saw it."

"It is serious, friends, it is very serious. Always before, we had a protection. It has failed."

The others shook, as with a sort of chill, and muttered those words over—"It has failed." "God has forsaken us."

"It is true," said Seppi Wohlmeyer's father; "there is nowhere to look for help."

"The people will realize this," said Nikolaus' father, the judge, "and despair will take away their courage and their energies. We have indeed fallen upon evil times."

He sighed, and Wohlmeyer said, in a troubled voice: "The report of it all will go about the country, and our village will be shunned as being under the displeasure of God. The Golden Stag will know hard times."

"True, neighbor," said my father; "all of us will suffer —all in repute, many in estate. And, good God!—"

"What is it?"

"That can come—to finish us!"

"Name it—*um Gottes Willen!*"

"The Interdict!"

It smote like a thunderclap, and they were like to swoon with the terror of it. Then the dread of this calamity roused their energies, and they stopped brooding and began to consider ways to avert it. They discussed this, that, and the other way, and talked till the afternoon was far spent, then confessed that at present they could arrive at no decision. So they parted sorrowfully, with oppressed hearts which were filled with bodings.

While they were saying their parting words I slipped out and set my course for Marget's house to see what was happening there. I met many people, but none of them greeted me. It ought to have been surprising, but it was not, for they were so distraught with fear and dread that they were not in their right minds, I think; they were white and haggard, and walked like persons in a dream, their eyes open but seeing nothing, their lips moving but uttering nothing, and worriedly clasping and unclasping their hands without knowing it.

At Marget's it was like a funeral. She and Wilhelm sat together on the sofa, but said nothing, not even holding hands. Both were steeped in gloom, and Marget's eyes were red from the crying she had been doing. She said:

"I have been begging him to go, and come no more, and so save himself alive. I cannot bear to be his murderer. This house is bewitched, and no inmate will escape the fire. But he will not go, and he will be lost with the rest."

Wilhelm said he would not go; if there was danger for her, his place was by her, and there he would remain. Then she began to cry again, and it was all so mournful that I wished I had stayed away. There was a knock, now, and Satan came in, fresh and cheery and beautiful, and brought that winy atmosphere of his and changed the whole thing. He never said a word about what had been happening, nor about the awful fears which were freezing the blood in the hearts of the community, but began to talk and rattle on about all manner of gay and pleasant things; and next about music—an artful stroke which cleared away the remnant of Marget's depression and brought her spirits and her interests broad awake. She had not heard anyone talk so well and so knowingly on that subject before, and she was so uplifted by it and so charmed that what she was feeling lit up her face and came out in her words; and Wilhelm noticed it and did not look as pleased as he ought to have done. And next Satan branched off into poetry, and recited some, and did it well, and Marget was charmed again; and again

Wilhelm was not as pleased as he ought to have been, and this time Marget noticed it and was remorseful.

I fell asleep to pleasant music that night—the patter of rain upon the panes and the dull growling of distant thunder. Away in the night Satan came and roused me and said: "Come with me. Where shall we go?"

"Anywhere—so it is with you."

Then there was a fierce glare of sunlight, and he said, "This is China."

That was a grand surprise, and made me sort of drunk with vanity and gladness to think I had come so far—so much, much farther than anybody else in our village, including Bartel Sperling, who had such a great opinion of his travels. We buzzed around over that empire for more than half an hour, and saw the whole of it. It was wonderful, the spectacles we saw; and some were beautiful, others too horrible to think. For instance— However, I may go into that by and by, and also why Satan chose China for this excursion instead of another place; it would interrupt my tale to do it now. Finally we stopped flitting and lit. We sat upon a mountain commanding a vast landscape of mountain range and gorge and valley and plain and river, with cities and villages slumbering in the sunlight, and a glimpse of blue sea on the farther verge. It was a tranquil and dreamy picture, beautiful to the eye and restful to the spirit. If we could only make a change like that whenever we wanted to, the world would be easier to live in than it is, for change of scene shifts the mind's burdens to the other shoulder and banishes old, shopworn wearinesses from mind and body both.

We talked together, and I had the idea of trying to reform Satan and persuade him to lead a better life. I told him about all those things he had been doing, and begged him to be more considerate and stop making people unhappy. I said I knew he did not mean any harm, but that he ought to stop and consider the possible consequences of a thing before launching it in that impulsive and random way of his; then he would not make so much trouble. He was not hurt by this plain speech; he only looked amused and surprised, and said:

"What? I do random things? Indeed, I never do. I

stop and consider possible consequences? Where is the need? I know what the consequences are going to be—always."

"Oh, Satan, then how could you do these things?"

"Well, I will tell you, and you must understand if you can. You belong to a singular race. Every man is a suffering-machine and a happiness-machine combined. The two functions work together harmoniously, with a fine and delicate precision, on the give-and-take principle. For every happiness turned out in the one department the other stands ready to modify it with a sorrow or a pain—maybe a dozen. In most cases the man's life is about equally divided between happiness and unhappiness. When this is not the case the unhappiness predominates—always; never the other. Sometimes a man's make and disposition are such that his misery-machine is able to do nearly all the business. Such a man goes through life almost ignorant of what happiness is. Everything he touches, everything he does, brings a misfortune upon him. You have seen such people? To that kind of a person life is not an advantage, is it? It is only a disaster. Sometimes for an hour's happiness a man's machinery makes him pay years of misery. Don't you know that? It happens every now and then. I will give you a case or two presently. Now the people of your village are nothing to me—you know that, don't you?"

I did not like to speak out too flatly, so I said I had suspected it.

"Well, it is true that they are nothing to me. It is not possible that they should be. The difference between them and me is abysmal, immeasurable. They have no intellect."

"No intellect?"

"Nothing that resembles it. At a future time I will examine what man calls his mind and give you the details of that chaos, then you will see and understand. Men have nothing in common with me—there is no point of contact; they have foolish little feelings and foolish little vanities and impertinences and ambitions; their foolish little life is but a laugh, a sigh, and extinction; and they have no sense. Only the Moral Sense. I will show you what I mean. Here is a red spider, not so big as a pin's head. Can you imagine an elephant being interested in

him—caring whether he is happy or isn't, or whether he
is wealthy or poor, or whether his sweetheart returns his
love or not, or whether his mother is sick or well, or
whether he is looked up to in society or not, or whether
his enemies will smite him or his friends desert him, or
whether his hopes will suffer blight or his political ambitions fail, or whether he shall die in the bosom of his
family or neglected and despised in a foreign land? These
things can never be important to the elephant; they are
nothing to him; he cannot shrink his sympathies to the
microscopic size of them. Man is to me as the red spider
is to the elephant. The elephant has nothing against the
spider—he cannot get down to that remote level; I have
nothing against man. The elephant is indifferent; I am
indifferent. The elephant would not take the trouble to do
the spider an ill turn; if he took the notion he might do
him a good turn, if it came in his way and cost nothing.
I have done men good service, but no ill turns.

"The elephant lives a century, the red spider a day; in
power, intellect, and dignity the one creature is separated
from the other by a distance which is simply astronom-
ical. Yet in these, as in all qualities, man is immeasur-
ably further below me than is the wee spider below the
elephant.

"Man's mind clumsily and tediously and laboriously
patches little trivialities together and gets a result—such
as it is. My mind creates! Do you get the force of that?
Creates anything it desires—and in a moment. Creates
without material. Creates fluids, solids, colors—anything,
everything—out of the airy nothing which is called
Thought. A man imagines a silk thread, imagines a machine to make it, imagines a picture, then by weeks of
labor embroiders it on canvas with the thread. I think the
whole thing, and in a moment it is before you—created.

"I think a poem, music, the record of a game of chess
—anything—and it is there. This is the immortal mind—
nothing is beyond its reach. Nothing can obstruct my
vision; the rocks are transparent to me, and darkness is
daylight. I do not need to open a book; I take the whole
of its contents into my mind at a single glance, through
the cover; and in a million years I could not forget a single word of it, or its place in the volume. Nothing goes

on in the skull of man, bird, fish, insect, or other creature which can be hidden from me. I pierce the learned man's brain with a single glance, and the treasures which cost him threescore years to accumulate are mine; he can forget, and he does forget, but I retain.

"Now, then, I perceive by your thoughts that you are understanding me fairly well. Let us proceed. Circumstances might so fall out that the elephant could like the spider—supposing he can see it—but he could not love it. His love is for his own kind—for his equals. An angel's love is sublime, adorable, divine, beyond the imagination of man—infinitely beyond it! But it is limited to his own august order. If it fell upon one of your race for only an instant, it would consume its object to ashes. No, we cannot love men, but we can be harmlessly indifferent to them; we can also like them, sometimes. I like you and the boys, I like Father Peter, and for your sakes I am doing all these things for the villagers."

He saw that I was thinking a sarcasm, and he explained his position.

"I have wrought well for the villagers, though it does not look like it on the surface. Your race never know good fortune from ill. They are always mistaking the one for the other. It is because they cannot see into the future. What I am doing for the villagers will bear good fruit some day; in some cases to themselves; in others, to unborn generations of men. No one will ever know that I was the cause, but it will be none the less true, for all that. Among you boys you have a game: you stand a row of bricks on end a few inches apart; you push a brick, it knocks its neighbor over, the neighbor knocks over the next brick—and so on till all the row is prostrate. That is human life. A child's first act knocks over the initial brick, and the rest will follow inexorably. If you could see into the future, as I can, you would see everything that was going to happen to that creature; for nothing can change the order of its life after the first event has determined it. That is, nothing will change it, because each act unfailingly begets an act, that act begets another, and so on to the end, and the seer can look forward down the line and see just when each act is to have birth, from cradle to grave."

"Does God order the career?"

"Foreordain it? No. The man's circumstances and environment order it. His first act determines the second and all that follow after. But suppose, for argument's sake, that the man should skip one of these acts; an apparently trifling one, for instance; suppose that it had been appointed that on a certain day, at a certain hour and minute and second and fraction of a second he should go to the well, and he didn't go. That man's career would change utterly, from that moment; thence to the grave it would be wholly different from the career which his first act as a child had arranged for him. Indeed, it might be that if he had gone to the well he would have ended his career on a throne, and that omitting to do it would set him upon a career that would lead to beggary and a pauper's grave. For instance: if at any time—say in boyhood—Columbus had skipped the triflingest little link in the chain of acts projected and made inevitable by his first childish act, it would have changed his whole subsequent life, and he would have become a priest and died obscure in an Italian village, and America could not have been discovered for two centuries afterward. I know this. To skip any one of the billion acts in Columbus's chain would have wholly changed his life. I have examined his billion of possible careers, and in only one of them occurs the discovery of America. You people do not suspect that all of your acts are of one size and importance, but it is true; to snatch at an appointed fly is as big with fate for you as in any other appointed act—"

"As the conquering of a continent, for instance?"

"Yes. Now, then, no man ever does drop a link—the thing has never happened! Even when he is trying to make up his mind as to whether he will do a thing or not, that itself is a link, an act, and has its proper place in his chain; and when he finally decides an act, that also was the thing which he was absolutely certain to do. You see, now, that a man will never drop a link in his chain. He cannot. If he made up his mind to try, that project would itself be an unavoidable link—a thought bound to occur to him at that precise moment, and made certain by the first act of his babyhood."

It seemed so dismal!

"He is a prisoner for life," I said sorrowfully, "and cannot get free."

"No, of himself he cannot get away from the consequences of his first childish act. But I can free him."

I looked up wistfully.

"I have changed the careers of a number of your villagers."

I tried to thank him, but found it difficult, and let it drop.

"I shall make some other changes. You know that little Lisa Brandt?"

"Oh yes, everybody does. My mother says she is so sweet and so lovely that she is not like any other child. She says she will be the pride of the village when she grows up; and its idol, too, just as she is now."

"I shall change her future."

"Make it better?" I asked.

"Yes. And I will change the future of Nikolaus."

I was glad, this time, and said, "I don't need to ask about his case; you will be sure to do generously by him."

"It is my intention."

Straight off I was building that great future of Nicky's in my imagination, and had already made a renowned general of him and *hofmeister* at the court, when I noticed that Satan was waiting for me to get ready to listen again. I was ashamed of having exposed my cheap imaginings to him, and was expecting some sarcasms, but it did not happen. He proceeded with his subject:

"Nicky's appointed life is sixty-two years."

"That's grand!" I said.

"Lisa's, thirty-six. But, as I told you, I shall change their lives and those ages. Two minutes and a quarter from now Nikolaus will wake out of his sleep and find the rain blowing in. It was appointed that he should turn over and go to sleep again. But I have appointed that he shall get up and close the window first. That trifle will change his career entirely. He will rise in the morning two minutes later than the chain of his life had appointed him to rise. By consequence, thenceforth nothing will ever happen to him in accordance with the details of the old chain." He took out his watch and sat looking at it a few moments, then said: "Nikolaus has risen to close the window. His life is changed, his new career has begun. There will be consequences."

It made me feel creepy; it was uncanny.

"But for this change certain things would happen twelve days from now. For instance, Nikolaus would save Lisa from drowning. He would arrive on the scene at exactly the right moment—four minutes past ten, the long-ago appointed instant of time—and the water would be shoal, the achievement easy and certain. But he will arrive some seconds too late, now; Lisa will have struggled into deeper water. He will do his best, but both will drown."

"Oh, Satan! oh, dear Satan!" I cried, with the tears rising in my eyes, "save them! Don't let it happen. I can't bear to lose Nikolaus, he is my loving playmate and friend; and think of Lisa's poor mother!"

I clung to him and begged and pleaded, but he was not moved. He made me sit down again, and told me I must hear him out.

"I have changed Nikolaus's life, and this has changed Lisa's. If I had not done this, Nikolaus would save Lisa, then he would catch cold from his drenching; one of your race's fantastic and desolating scarlet fevers would follow, with pathetic aftereffects; for forty-six years he would lie in his bed a paralytic log, deaf, dumb, blind, and praying night and day for the blessed relief of death. Shall I change his life back?"

"Oh no! Oh, not for the world! In charity and pity leave it as it is."

"It is best so. I could not have changed any other link in his life and done him so good a service. He had a billion possible careers, but not one of them was worth living; they were charged full with miseries and disasters. But for my intervention he would do his brave deed twelve days from now—a deed begun and ended in six minutes—and get for all reward those forty-six years of sorrow and suffering I told you of. It is one of the cases I was thinking of a while ago when I said that sometimes an act which brings the actor an hour's happiness and self-satisfaction is paid for—or punished—by years of suffering."

I wondered what poor little Lisa's early death would save her from. He answered the thought:

"From ten years of pain and slow recovery from an accident, and then from nineteen years' pollution, shame, depravity, crime, ending with death at the hands of the executioner. Twelve days hence she will die; her mother would save her life if she could. Am I not kinder than her mother?"

"Yes—oh, indeed yes; and wiser."

"Father Peter's case is coming on presently. He will be acquitted, through unassailable proofs of his innocence."

"Why, Satan, how can that be? Do you really think it?"

"Indeed, I know it. His good name will be restored, and the rest of his life will be happy."

"I can believe it. To restore his good name will have that effect."

"His happiness will not proceed from that cause. I shall change his life that day, for his good. He will never know his good name has been restored."

In my mind—and modestly—I asked for particulars, but Satan paid no attention to my thought. Next, my mind wandered to the astrologer, and I wondered where he might be.

"In the moon," said Satan, with a fleeting sound which I believed was a chuckle. "I've got him on the cold side of it, too. He doesn't know where he is, and is not having a pleasant time; still, it is good enough for him, a good place for his star studies. I shall need him presently; then I shall bring him back and possess him again. He has a long and cruel and odious life before him, but I will change that, for I have no feeling against him and am quite willing to do him a kindness. I think I shall get him burned."

He had such strange notions of kindness! But angels are made so, and do not know any better. Their ways are not like our ways; and, besides, human beings are nothing to them; they think they are only freaks. It seemed to me odd that he should put the astrologer so far away; he could have dumped him in Germany just as well, where he would be handy.

"Far away?" said Satan. "To me no place is far away; distance does not exist for me. The sun is less than a hundred million miles from here, and the light that is falling upon us has taken eight minutes to come; but I can make that flight, or any other, in a fraction of time so minute that it cannot be measured by a watch. I have but to think the journey, and it is accomplished."

I held out my hand and said, "The light lies upon it; think it into a glass of wine, Satan."

He did it. I drank the wine.

"Break the glass," he said.

I broke it.

"There—you see it is real. The villagers thought the brass balls were magic stuff and as perishable as smoke. They were afraid to touch them. You are a curious lot—your race. But come along; I have business. I will put you to bed." Said and done. Then he was gone; but his voice came back to me through the rain and darkness saying, "Yes, tell Seppi, but no other."

It was the answer to my thought.

CHAPTER VIII

SLEEP would not come. It was not because I was proud of my travels and excited about having been around the big world to China, and feeling contemptuous of Bartel Sperling, "the traveler," as he called himself, and looked down upon us others because he had been to Vienna once and was the only Eseldorf boy who had made such a journey and seen the world's wonders. At another time that would have kept me awake, but it did not affect me now. No, my mind was filled with Nikolaus, my thoughts ran upon him only, and the good days we had seen together at romps and frolics in the woods and the fields and the river in the long summer days, and skating and sliding in the winter when our parents thought we were in school. And now he was going out of this young life, and the summers and winters would come and go, and we others would rove and play as before, but his place would be vacant; we should see him no more. To-morrow he would not suspect, but would be as he had always been, and it would shock me to hear him laugh, and see him do lightsome and frivolous things, for to me he would be a corpse, with waxen hands and dull eyes, and I should see the shroud around his face; and next day he would not suspect, nor the next, and all the time his handful of days would be wasting swiftly away and that awful thing coming nearer and nearer, his fate closing steadily around him and no one knowing it but Seppi and me. Twelve days—only twelve days. It was awful to think of. I noticed that in my thoughts I was not calling him by his familiar names, Nick and Nicky, but was speaking of him by his full name, and reverently, as one speaks of the dead. Also, as incident after incident of our comradeship came thronging into my mind out of the past, I noticed that they were mainly cases where I had wronged him or hurt him, and they rebuked me and reproached me, and my heart was wrung with remorse, just as it is when we remember our unkindnesses to friends who have passed beyond the veil, and we wish we could have them back again, if only for a moment, so that we could go on our knees to them and say, "Have pity, and forgive."

Once when we were nine years old he went a long errand of nearly two miles for the fruiterer, who gave him a splendid big apple for reward, and he was flying home with it, almost beside himself with astonishment and delight, and I met him, and he let me look at the apple, not thinking of treachery, and I ran off with it, eating it as I ran, he following me and begging; and when he overtook me I offered him the core, which was all that was left; and I laughed. Then he turned away, crying, and said he had meant to give it to his little sister. That smote me, for she was slowly getting well of a sickness, and it would have been a proud moment for him, to see her joy and surprise and have her caresses. But I was ashamed to say I was ashamed, and only said something rude and mean, to pretend I did not care, and he made no reply in words, but there was a wounded look in his face as he turned away toward his home which rose before me many times in after years, in the night, and reproached me and made me ashamed again. It had grown dim in my mind, by and by, then it disappeared; but it was back now, and not dim.

Once at school, when we were eleven, I upset my ink and spoiled four copybooks, and was in danger of severe punishment; but I put it upon him, and he got the whipping.

And only last year I had cheated him in a trade, giving him a large fishhook which was partly broken through for three small sound ones. The first fish he caught broke the hook, but he did not know I was blamable, and he refused to take back one of the small hooks which my conscience forced me to offer him, but said, "A trade is a trade; the hook was bad, but that was not your fault."

No, I could not sleep. These little, shabby wrongs upbraided me and tortured me, and with a pain much sharper than one feels when the wrongs have been done to the living. Nikolaus was living, but no matter; he was to me as one already dead. The wind was still moaning about the eaves, the rain still pattering upon the panes.

In the morning I sought out Seppi and told him. It was down by the river. His lips moved, but he did not say anything, he only looked dazed and stunned, and his face turned very white. He stood like that a few moments, the tears welling into his eyes, then he turned away and I locked my arm in his and we walked along thinking, but not speaking. We crossed the bridge and wandered through the meadows and up among the hills and the woods, and at last the talk came and flowed freely, and it was all about Nikolaus and was a recalling of the life we had lived with him. And every now and then Seppi said, as if to himself:

"Twelve days!—less than twelve."

We said we must be with him all the time; we must have all of him we could; the days were precious now. Yet we did not go to seek him. It would be like meeting the dead, and we were afraid. We did not say it, but that was what we were feeling. And so it gave us a shock when we turned a curve and came upon Nikolaus face to face. He shouted, gaily:

"Hi-hi! What is the matter? Have you seen a ghost?"

We couldn't speak, but there was no occasion, he was willing to talk for us all, for he had just seen Satan and was in high spirits about it. Satan had told him about our trip to China, and he had begged Satan to take him a journey, and Satan had promised. It was to be a far journey, and wonderful and beautiful; and Nikolaus had begged him to take us, too, but he said no, he would take us some day, maybe, but not now. Satan would come for him on the 13th, and Nikolaus was already counting the hours, he was so impatient.

That was the fatal day. We were already counting the hours, too.

We wandered many a mile, always following paths which had been our favorites from the days when we were little, and always we talked about the old times. All the blitheness was with Nikolaus; we others could not shake off our depression. Our tone toward Nikolaus was so strangely gentle and tender and yearning that he noticed it, and was pleased; and we were constantly doing him deferential little offices of courtesy, and saying, "Wait, let me do that for you," and that pleased him, too. I gave him seven fishhooks—all I had—and made him take them; and Seppi gave him his new knife and a humming-top painted red and yellow—atonements for swindles practiced upon him formerly, as I learned later, and probably no longer remembered by Nikolaus now. These things touched him, and he said he could not have believed that we loved him so; and his pride in it and gratefulness for it cut us to the heart, we were so undeserving of them. When we parted at last, he was radiant, and said he had never had such a happy day.

As we walked along homeward, Seppi said, "We always prized him, but never so much as now, when we are going to lose him."

Next day and every day we spent all of our spare time with Nikolaus; and also added to it time which we (and he) stole from work and other duties, and this cost the three of us some sharp scoldings, and some threats of punishment. Every morning two of us woke with a start and a shudder, saying, as the days flew along, "Only ten days left"; "only nine days left"; "only eight"; "only seven." Always it was narrowing. Always Nikolaus was gay and happy, and always puzzled because we were not. He wore his invention to the bone trying to invent ways to cheer us up, but it was only a hollow success; he could see that our jollity had no heart in it, and that the laughs

we broke into came up against some obstruction or other
and suffered damage and decayed into a sigh. He tried to
find out what the matter was, so that he could help us
out of our trouble or make it lighter by sharing it
with us; so we had to tell many lies to deceive him and
appease him.

But the most distressing thing of all was that he was
always making plans, and often they went beyond the
13th! Whenever that happened it made us groan in spirit.
All his mind was fixed upon finding some way to conquer
our depression and cheer us up; and at last, when he
had but three days to live, he fell upon the right idea
and was jubilant over it—a boys-and-girls' frolic and
dance in the woods, up there where we first met Satan,
and this was to occur on the 14th. It was ghastly, for that
was his funeral day. We couldn't venture to protest; it
would only have brought a "Why?" which we could not
answer. He wanted us to help him invite his guests, and
we did it—one can refuse nothing to a dying friend. But
it was dreadful, for really we were inviting them to his
funeral.

It was an awful eleven days; and yet, with a lifetime
stretching back between today and then, they are still a
grateful memory to me, and beautiful. In effect they were
days of companionship with one's sacred dead, and I have
known no comradeship that was so close or so precious.
We clung to the hours and the minutes, counting them as
they wasted away, and parting with them with that pain
and bereavement which a miser feels who sees his hoard
filched from him coin by coin by robbers and is helpless to prevent it.

When the evening of the last day came we stayed out
too long; Seppi and I were in fault for that; we could
not bear to part with Nikolaus; so it was very late when we
left him at his door. We lingered near awhile, listening;
and that happened which we were fearing. His father
gave him the promised punishment, and we heard his
shrieks. But we listened only a moment, then hurried
away, remorseful for this thing which we had caused.
And sorry for the father, too; our thought being, "If
he only knew—if he only knew!"

In the morning Nikolaus did not meet us at the appointed place, so we went to his home to see what the matter was. His mother said:

"His father is out of all patience with these goings-on, and will not have any more of it. Half the time when Nick is needed he is not to be found; then it turns out that he has been gadding around with you two. His father gave him a flogging last night. It always grieved me before, and many's the time I have begged him off and saved him, but this time he appealed to me in vain, for I was out of patience myself."

"I wish you had saved him just this one time," I said, my voice trembling a little; "it would ease a pain in your heart to remember it some day."

She was ironing at the time, and her back was partly toward me. She turned about with a startled or wondering look in her face and said, "What do you mean by that?"

I was not prepared, and didn't know anything to say; so it was awkward, for she kept looking at me; but Seppi was alert and spoke up:

"Why, of course it would be pleasant to remember, for the very reason we were out so late was that Nikolaus got to telling how good you are to him, and how he never got whipped when you were by to save him; and he was so full of it, and we were so full of the interest of it, that none of us noticed how late it was getting."

"Did he say that? Did he?" and she put her apron to her eyes.

"You can ask Theodor—he will tell you the same."

"It is a dear, good lad, my Nick," she said. "I am sorry I let him get whipped; I will never do it again. To think—all the time I was sitting here last night, fretting and angry at him, he was loving me and praising me! Dear, dear, if we could only know! Then we shouldn't ever go wrong; but we are only poor, dumb beasts groping around and making mistakes. I shan't ever think of last night without a pang."

She was like all the rest; it seemed as if nobody could open a mouth, in these wretched days, without saying something that made us shiver. They were "groping around," and did not know what true, sorrowfully true things they were saying by accident.

Seppi asked if Nikolaus might go out with us.

"I am sorry," she answered, "but he can't. To punish him further, his father doesn't allow him to go out of the house today."

We had a great hope! I saw it in Seppi's eyes. We thought, "If he cannot leave the house, he cannot be drowned." Seppi asked, to make sure:

"Must he stay in all day, or only the morning?"

"All day. It's such a pity, too; it's a beautiful day, and he is so unused to being shut up. But he is busy planning his party, and maybe that is company for him. I do hope he isn't too lonesome."

Seppi saw that in her eye which emboldened him to ask if we might go up and help him pass his time.

"And welcome!" she said, right heartily. "Now I call that real friendship, when you might be abroad in the fields and the woods, having a happy time. You are good boys, I'll allow that, though you don't always find satisfactory ways of improving it. Take these cakes—for yourselves—and give him this one, from his mother."

The first thing we noticed when we entered Nikolaus's room was the time—a quarter to ten. Could that be correct? Only such a few minutes to live! I felt a contraction at my heart. Nikolaus jumped up and gave us a glad welcome. He was in good spirits over his plannings for his party and had not been lonesome.

"Sit down," he said, "and look at what I've been doing. And I've finished a kite that you will say is a beauty. It's drying, in the kitchen; I'll fetch it.'

He had been spending his penny savings in fanciful trifles of various kinds, to go as prizes in the games, and they were marshaled with fine and showy effect upon the table. He said:

"Examine them at your leisure while I get mother to touch up the kite with her iron if it isn't dry enough yet."

Then he tripped out and went clattering downstairs, whistling.

We did not look at the things; we couldn't take any interest in anything but the clock. We sat staring at it in silence, listening to the ticking, and every time the minute hand jumped we nodded recognition—one minute fewer to cover in the race for life or for death. Finally Seppi drew a deep breath and said:

"Two minutes to ten. Seven minutes more and he will pass the death-point. Theodor, he is going to be saved! He's going to—"

"Hush! I'm on needles. Watch the clock and keep still."

Five minutes more. We were panting with the strain and the excitement. Another three minutes, and there was a footstep on the stair.

"Saved!" And we jumped up and faced the door.

The old mother entered, bringing the kite. "Isn't it a beauty?" she said. "And, dear me, how he has slaved over it—ever since daylight, I think, and only finished it awhile before you came." She stood it against the wall, and stepped back to take a view of it. "He drew the pictures his own self, and I think they are very good. The church isn't so very good, I'll have to admit, but look at the bridge—anyone can recognize the bridge in a minute. He asked me to bring it up. . . . Dear me! it's seven minutes past ten, and I—"

"But where is he?"

"He? Oh, he'll be here soon; he's gone out a minute."

"Gone out?"

"Yes. Just as he came downstairs little Lisa's mother came in and said the child had wandered off somewhere, and as she was a little uneasy I told Nikolaus to never mind about his father's orders—go and look her up. . . . Why, how white you two do look! I do believe you are sick. Sit down; I'll fetch something. That cake has disagreed with you. It is a little heavy, but I thought—"

She disappeared without finishing her sentence, and we hurried at once to the back window and looked toward the river. There was a great crowd at the other end of the bridge, and people were flying toward that point from every direction.

"Oh, it is all over—poor Nikolaus! Why, oh, why did she let him get out of the house!"

"Come away," said Seppi, half sobbing, "come quick— we can't bear to meet her; in five minutes she will know."

But we were not to escape. She came upon us at the foot of the stairs, with her cordials in her hands, and made us come in and sit down and take the medicine.

Then she watched the effect, and it did not satisfy her; so she made us wait longer, and kept upbraiding herself for giving us the unwholesome cake.

Presently the thing happened which we were dreading. There was a sound of tramping and scraping outside, and a crowd came solemnly in, with heads uncovered, and laid the two drowned bodies on the bed.

"Oh, my God!" that poor mother cried out, and fell on her knees, and put her arms about her dead boy and began to cover the wet face with kisses. "Oh, it was I that sent him, and I have been his death. If I had obeyed, and kept him in the house, this would not have happened. And I am rightly punished; I was cruel to him last night, and him begging me, his own mother, to be his friend."

And so she went on and on, and all the women cried and pitied her, and tried to comfort her, but she could not forgive herself and could not be comforted, and kept on saying if she had not sent him out he would be alive and well now, and she was the cause of his death.

It shows how foolish people are when they blame themselves for anything they have done. Satan knows, and he said nothing happens that your first act hasn't arranged to happen and made inevitable; and so, of your own motion you can't ever alter the scheme or do a thing that will break a link. Next we heard screams, and Frau Brandt came wildly plowing and plunging through the crowd with her dress in disorder and hair flying loose, and flung herself upon her dead child with moans and kisses and pleadings and endearments; and by and by she rose up almost exhausted with her outpourings of passionate emotion, and clenched her fist and lifted it toward the sky, and her tear-drenched face grew hard and resentful, and she said:

"For nearly two weeks I have had dreams and presentiments and warnings that death was going to strike what was most precious to me, and day and night and night and day I have groveled in the dirt before Him praying Him to have pity on my innocent child and save it from harm—and here is His answer!"

Why, He had saved it from harm—but she did not know.

She wiped the tears from her eyes and cheeks, and stood awhile gazing down at the child and caressing its face and its hair with her hand; then she spoke again in that bitter tone: "But in His hard heart is no compassion. I will never pray again."

She gathered her dead child to her bosom and strode away, the crowd falling back to let her pass, and smitten dumb by the awful words they had heard. Ah, that poor woman! It is as Satan said, we do not know good fortune from bad, and are always mistaking the one for the other. Many a time since then I have heard people pray to God to spare the life of sick persons, but I have never done it.

Both funerals took place at the same time in our little church next day. Everybody was there, including the party guests. Satan was there, too; which was proper, for it was on account of his efforts that the funerals had happened. Nikolaus had departed this life without absolution, and a collection was taken up for masses, to get him out of purgatory. Only two-thirds of the required money was gathered, and the parents were going to try to borrow the rest, but Satan furnished it. He told us privately that there was no purgatory, but he had contributed in order that Nikolaus' parents and their friends might be saved from worry and distress. We thought it very good of him, but he said money did not cost him anything.

At the graveyard the body of little Lisa was seized for debt by a carpenter to whom the mother owed fifty groschen for work done the year before. She had never been able to pay this, and was not able now. The carpenter took the corpse home and kept it four days in his cellar, the mother weeping and imploring about his house all the time; then he buried it in his brother's cattle yard, without religious ceremonies. It drove the mother wild with grief and shame, and she forsook her work and went daily about the town, cursing the carpenter and blaspheming the laws of the emperor and the church, and it was pitiful to see. Seppi asked Satan to interfere, but he said the carpenter and the rest were members of the human race and were acting quite neatly for that species of animal. He would interfere if he found a horse acting in such a way, and we must inform him when we came across that kind of horse doing that kind of a human thing, so that he could stop it. We believed this was sarcasm, for of course there wasn't any such horse.

But after a few days we found that we could not abide that poor woman's distress, so we begged Satan to examine her several possible careers, and see if he could not change her, to her profit, to a new one. He said the longest of her careers as they now stood gave her forty-two years to live, and her shortest one twenty-nine, and that both were charged with grief and hunger and cold and pain. The only improvement he could make would be to enable her to skip a certain three minutes from now; and he asked us if he should do it. This was such a short time to decide in that we went to pieces with nervous excitement, and before we could pull ourselves together and ask for particulars he said the time would be up in a few more seconds; so then we gasped out, "Do it!"

"It is done," he said; "she was going around a corner; I have turned her back; it has changed her career."

"Then what will happen, Satan?"

"It is happening now. She is having words with Fischer, the weaver. In his anger Fischer will straightway do what he would not have done but for this accident. He was present when she stood over her child's body and uttered those blasphemies."

"What will he do?"

"He is doing it now—betraying her. In three days she will go to the stake."

We could not speak; we were frozen with horror, for if we had not meddled with her career she would have been spared this awful fate. Satan noticed these thoughts, and said:

"What you are thinking is strictly human-like—that is to say, foolish. The woman is advantaged. Die when she might, she would go to heaven. By this prompt death she gets twenty-nine years more of heaven than she is entitled to, and escapes twenty-nine years of misery here."

A moment before we were bitterly making up our minds that we would ask no more favors of Satan for friends of ours, for he did not seem to know any way to do a person a kindness but by killing him; but the whole aspect of the case was changed now, and we were glad of what we had done and full of happiness in the thought of it.

After a little I began to feel troubled about Fischer, and asked, timidly, "Does this episode change Fischer's life-scheme, Satan?"

"Change it? Why, certainly. And radically. If he had not met Frau Brandt awhile ago he would die next year, thirty-four years of age. Now he will live to be ninety, and have a pretty prosperous and comfortable life of it, as human lives go."

We felt a great joy and pride in what we had done for Fischer, and were expecting Satan to sympathize with this feeling; but he showed no sign, and this made us uneasy. We waited for him to speak, but he didn't; so, to assuage our solicitude we had to ask him if there was any defect in Fischer's good luck. Satan considered the question a moment, then said, with some hesitation:

"Well, the fact is, it is a delicate point. Under his several former possible life-careers he was going to heaven."

We were aghast. "Oh, Satan! and under this one—"

"There, don't be so distressed. You were sincerely trying to do him a kindness; let that comfort you."

"Oh, dear, dear, that cannot comfort us. You ought to have told us what we were doing, then we wouldn't have acted so."

But it made no impression on him. He had never felt a pain or a sorrow, and did not know what they were, in any really informing way. He had no knowledge of them except theoretically—that is to say, intellectually. And of course that is no good. One can never get any but a loose and ignorant notion of such things except by experience. We tried our best to make him comprehend the awful thing that had been done and how we were compromised by it, but he couldn't seem to get hold of it. He said he did not think it important where Fischer went to; in heaven he would not be missed, there were "plenty there." We tried to make him see that he was missing the point entirely; that Fischer, and not other people, was the proper one to decide about the importance of it; but it all went for nothing; he said he did not care for Fischer—there were plenty more Fischers.

The next minute Fischer went by on the other side of the way, and it made us sick and faint to see him, remembering the doom that was upon him, and we the cause of it. And how unconscious he was that anything had happened to him! You could see by his elastic step and his alert manner that he was well satisfied with himself for doing that hard turn for poor Frau Brandt. He kept glancing back over his shoulder expectantly. And, sure enough, pretty soon Frau Brandt followed after, in charge of the officers and wearing jingling chains. A mob was in her wake, jeering and shouting, "Blasphemer and heretic!" and some among them were neighbors and friends of her happier days. Some were trying to strike her, and the officers were not taking as much trouble as they might to keep them from it.

"Oh, stop them, Satan!" It was out before we remembered that he could not interrupt them for a moment without changing their whole afterlives. He puffed a little puff toward them with his lips and they began to reel and stagger and grab at the empty air; then they broke apart and fled in every direction, shrieking, as if in intolerable pain. He had crushed a rib of each of them with that little puff. We could not help asking if their life-chart was changed.

"Yes, entirely. Some have gained years, some have lost them. Some few will profit in various ways by the change, but only that few."

We did not ask if we had brought poor Fischer's luck to any of them. We did not wish to know. We fully believed in Satan's desire to do us kindnesses, but we were losing confidence in his judgment. It was at this time that our growing anxiety to have him look over our life-charts and suggest improvements began to fade out and give place to other interests.

For a day or two the whole village was a chattering turmoil over Frau Brandt's case and over the mysterious calamity that had overtaken the mob, and at her trial the place was crowded. She was easily convicted of her blasphemies, for she uttered those terrible words again and said she would not take them back. When warned that she was imperiling her life, she said they could take it in welcome, she did not want it, she would rather live with the professional devils in perdition than with these imitators in the village. They accused her of breaking all those ribs by witchcraft, and asked her if she was not a witch? She answered scornfully:

"No. If I had·that power would any of you holy hypocrites be alive five minutes? No; I would strike you all dead. Pronounce your sentence and let me go; I am tired of your society."

So they found her guilty, and she was excommunicated and cut off from the joys of heaven and doomed to the fires of hell; then she was clothed in a coarse robe and delivered to the secular arm, and conducted to the market place, the bell solemnly tolling the while. We saw her chained to the stake, and saw the first thin film of blue smoke rise on the still air. Then her hard face softened, and she looked upon the packed crowd in front of her and said, with gentleness:

"We played together once, in long-agone days when we were innocent little creatures. For the sake of that, I forgive you."

We went away then, and did not see the fires consume her, but we heard the shrieks, although we put our fingers in our ears. When they ceased we knew she was in heaven, notwithstanding the excommunication; and we were glad of her death and not sorry that we had brought it about.

One day, a little while after this, Satan appeared again. We were always watching out for him, for life was never very stagnant when he was by. He came upon us at that place in the woods where we had first met him. Being boys, we wanted to be entertained; we asked him to do a show for us.

"Very well," he said. "Would you like to see a history of the progress of the human race?—its development of that product which it calls civilization?"

We said we should.

So, with a thought, he turned the place into the Garden of Eden, and we saw Abel praying by his altar; then Cain came walking toward him with his club, and did not seem to see us, and would have stepped on my foot if I had not drawn it in. He spoke to his brother in a language which we did not understand; then he grew violent and threatening, and we knew what was going to happen, and turned away our heads for the moment; but we heard the crash of the blows and heard the shrieks and the groans; then there was silence, and we saw Abel lying in his blood and gasping out his life, and Cain standing over him and looking down at him, vengeful and unrepentant.

Then the vision vanished, and was followed by a long series of unknown wars, murders, and massacres. Next we had the Flood, and the Ark tossing around in the stormy waters, with lofty mountains in the distance showing veiled and dim through the rain. Satan said:

"The progress of your race was not satisfactory. It is to have another chance now."

The scene changed, and we saw Noah overcome with wine.

Next, we had Sodom and Gomorrah, and "the attempt to discover two or three respectable persons there," as Satan described it. Next, Lot and his daughters in the cave.

Next came the Hebraic wars, and we saw the victors massacre the survivors and their cattle, and save the young girls alive and distribute them around.

Next we had Jael; and saw her slip into the tent and drive the nail into the temple of her sleeping guest; and we were so close that when the blood gushed out it trickled in a little, red stream to our feet, and we could have stained our hands in it if we had wanted to.

Next we had Egyptian wars, Greek wars, Roman wars, hideous drenchings of the earth with blood; and we saw the treacheries of the Romans toward the Carthaginians, and the sickening spectacle of the massacre of those brave people. Also we saw Cæsar invade Britain—"not that those barbarians had done him any harm, but because he wanted their land, and desired to confer the blessings of civilization upon their widows and orphans," as Satan explained.

Next, Christianity was born. Then ages of Europe passed in review before us, and we saw Christianity and Civilization march hand in hand through those ages, "leaving famine and death and desolation in their wake, and other signs of the progress of the human race," as Satan observed.

And always we had wars, and more wars, and still other wars—all over Europe, all over the world. "Sometimes in the private interest of royal families," Satan said, "sometimes to crush a weak nation; but never a war started by the aggressor for any clean purpose—there is no such war in the history of the race."

"Now," said Satan, "you have seen your progress down to the present, and you must confess that it is wonderful —in its way. We must now exhibit the future."

He showed us slaughters more terrible in their destruction of life, more devastating in their engines of war, than any we had seen.

"You perceive," he said, "that you have made continual progress. Cain did his murder with a club; the Hebrews did their murders with javelins and swords; the Greeks and Romans added protective armor and the fine arts of military organization and generalship; the Christian has added guns and gunpowder; a few centuries from now he will have so greatly improved the deadly effectiveness of his weapons of slaughter that all men will confess that without Christian civilization war must have remained a poor and trifling thing to the end of time."

Then he began to laugh in the most unfeeling way, and make fun of the human race, although he knew that what he had been saying shamed us and wounded us. No one but an angel could have acted so; but suffering is nothing to them; they do not know what it is, except by hearsay.

More than once Seppi and I had tried in a humble and diffident way to convert him, and as he had remained silent we had taken his silence as a sort of encouragement; necessarily, then, this talk of his was a disappointment to us, for it showed that we had made no deep impression upon him. The thought made us sad, and we knew then how the missionary must feel when he has been cherishing a glad hope and has seen it blighted. We kept our grief to ourselves, knowing that this was not the time to continue our work.

Satan laughed his unkind laugh to a finish; then he said:

"It is a remarkable progress. In five or six thousand years five or six high civilizations have risen, flourished, commanded the wonder of the world, then faded out and disappeared; and not one of them except the latest ever invented any sweeping and adequate way to kill people. They all did their best—to kill being the chiefest ambition of the human race and the earliest incident in its history—but only the Christian civilization has scored a triumph to be proud of. Two or three centuries from now it will be recognized that all the competent killers are Christians; then the pagan world will go to school to the Christian—not to acquire his religion, but his guns. The Turk and the Chinaman will buy those to kill missionaries and converts with."

By this time his theater was at work again, and before our eyes nation after nation drifted by, during two or three centuries, a mighty procession, an endless procession, raging, struggling, wallowing through seas of blood, smothered in battle smoke through which the flags glinted and the red jets from the cannon darted; and always we heard the thunder of the guns and the cries of the dying.

"And what does it amount to?" said Satan, with his evil chuckle. "Nothing at all. You gain nothing; you always come out where you went in. For a million years the race has gone on monotonously propagating itself and monotonously reperforming this dull nonsense—to what end? No wisdom can guess! Who gets a profit out of it? Nobody but a parcel of usurping little monarchs and nobilities who despise you; would feel defiled if you touched them; would shut the door in your face if you proposed to call; whom you slave for, fight for, die for, and are not ashamed of it, but proud; whose existence is a perpetual insult to you and you are afraid to resent it; who are mendicants supported by your alms, yet assume toward you the airs of benefactor toward beggar; who address you in the language of master to slave, and are answered in the language of slave to master; who are worshiped by you with your mouth, while in your heart—if you have one—you despise yourselves for it. The first man was a hypocrite and a coward, qualities which have not yet failed in his line; it is the foundation upon which all civilizations have been built. Drink to their

perpetuation! Drink to their augmentation! Drink to—"
Then he saw by our faces how much we were hurt,
and he cut his sentence short and stopped chuckling,
and his manner changed. He said, gently: "No, we will
drink one another's health, and let civilization go. The
wine which has flown to our hands out of space by desire
is earthly, and good enough for that other toast; but
throw away the glasses; we will drink this one in wine
which has not visited this world before."

We obeyed, and reached up and received the new cups
as they descended. They were shapely and beautiful goblets, but they were not made of any material that we
were acquainted with. They seemed to be in motion, they
seemed to be alive; and certainly the colors in them were
in motion. They were very brilliant and sparkling, and of
every tint, and they were never still, but flowed to and
fro in rich tides which met and broke and flashed out
dainty explosions of enchanting color. I think it was most
like opals washing about in waves and flashing out their
splendid fires. But there is nothing to compare the wine
with. We drank it, and felt a strange and witching ecstasy
as of heaven go stealing through us, and Seppi's eyes
filled and he said, worshipingly:

"We shall be there some day, and then—"

He glanced furtively at Satan, and I think he hoped
Satan would say, "Yes, you will be there some day," but
Satan seemed to be thinking about something else, and
said nothing. This made me feel ghastly, for I knew he
had heard; nothing, spoken or unspoken, ever escaped
him. Poor Seppi looked distressed, and did not finish his
remark. The goblets rose and clove their way into the
sky, a triplet of radiant sundogs, and disappeared. Why
didn't they stay? It seemed a bad sign, and depressed me.
Should I ever see mine again? Would Seppi ever see his?

CHAPTER IX

IT was wonderful, the mastery Satan had over time and
distance. For him they did not exist. He called them
human inventions, and said they were artificialities. We
often went to the most distant parts of the globe with
him, and stayed weeks and months, and yet were gone

only a fraction of a second, as a rule. You could prove it by the clock. One day when our people were in such awful distress because the witch commission were afraid to proceed against the astrologer and Father Peter's household, or against any, indeed, but the poor and the friendless, they lost patience and took to witch-hunting on their own score, and began to chase a born lady who was known to have the habit of curing people by devilish arts, such as bathing them, washing them, and nourishing them instead of bleeding them and purging them through the ministrations of a barber-surgeon in the proper way. She came flying down, with the howling and cursing mob after her, and tried to take refuge in houses, but the doors were shut in her face. They chased her more than half an hour, we following to see it, and at last she was exhausted and fell, and they caught her. They dragged her to a tree and threw a rope over the limb, and began to make a noose of it, some holding her, meantime, and she crying and begging, and her young daughter looking on and weeping, but afraid to say or do anything.

They hanged the lady, and I threw a stone at her, although in my heart I was sorry for her; but all were throwing stones and each was watching his neighbor, and if I had not done as the others did it would have been noticed and spoken of. Satan burst out laughing.

All that were near by turned upon him, astonished and not pleased. It was an ill time to laugh, for his free and scoffing ways and his supernatural music had brought him under suspicion all over the town and turned many privately against him. The big blacksmith called attention to him now, raising his voice so that all should hear, and said:

"What are you laughing at? Answer! Moreover, please explain to the company why you threw no stone."

"Are you sure I did not throw a stone?"

"Yes. You needn't try to get out of it; I had my eye on you."

"And I—I noticed you!" shouted two others.

"Three witnesses," said Satan: "Mueller, the blacksmith; Klein, the butcher's man; Pfeiffer, the weaver's journeyman. Three very ordinary liars. Are there any more?"

"Never mind whether there are others or not, and

never mind about what you consider us—three's enough to settle your matter for you. You'll prove that you threw a stone, or it shall go hard with you."

"That's so!" shouted the crowd, and surged up as closely as they could to the center of interest.

"And first you will answer that other question," cried the blacksmith, pleased with himself for being mouthpiece to the public and hero of the occasion. "What are you laughing at?"

Satan smiled and answered, pleasantly: "To see three cowards stoning a dying lady when they were so near death themselves."

You could see the superstitious crowd shrink and catch their breath, under the sudden shock. The blacksmith, with a show of bravado, said:

"Pooh! What do you know about it?"

"I? Everything. By profession I am a fortuneteller, and I read the hands of you three—and some others—when you lifted them to stone the woman. One of you will die tomorrow week; another of you will die to-night; the third has but five minutes to live—and yonder is the clock!"

It made a sensation. The faces of the crowd blanched, and turned mechanically toward the clock. The butcher and the weaver seemed smitten with an illness, but the blacksmith braced up and said, with spirit:

"It is not long to wait for prediction number one. If it fails, young master, you will not live a whole minute after, I promise you that."

No one said anything; all watched the clock in a deep stillness which was impressive. When four and a half minutes were gone the blacksmith gave a sudden gasp and clapped his hand upon his heart, saying, "Give me breath! Give me room!" and began to sink down. The crowd surged back, no one offering to support him, and he fell lumbering to the ground and was dead. The people stared at him, then at Satan, then at one another; and their lips moved, but no words came. Then Satan said:

"Three saw that I threw no stone. Perhaps there are others; let them speak."

It struck a kind of panic into them, and, although no one answered him, many began to violently accuse one another, saying, "You said he didn't throw," and getting for reply, "It is a lie, and I will make you eat it!" And so in a moment they were in a raging and noisy turmoil, and beating and banging one another; and in the midst was the only indifferent one—the dead lady hanging from her rope, her troubles forgotten, her spirit at peace.

So we walked away, and I was not at ease, but was saying to myself, "He told them he was laughing at them, but it was a lie—he was laughing at me."

That made him laugh again, and he said, "Yes, I was laughing at you, because, in fear of what others might report about you, you stoned the woman when your heart revolted at the act—but I was laughing at the others, too."

"Why?"

"Because their case was yours."

"How is that?"

"Well, there were sixty-eight people there, and sixty-two of them had no more desire to throw a stone than you had."

"Satan!"

"Oh, it's true. I know your race. It is made up of sheep. It is governed by minorities, seldom or never by majorities. It suppresses its feelings and its beliefs and follows the handful that makes the most noise. Sometimes the noisy handful is right, sometimes wrong; but no matter, the crowd follows it. The vast majority of the race, whether savage or civilized, are secretly kindhearted and shrink from inflicting pain, but in the presence of the aggressive and pitiless minority they don't dare to assert themselves. Think of it! One kindhearted creature spies upon another, and sees to it that he loyally helps in iniquities which revolt both of them. Speaking as an expert, I know that ninety-nine out of a hundred of your race were strongly against the killing of witches when that foolishness was first agitated by a handful of pious lunatics in the long ago. And I know that even today, after ages of transmitted prejudice and silly teaching, only one person in twenty puts any real heart into the harrying of a witch. And yet apparently everybody hates witches and wants them killed. Some day a handful will rise up on the other side and make the most noise

—perhaps even a single daring man with a big voice and a determined front will do it—and in a week all the sheep will wheel and follow him, and witch-hunting will come to a sudden end.

"Monarchies, aristocracies, and religions are all based upon that large defect in your race—the individual's distrust of his neighbor, and his desire, for safety's or comfort's sake, to stand well in his neighbor's eye. These institutions will always remain, and always flourish, and always oppress you, affront you, and degrade you, because you will always be and remain slaves of minorities. There was never a country where the majority of the people were in their secret hearts loyal to any of these institutions."

I did not like to hear our race called sheep, and said I did not think they were.

"Still, it is true, lamb," said Satan. "Look at you in war —what mutton you are, and how ridiculous!"

"In war? How?"

"There has never been a just one, never an honorable one—on the part of the instigator of the war. I can see a million years ahead, and this rule will never change in so many as half a dozen instances. The loud little handful— as usual—will shout for the war. The pulpit will—warily and cautiously—object—at first; the great, big, dull bulk of the nation will rub its sleepy eyes and try to make out why there should be a war, and will say, earnestly and indignantly, 'It is unjust and dishonorable, and there is no necessity for it.' Then the handful will shout louder. A few fair men on the other side will argue and reason against the war with speech and pen, and at first will have a hearing and be applauded; but it will not last long; those others will outshout them, and presently the antiwar audiences will thin out and lose popularity. Before long you will see this curious thing: the speakers stoned from the platform, and free speech strangled by hordes of furious men who in their secret hearts are still at one with those stoned speakers—as earlier—but do not dare to say so. And now the whole nation—pulpit and all— will take up the war cry, and shout itself hoarse, and mob any honest man who ventures to open his mouth; and presently such mouths will cease to open. Next the statesmen will invent cheap lies, putting the blame upon the nation that is attacked, and every man will be glad of those conscience-soothing falsities, and will diligently study them, and refuse to examine any refutations of them; and thus he will by and by convince himself that the war is just, and will thank God for the better sleep he enjoys after this process of grotesque self-deception."

CHAPTER X

Days and days went by now, and no Satan. It was dull without him. But the astrologer, who had returned from his excursion to the moon, went about the village, braving public opinion, and getting a stone in the middle of his back now and then when some witch-hater got a safe chance to throw it and dodge out of sight. Meantime two influences had been working well for Marget. That Satan, who was quite indifferent to her, had stopped going to her house after a visit or two had hurt her pride, and she had set herself the task of banishing him from her heart. Reports of Wilhelm Meidling's dissipation brought to her from time to time by old Ursula had touched her with remorse, jealousy of Satan being the cause of it; and so now, these two matters working upon her together, she was getting a good profit out of the combination—her interest in Satan was steadily cooling, her interest in Wilhelm as steadily warming. All that was needed to complete her conversion was that Wilhelm should brace up and do something that should cause favorable talk and incline the public toward him again.

The opportunity came now. Marget sent and asked him to defend her uncle in the approaching trial, and he was greatly pleased, and stopped drinking and began his preparations with diligence. With more diligence than hope, in fact, for it was not a promising case. He had many interviews in his office with Seppi and me, and threshed out our testimony pretty thoroughly, thinking to find some valuable grains among the chaff, but the harvest was poor, of course.

If Satan would only come! That was my constant thought. He could invent some way to win the case; for he had said it would be won, so he necessarily knew

how it could be done. But the days dragged on, and still
he did not come. Of course I did not doubt that it would
win, and that Father Peter would be happy for the rest
of his life, since Satan had said so; yet I knew I should be
much more comfortable if he would come and tell us
how to manage it. It was getting high time for Father
Peter to have a saving change toward happiness, for by
general report he was worn out with his imprisonment
and the ignominy that was burdening him, and was like
to die of his miseries unless he got relief soon.

At last the trial came on, and the people gathered from
all around to witness it; among them many strangers
from considerable distances. Yes, everybody was there except the accused. He was too feeble in body for the strain.
But Marget was present, and keeping up her hope and her
spirit the best she could. The money was present, too.
It was emptied on the table, and was handled and ca-
ressed and examined by such as were privileged.

The astrologer was put in the witness box. He had
on his best hat and robe for the occasion.

Question. You claim that this money is yours?

Answer. I do.

Q. How did you come by it?

A. I found the bag in the road when I was returning
from a journey.

Q. When?

A. More than two years ago.

Q. What did you do with it?

A. I brought it home and hid it in a secret place in
my observatory, intending to find the owner if I could.

Q. You endeavored to find him?

A. I made diligent inquiry during several months, but
nothing came of it.

Q. And then?

A. I thought it not worth while to look further, and
was minded to use the money in finishing the wing of the
foundling asylum connected with the priory and nunnery.
So I took it out of its hiding place and counted it to see if
any of it was missing. And then—

Q. Why do you stop? Proceed.

A. I am sorry to have to say this, but just as I had

finished and was restoring the bag to its place, I looked
up and there stood Father Peter behind me.

Several murmured, "That looks bad," but others answered, "Ah, but he is such a liar!"

Q. That made you uneasy?

A. No; I thought nothing of it at the time, for Father
Peter often came to me unannounced to ask for a little
help in his need.

Marget blushed crimson at hearing her uncle falsely and
impudently charged with begging, especially from one he
had always denounced as a fraud, and was going to speak,
but remembered herself in time and held her peace.

Q. Proceed.

A. In the end I was afraid to contribute the money to
the foundling asylum, but elected to wait yet another year
and continue my inquiries. When I heard of Father Peter's
find I was glad, and no suspicions entered my mind; when
I came home a day or two later and discovered that my
own money was gone I still did not suspect until three
circumstances connected with Father Peter's good fortune
struck me as being singular coincidences.

Q. Pray name them.

A. Father Peter had found his money in a path—I
had found mine in a road. Father Peter's find consisted exclusively of gold ducats—mine also. Father Peter
found eleven hundred and seven ducats—I exactly the
same.

This closed his evidence, and certainly it made a strong
impression on the house; one could see that.

Wilhelm Meidling asked him some questions, then
called us boys, and we told our tale. It made the people
laugh, and we were ashamed. We were feeling pretty
badly, anyhow, because Wilhelm was hopeless, and
showed it. He was doing as well as he could, poor young
fellow, but nothing was in his favor, and such sympathy
as there was was now plainly not with his client. It might
be difficult for court and people to believe the astrologer's
story, considering his character, but it was almost impossible to believe Father Peter's. We were already feeling badly enough, but when the astrologer's lawyer
said he believed he would not ask us any questions—for
our story was a little delicate and it would be cruel for

him to put any strain upon it—everybody tittered, and it was almost more than we could bear. Then he made a sarcastic little speech, and got so much fun out of our tale, and it seemed so ridiculous and childish and every way impossible and foolish, that it made everybody laugh till the tears came; and at last Marget could not keep up her courage any longer, but broke down and cried, and I was so sorry for her.

Now I noticed something that braced me up. It was Satan standing alongside of Wilhelm! And there was such a contrast!—Satan looked so confident, had such a spirit in his eyes and face, and Wilhelm looked so depressed and despondent. We two were comfortable now, and judged that he would testify and persuade the bench and the people that black was white and white black, or any other color he wanted it. We glanced around to see what the strangers in the house thought of him, for he was beautiful, you know—stunning, in fact—but no one was noticing him; so we knew by that that he was invisible.

The lawyer was saying his last words; and while he was saying them Satan began to melt into Wilhelm. He melted into him and disappeared; and then there was a change, when his spirit began to look out of Wilhelm's eyes.

That lawyer finished quite seriously, and with dignity. He pointed to the money, and said:

"The love of it is the root of all evil. There it lies, the ancient tempter, newly red with the shame of its latest victory—the dishonor of a priest of God and his two poor juvenile helpers in crime. If it could but speak, let us hope that it would be constrained to confess that of all its conquests this was the basest and the most pathetic."

He sat down. Wilhelm rose and said:

"From the testimony of the accuser I gather that he found this money in a road more than two years ago. Correct me, sir, if I misunderstood you."

The astrologer said his understanding of it was correct.

"And the money so found was never out of his hands thenceforth up to a certain definite date—the last day of last year. Correct me, sir, if I am wrong."

The astrologer nodded his head. Wilhelm turned to the bench and said:

"If I prove that this money here was not that money, then it is not his?"

"Certainly not; but this is irregular. If you had such a witness it was your duty to give proper notice of it and have him here to—" He broke off and began to consult with the other judges. Meantime that other lawyer got up excited and began to protest against allowing new witnesses to be brought into the case at this late stage.

The judges decided that his contention was just and must be allowed.

"But this is not a new witness," said Wilhelm. "It has already been partly examined. I speak of the coin."

"The coin? What can the coin say?"

"It can say it is not the coin that the astrologer once possessed. It can say it was not in existence last December. By its date it can say this."

And it was so! There was the greatest excitement in the court while that lawyer and the judges were reaching for coins and examining them and exclaiming. And everybody was full of admiration of Wilhelm's brightness in happening to think of that neat idea. At last order was called and the court said:

"All of the coins but four are of the date of the present year. The court tenders its sincere sympathy to the accused, and its deep regret that he, an innocent man, through an unfortunate mistake, has suffered the undeserved humiliation of imprisonment and trial. The case is dismissed."

So the money could speak, after all, though that lawyer thought it couldn't. The court rose, and almost everybody came forward to shake hands with Marget and congratulate her, and then to shake with Wilhelm and praise him; and Satan had stepped out of Wilhelm and was standing around looking on full of interest, and people walking through him every which way, not knowing he was there. And Wilhelm could not explain why he only thought of the date on the coins at the last moment, instead of earlier; he said it just occurred to him, all of a sudden, like an inspiration, and he brought it right out without any hesitation, for, although he didn't examine the coins, he seemed, somehow, to know it was true. That was honest of him, and like him; another would have pretended he had thought of it earlier, and was keeping it back for a surprise.

He had dulled down a little now; not much, but still you could notice that he hadn't that luminous look in his eyes that he had while Satan was in him. He nearly got it back, though, for a moment when Marget came and praised him and thanked him and couldn't keep him from seeing how proud she was of him. The astrologer went off dissatisfied and cursing, and Solomon Isaacs gathered up the money and carried it away. It was Father Peter's for good and all, now.

Satan was gone. I judged that he had spirited himself away to the jail to tell the prisoner the news; and in this I was right. Marget and the rest of us hurried thither at our best speed, in a great state of rejoicing.

Well, what Satan had done was this: he had appeared before that poor prisoner, exclaiming, "The trial is over, and you stand forever disgraced as a thief—by verdict of the court!"

The shock unseated the old man's reason. When we arrived, ten minutes later, he was parading pompously up and down and delivering commands to this and that and the other constable or jailer, and calling them Grand Chamberlain, and Prince This and Prince That, and Admiral of the Fleet, Field Marshal in Command, and all such fustian, and was as happy as a bird. He thought he was the Emperor!

Marget flung herself on his breast and cried, and indeed everybody was moved almost to heartbreak. He recognized Marget, but could not understand why she should cry. He patted her on the shoulder and said:

"Don't do it, dear; remember, there are witnesses, and it is not becoming in the Crown Princess. Tell me your trouble—it shall be mended; there is nothing the Emperor cannot do." Then he looked around and saw old Ursula with her apron to her eyes. He was puzzled at that, and said, "And what is the matter with you?"

Through her sobs she got out words explaining that she was distressed to see him—"so." He reflected over that a moment, then muttered, as if to himself: "A singular old thing, the Dowager Duchess—means well, but is always snuffling and never able to tell what it is about. It is because she doesn't know." His eye fell on Wilhelm. "Prince of India," he said, "I divine that it is you that the Crown Princess is concerned about. Her tears shall be dried; I will no longer stand between you; she shall share your throne; and between you you shall inherit mine. There little lady, have I done well? You can smile now—isn't it so?"

He petted Marget and kissed her, and was so contented with himself and with everybody that he could not do enough for us all, but began to give away kingdoms and such things right and left, and the least that any of us got was a principality. And so at last, being persuaded to go home, he marched in imposing state; and when the crowds along the way saw how it gratified him to be hurrahed at, they humored him to the top of his desire, and he responded with condescending bows and gracious smiles, and often stretched out a hand and said, "Bless you, my people!"

As pitiful a sight as ever I saw. And Marget, and old Ursula crying all the way.

On my road home I came upon Satan, and reproached him with deceiving me with that lie. He was not embarrassed, but said, quite simply and composedly:

"Ah, you mistake; it was the truth. I said he would be happy the rest of his days, and he will, for he will always think he is the Emperor, and his pride in it and his joy in it will endure to the end. He is now, and will remain, the one utterly happy person in this empire."

"But the method of it, Satan, the method! Couldn't you have done it without depriving him of his reason?"

It was difficult to irritate Satan, but that accomplished it.

"What an ass you are!" he said. "Are you so unobservant as not to have found out that sanity and happiness are an impossible combination? No sane man can be happy, for to him life is real, and he sees what a fearful thing it is. Only the mad can be happy, and not many of those. The few that imagine themselves kings or gods are happy, the rest are no happier than the sane. Of course, no man is entirely in his right mind at any time, but I have been referring to the extreme cases. I have taken from this man that trumpery thing which the race regards as a Mind; I have replaced his tin life with a silver-gilt fiction; you see the result—and you criticize! I said I would make him permanently happy, and I have done it. I have made him happy by the only means possible to his race—and you are not satisfied!" He heaved a discouraged sigh, and said, "It seems to me that this race is hard to please."

There it was, you see. He didn't seem to know any way to do a person a favor except by killing him or making a lunatic out of him. I apologized, as well as I could; but privately I did not think much of his processes—at that time.

Satan was accustomed to say that our race lived a life of continuous and uninterrupted self-deception. It duped itself from cradle to grave with shams and delusions which it mistook for realities, and this made its entire life a sham. Of the score of fine qualities which it imagined it had and was vain of, it really possessed hardly one. It regarded itself as gold, and was only brass. One day when he was in this vein he mentioned a detail—the sense of humor. I cheered up then, and took issue. I said we possessed it.

"There spoke the race!" he said; "always ready to claim what it hasn't got, and mistake its ounce of brass filings for a ton of gold dust. You have a mongrel perception of humor, nothing more; a multitude of you possess that. This multitude see the comic side of a thousand low-grade and trivial things—broad incongruities, mainly; grotesqueries, absurdities, evokers of the horselaugh. The ten thousand high-grade comicalities which exist in the world are sealed from their dull vision. Will a day come when the race will detect the funniness of these juvenilities and laugh at them—and by laughing at them destroy them? For your race, in its poverty, has unquestionably one really effective weapon—laughter. Power, money, persuasion, supplication, persecution—these can lift at a colossal humbug—push it a little—weaken it a little, century by century; but only laughter can blow it to rags and atoms at a blast. Against the assault of laughter nothing can stand. You are always fussing and fighting with your other weapons. Do you ever use that one? No; you leave it lying rusting. As a race, do you ever use it at all? No; you lack sense and the courage."

We were traveling at the time and stopped at a little city in India and looked on while a juggler did his tricks before a group of natives. They were wonderful, but I knew Satan could beat that game, and I begged him to show off a little, and he said he would. He changed himself into a native in turban and breechcloth, and very considerately conferred on me a temporary knowledge of the language.

The juggler exhibited a seed, covered it with earth in a small flowerpot, then put a rag over the pot; after a minute the rag began to rise; in ten minutes it had risen a foot; then the rag was removed and a little tree was exposed, with leaves upon it and ripe fruit. We ate the fruit, and it was good. But Satan said:

"Why do you cover the pot? Can't you grow the tree in the sunlight?"

"No," said the juggler; "no one can do that."

"You are only an apprentice; you don't know your trade. Give me the seed. I will show you." He took the seed and said, "What shall I raise from it?"

"It is a cherry seed; of course you will raise a cherry."

"Oh no; that is a trifle; any novice can do that. Shall I raise an orange tree from it?"

"Oh yes!" and the juggler laughed.

"And shall I make it bear other fruits as well as oranges?"

"If God wills!" and they all laughed.

Satan put the seed in the ground, put a handful of dust on it, and said, "Rise!"

A tiny stem shot up and began to grow, and grew so fast that in five minutes it was a great tree, and we were sitting in the shade of it. There was a murmur of wonder, then all looked up and saw a strange and pretty sight, for the branches were heavy with fruits of many kinds and colors—oranges, grapes, bananas, peaches, cherries, apricots, and so on. Baskets were brought, and the unlading of the tree began; and the people crowded around Satan and kissed his hand, and praised him, calling him the prince of jugglers. The news went about the town, and everybody came running to see the wonder—and they remembered to bring baskets, too. But the tree was equal to the occasion; it put out new fruits as fast as any were removed; baskets were filled by the score and by the hundred, but always the supply remained undiminished. At last a foreigner in white linen and sun helmet arrived, and exclaimed angrily:

"Away from here! Clear out, you dogs; the tree is on my lands and is my property."

The natives put down their baskets and made humble obeisance. Satan made humble obeisance, too, with his fingers to his forehead, in the native way, and said:

"Please let them have their pleasure for an hour, sir—only that, and no longer. Afterward you may forbid them; and you will still have more fruit than you and the state together can consume in a year."

This made the foreigner very angry, and he cried out, "Who are you, you vagabond, to tell your betters what they may do and what they mayn't!" and he struck Satan with his cane and followed this error with a kick.

The fruits rotted on the branches, and the leaves withered and fell. The foreigner gazed at the bare limbs with the look of one who is surprised, and not gratified. Satan said:

"Take good care of the tree, for its health and yours are bound together. It will never bear again, but if you tend it well it will live long. Water its roots once in each hour every night—and do it yourself; it must not be done by proxy, and to do it in daylight will not answer. If you fail only once in any night, the tree will die, and you likewise. Do not go home to your own country any more—you would not reach there; make no business or pleasure engagements which require you to go outside your gate at night—you cannot afford the risk; do not rent or sell this place—it would be injudicious."

The foreigner was proud and wouldn't beg, but I thought he looked as if he would like to. While he stood gazing at Satan we vanished away and landed in Ceylon.

I was sorry for that man; sorry Satan hadn't been his

customary self and killed him or made him a lunatic. It would have been a mercy. Satan overheard the thought, and said:

"I would have done it but for his wife, who has not offended me. She is coming to him presently from their native land, Portugal. She is well, but has not long to live, and has been yearning to see him and persuade him to go back with her next year. She will die without knowing he can't leave that place."

"He won't tell her?"

"He? He will not trust that secret with anyone; he will reflect that it could be revealed in sleep, in the hearing of some Portuguese guest's servant some time or other."

"Did none of those natives understand what you said to him?"

"None of them understood, but he will always be afraid that some of them did. That fear will be torture to him, for he has been a harsh master to them. In his dreams he will imagine them chopping his tree down. That will make his days uncomfortable—I have already arranged for his nights."

It grieved me, though not sharply, to see him take such a malicious satisfaction in his plans for this foreigner.

"Does he believe what you told him, Satan?"

"He thought he didn't, but our vanishing helped. The tree, where there had been no tree before—that helped. The insane and uncanny variety of fruits—the sudden withering—all these things are helps. Let him think as he may, reason as he may, one thing is certain, he will water the tree. But between this and night he will begin his changed career with a very natural precaution—for him."

"What is that?"

"He will fetch a priest to cast out the tree's devil. You are such a humorous race—and don't suspect it."

"Will he tell the priest?"

"No. He will say a juggler from Bombay created it, and that he wants the juggler's devil driven out of it, so that it will thrive and be fruitful again. The priest's incantations will fail; then the Portuguese will give up that scheme and get his watering pot ready."

"But the priest will burn the tree. I know it; he will not allow it to remain."

"Yes, and anywhere in Europe he would burn the man, too. But in India the people are civilized, and these things will not happen. The man will drive the priest away and take care of the tree."

I reflected a little, then said, "Satan, you have given him a hard life, I think."

"Comparatively. It must not be mistaken for a holiday."

We flitted from place to place around the world as we had done before, Satan showing me a hundred wonders, most of them reflecting in some way the weakness and triviality of our race. He did this now every few days—not out of malice—I am sure of that—it only seemed to amuse and interest him, just as a naturalist might be amused and interested by a collection of ants.

CHAPTER XI

FOR as much as a year Satan continued these visits, but at last he came less often, and then for a long time he did not come at all. This always made me lonely and melancholy. I felt that he was losing interest in our tiny world and might at any time abandon his visits entirely. When one day he finally came to me I was overjoyed, but only for a little while. He had come to say goodbye, he told me, and for the last time. He had investigations and undertakings in other corners of the universe, he said, that would keep him busy for a longer period than I could wait for his return.

"And you are going away, and will not come back any more?"

"Yes," he said. "We have comraded long together, and it has been pleasant—pleasant for both; but I must go now, and we shall not see each other any more."

"In this life, Satan, but in another? We shall meet in another, surely?"

Then, all tranquilly and soberly, he made the strange answer, *"There is no other."*

A subtle influence blew upon my spirit from his, bringing with it a vague, dim, but blessed and hopeful feeling that the incredible words might be true—even *must* be true.

"Have you never suspected this, Theodor?"

"No. How could I? But if it can only be true—"

"It is true."

A gust of thankfulness rose in my breast, but a doubt checked it before it could issue in words, and I said, "But —but—we have seen that future life—seen it in its actuality, and so—"

"It was a vision—it had no existence."

I could hardly breathe for the great hope that was struggling in me. "A vision?—a vi—"

"Life itself is only a vision, a dream."

It was electrical. By God! I had had that very thought a thousand times in my musings!

"Nothing exists; all is a dream. God—man—the world —the sun, the moon, the wilderness of stars—a dream, all a dream; they have no existence. *Nothing exists save empty space—and you!"*

"I!"

"And you are not you—you have no body, no blood, no bones, you are but a *thought.* I myself have no existence; I am but a dream—your dream, creature of your imagination. In a moment you will have realized this, then you will banish me from your visions and I shall dissolve into the nothingness out of which you made me. . . .

"I am perishing already—I am failing—I am passing away. In a little while you will be alone in shoreless space, to wander its limitless solitudes without friend or comrade forever—for you will remain a *thought,* the only existent thought, and by your nature inextinguishable, indestructible. But I, your poor servant, have revealed you to yourself and set you free. Dream other dreams, and better!

"Strange! that you should not have suspected years ago—centuries, ages, eons ago!—for you have existed, companionless, through all the eternities. Strange, indeed, that you should not have suspected that your universe and its contents were only dreams, visions, fiction! Strange, because they are so frankly and hysterically insane—like all dreams: a God who could make good children as easily as bad, yet preferred to make bad ones; who could have made every one of them happy, yet never made a single happy one; who made them prize their bitter life, yet stingily cut it short; who gave his angels eternal happiness unearned, yet required his other children to earn it; who gave his angels painless lives, yet cursed his other children with biting miseries and maladies of mind and body; who mouths justice and invented hell—mouths mercy and invented hell—mouths Golden Rules, and forgiveness multiplied by seventy times seven, and invented hell; who mouths morals to other people and has none himself; who frowns upon crimes, yet commits them all; who created man without invitation, then tries to shuffle the responsibility for man's acts upon man, instead of honorably placing it where it belongs, upon himself; and finally, with altogether divine obtuseness, invites this poor, abused slave to worship him! . . .

"You perceive, *now*, that these things are all impossible except in a dream. You perceive that they are pure and puerile insanities, the silly creations of an imagination that is not conscious of its freaks—in a word, that they are a dream, and you the maker of it. The dream-marks are all present; you should have recognized them earlier.

"It is true, that which I have revealed to you: there is no God, no universe, no human race, no earthly life, no heaven, no hell. It is all a dream—a grotesque and foolish dream. Nothing exists but you. And you are but a *thought*—a vagrant thought, a useless thought, a homeless thought, wandering forlorn among the empty eternities!"

He vanished, and left me appalled; for I knew, and realized, that all he had said was true.

SELECTED BIBLIOGRAPHY

Works by Mark Twain

The Celebrated Jumping Frog of Calaveras County, 1865 Story (Signet Classic 0451-520696)

The Innocents Abroad, 1869 Travel (Signet Classic 0451-523245

Roughing It, 1872 Travel (Signet Classic 0451-524071)

The Gilded Age (with Charles Dudley Warner), 1873 Novel (Meridian Classic 0452-009995)

The Adventures of Tom Sawyer, 1876 Novel (Signet Classic 0451-519620)

The Facts Concerning the Recent Carnival of Crime in Connecticut, 1876 Story (Signet Classic 0451-520696)

A Tramp Abroad, 1880 Travel

The Prince and the Pauper, 1882 Novel (Signet Classic 0451-521935)

The Stolen White Elephant, 1882 Story (Signet Classic 0451-520696)

Life on the Mississippi, 1883 Travel (Signet Classic 0451-521722)

The Adventures of Huckleberry Finn, 1884 Novel (Signet Classic 0451-519124)

A Connecticut Yankee in King Arthur's Court, 1889 Novel (Signet Classic 0451-523539)

Luck, 1891 Story (Signet Classic 0451-520696)

The American Claimant, 1892 Novel

The £1,000,000 Bank Note, 1893 Story (Signet Classic 0451-520696)

The Tragedy of Pudd'nhead Wilson and the Comedy of Those Extraordinary Twins, 1894 Novel (Signet Classic 0451-523741)

Personal Recollections of Joan of Arc, 1896 Novel

Tom Sawyer Abroad, Tom Sawyer, Detective, and Other Stories, 1896 Novels and Stories

How to Tell a Story and Other Essays, 1897 Essays

The Man that Corrupted Hadleyburg, 1899 Story (Signet Classic 0451-520696)

The Five Boons of Life, 1902 Story (Signet Classic 0451-520696)

Was It Heaven? Or Hell?, 1902 Story (Signet Classic 0451-520696)

The Mysterius Stranger, 1916 Short Novel (Signet Classic 0451-520696)

Biography and Criticism

Anderson, Frederick, ed. with Kenneth M. Sanderson. *Mark Twain: The Critical Heritage.* New York: Barnes and Noble, 1971.

Andrews, Kenneth R. *Nook Farm: Mark Twain's Hartford Circle.* Cambridge: Harvard Univ. Press, 1950.

Bellamy, Gladys Carmen. *Mark Twain as Literary Artist.* Norman: Univ. of Oklahoma Press, 1950.

Branch, Edgar M. *The Literary Apprenticeship of Mark Twain: With Selections from his Apprentice Writing*. Urbana: Univ. of Illinois Press, 1950.

Cox, James M. *Mark Twain: The Fate of Humor*. Princeton: Princeton Univ. Press, 1966.

DeVoto, Bernard. *Mark Twain at Work*. Cambridge: Harvard Univ. Press, 1942.

———. *Mark Twain's America*. Boston: Little, Brown, 1932.

Fench, Bryant M. *Mark Twain and "The Gilded Age."* Dallas: Southern Methodist Univ. Press, 1965.

Ferguson, DeLancey. *Mark Twain: Man and Legend*. Indianapolis: Bobbs-Merrill, 1943.

Gibson, William M. *The Art of Mark Twain*. New York: Oxford Univ. Press, 1976.

Hill, Hamlin. *Mark Twain: God's Fool*. New York: Harper and Row, 1973.

Howells, William Dean. *My Mark Twain: Reminiscences and Criticisms*. Ed. Marilyn Austin Baldwin. Baton Rouge: Louisiana State Univ. Press, 1967.

Kaplan, Justin. *Mark Twain and His World*. New York: Simon and Schuster, 1974.

———. *Mr. Clemens and Mark Twain*. New York: Simon and Schuster, 1966.

Leary, Lewis, ed. *A Casebook on Mark Twain's Wound*. New York: Thomas Y. Crowell, 1962.

———. *Southern Excursions: Essays on Mark Twain and Others*. Baton Rouge: Louisiana State Univ. Press, 1971.

Lynn, Kenneth S. *Mark Twain and Southwestern Humor*. Boston: Little, Brown, 1960.

MacDonald, Dwight. "Mark Twain." *The New Yorker*, 9 April, 1960, pp. 160–96. Rpt. in *Against The American Grain*. New York: Random House, 1962, pp. 79–123.

Paine, Albert Bigelow. *Mark Twain: A Biography*. 3 vols. New York: Harper and Brothers, 1912.

Schmitter, Dean Morgan, ed. *Mark Twain*. New York: McGraw-Hill, 1974.

Smith, Henry Nash, ed. *Mark Twain: A Collection of Critical Essays*. Englewood Cliffs, N.J.: Prentice-Hall, 1968.

———. *Mark Twain: The Development of a Writer*. Cambridge: Harvard Univ. Press, 1962.

Spengemann, William C. *Mark Twain and the Backwoods Angel: The Matter of Innocence in the Works of Samuel L. Clemens*. Kent, Ohio: Kent State Univ. Press, 1966.

Stone, Albert E. *The Innocent Eye: Childhood in Mark Twain's Imagination*. New Haven: Yale Univ. Press, 1961.

Wagenknecht, Edward. *Mark Twain: The Man and His Work*, 3rd ed. Norman: Univ. of Oklahoma Press, 1967.

Wector, Dixon. *Sam Clemens of Hannibal*. Boston: Houghton Mifflin, 1952.

A NOTE ON THE TEXT

The texts of the stories are based on the following sources. (Dates of first printings are shown on the Contents page.)

"The Celebrated Jumping Frog of Calaveras County," from *The Celebrated Jumping Frog of Calaveras County and Other Sketches*. New York: C. H. Webb, Publisher, 1867.

"The Facts Concerning the Recent Carnival of Crime in Connecticut," from *Tom Sawyer Abroad,* 1894.

"The Stolen White Elephant," from *The Stolen White Elephant, etc.* New York: Charles L. Webster & Company, 1894.

"Luck," from *Harper's New Monthly Magazine,* August, 1891.

"The £1,000,000 Bank-Note," from *The Century Magazine,* 1893.

"The Man That Corrupted Hadleyburg," from *The Man That Corrupted Hadleyburg and Other Stories and Essays.* New York and London: Harper & Brothers, 1904.

"The Five Boons of Life," from *Harper's Weekly,* July 5, 1902.

"Was It Heaven? Or Hell?" from *Harper's Monthly Magazine,* December, 1902.

The Mysterious Stranger, from *The Mysterious Stranger, a Romance.* New York and London: Harper & Brothers, 1916.